Shafter Range

OTHER FIVE STAR WESTERNS BY T. T. FLYNN:

Night of the Comanche Moon (1995)
Rawhide (1996)
Long Journey to Deep Cañon (1997)
Death Marks Time in Trampas (1998)
The Devil's Lode (1999)
Ride to Glory (2000)
Prodigal of Death (2001)
Hell's Cañon (2002)
Reunion at Cottonwood Station (2003)
Outlaws (2004)
Noose of Fate (2005)
Dead Man's Gold (2006)
Gunsmoke (2007)
Last Waltz on Wild Horse (2008)

Shafter Range

A Western Duo

T. T. Flynn

FIVE STAR
A part of Gale, Cengage Learning

Detroit • New York • San Francisco • New Haven, Conn • Waterville, Maine • London

Five Star Publishing, a part of Gale, Cengage Learning.

Set in 11 pt. Plantin.
Printed on permanent paper.

LIBRARY OF CONGRESS CATALOGING-IN-PUBLICATION DATA

Flynn, T. T.
Shafter range : a western duo / by T. T. Flynn. — 1st ed.
p. cm.
ISBN-13: 978-1-59414-798-2 (alk. paper)
ISBN-10: 1-59414-798-1 (alk. paper)
I. Flynn, T. T. What color is heaven. II. Title.
PS3556.L93S5 2009
813′.54—dc22 2009016126

First Edition. First Printing: September 2009.
Published in 2009 in conjunction with Golden West Literary Agency.

Printed in the United States of America
1 2 3 4 5 6 7 13 12 11 10 09

CONTENTS

★ ★ ★ ★ ★

"What Color Is Heaven?"

★ ★ ★ ★ ★

I

When the stage guard opened fire at the piled and tumbled rocks on the side of the road, Rick Candleman had the quick feeling that once more the Iron Hat range held bad luck for him. Eight years had passed since that night he had tangled with Rufus Madden and then had lathered a horse away from the Iron Hat country. And the news that Rufus Madden hadn't died after all caught up with Rick in the Argentine. He had stayed on down there under the Southern Cross. Now he was visiting home again—and, before the stage got him to Laguna, trouble was breaking in his face. The stage guard's roaring shotgun was the signal.

Rifles among the rocks answered the guard's gun. A bullet dropped one of the four stage horses. The tangled mêlée in the harness brought the stage to a swerving, reeling stop. The girl sitting opposite Rick exclaimed under her breath. Through the dust swirling around the stage they could hear the driver swearing as he fought the reins.

The other two passengers were men. The wizened, nattily dressed little man at the girl's side was a drummer for the hardware trade. Beside Rick was a blocky, broad-shouldered cowman with a black mustache and black, challenging brows. As the stage stopped, the cowman reached under his coat.

"Better not, friend," Rick warned. "They mean business. We got a lady here."

The cowman blurted: "Don't sit there an' be yellow! Grab a gun!"

"Haven't got a gun. You'll have it all to swing . . . and get us shot up, too, if you play it like this."

The wizened drummer sat with open mouth. The cowman glared at Rick. The girl eyed him with an intent, tense look. She wasn't afraid, Rick decided. He might have expected it from the hot red glint of her hair, and from the provocation in her look when the cowman had climbed on the stage at Mission Wells and ogled her. Now, while the stage still rocked and the driver fought the plunging horses, the guard's body rolled off the top, struck the road hard, and stayed where it landed.

"One dead already," Rick said curtly.

The cowman half rose to his feet, looked out at the body. The fight went out of him and he sat back heavily.

"Couple of rifles lined on us over there in the rocks," Rick said, looking out. "Only one man showing himself. You wouldn't have had a chance."

"Plenty of chance if I'd half a man to help me," the big fellow snapped under his breath.

One outlaw was running out from the rocks to the stage. He carried a six-shooter and wore a shapeless yellow slicker in the blistering midday heat. An old black hat was pulled low over a bandanna mask. He knew what he was about.

"Toss down that Laguna bank box!" he called to the driver as he came down through the big rocks.

The driver's voice cut back through the settling dust. "Ain't no bank box for you this trip!"

"One started from the railroad! It better hit the ground fast or the boys'll open up! Half a minute's all you get!"

"That's half a minute too long, damn you! Ain't no box here for a pack of low-down thieves an' killers!"

Rick had noticed the driver as the stage loaded at Mission

Wells. A lean, dried-out old fellow with a huge drooping mustache, the driver was the type to take a stubborn stand and hold to it.

The little dude drummer shrank back in the seat. "They'll k-kill him, won't they? They'll kill all of us if they start shooting?"

"Likely," Rick agreed.

The gunman outside the stage spoke venomously behind the bandanna. "Time's almost up!" He had no interest in the passengers.

The drummer whimpered: "Ought to be something we can do."

"Not much," Rick told him. "That dead horse has got us hog-tied."

The cowman snorted.

The red-headed girl said suddenly: "They'll kill that driver if he stays stubborn."

"Maybe not," Rick answered without much conviction.

"Of course they will. And maybe us, too." She was off the seat as she spoke. "I'll stop it. If he won't tell them about that box, I will."

Rick caught her arm as she opened the door. But she jerked away and stepped quickly out into the open. Rick followed her out irritably. This was a hair-trigger business. She could make it worse with a word.

"They put an old carpetbag on top that was heavy enough to have gold inside!" she called rapidly to the gunman. She stepped away from the stage, pointing to the top. "It's that green bag, between the two leather cases!"

The six-shooter threatened Rick to a stop. But the gunman chuckled behind his bandanna to the girl. "If every stage carried something purty an' helpful like you, lady, it'd make this business a cinch." Then the venomous threat snapped in his voice again as he addressed the driver: "Throw off that carpet-bag!"

Dust spurted as the carpetbag landed heavily a foot from the dead man.

The gunman kicked the bag, nodded satisfaction. "You saved the stubborn old coot's skin," he told the girl. "Set over there on a rock while he cuts that dead horse loose an' rolls on."

She started to obey, then stopped at Rick's cold voice. "The lady's riding the stage with us."

"She *was,* you mean. Git back in there. The lady's stayin' here."

Rick hesitated, shrugged, climbed back into the stage, and slammed the door. Without sitting down he snapped under his breath to the blocky cowman: "Give me that gun."

Startled, the man reached under his coat without asking a question. Rick caught the gun from his hand, turned quickly in the cramped space between the seats. His shoulder drove the stage door open, and he plunged out to what was probably the end of Rick Candleman.

Two rifles, maybe more, were lined on the stage. But Rick was counting on one slight advantage as he catapulted back into the open. None of the outlaws was expecting a play like this. The gunman in the slicker had half turned to look at the girl. Rick was on the ground, crouching, dodging, before a rifle up the long, boulder-strewn slope fired to bring him down.

The bullet missed, screamed off the rim of the back wheel, and the gunman, not half a dozen steps away, whirled for trouble. By then Rick was where he wanted to be. The slicker-clad figure was shielding him somewhat from the rifles, and he had hit the ground with six-gun cocked and ready. He fired first, two shots almost as one. He hit the man's gun arm, shattering it.

Rick heard the girl cry out as he plunged forward. He knew

her fear and it couldn't be helped. Better to frighten her a little now, better to put her in some danger than to let the stage roll on and leave her here. The man in the slicker had dropped his gun. He was hurt and rattled. He turned to run, inviting a shot in the back. Rick held back the shot, caught him, grabbed the slicker collar, and yanked him to a stop.

"Tell 'em to hold those rifles," Rick panted, gouging the gun muzzle into the man's back and holding him close for a shield.

The rifles stayed silent and the man in the slicker bawled: "He's got a gun in my back! Hold it, boys!"

Rick backed his prisoner toward the stage and called to the driver: "Cut that dead horse out of the harness!" The girl had not moved. Rick blurted at her: "Climb in the coach! You're all right now!"

But he wasn't so sure she was all right. A rifle bullet could drop the prisoner and Rick Candleman, too. The gunners hidden up there in the rocks might think the Laguna bank shipment was worth losing one man. But the guns were silent as Rick backed to the stagecoach. The girl came to his side.

"Get in!" Rick snapped at her.

Standing at the stage step, she said a queer thing. "You look like a Candleman. You're Rick Candleman, aren't you?"

"Yes," Rick answered, wondering why she hadn't asked the question before. He was struck again by her coolness, her self-possession. And then the last thing he expected to happen caught him off guard and stunned him. The red-headed girl spoke in husky warning and put a gun muzzle in his back. "I'll stay here. Drop your gun and the stage can go on."

She had gotten out of the stage with a woman's leather hand purse that must have held a small gun. Because he had looked into her face and eyes and judged her, Rick did not doubt her warning. An instant later he was blindly angry at the fool figure he'd cut. She had intended all along to stay here with the outlaws. She'd known there would be a hold-up. And because she was pretty as a red-headed jungle cat and probably twice as merciless, Rick did not try to argue.

"I'll drop nothing," he said savagely. "Pull that damned trigger and I'll still have time to get this curly wolf in front of me."

"He should be killed anyway for letting you cripple him," she answered with a lack of emotion that made Rick's nerves crawl. She spoke past Rick's shoulder in the same unmoved tone: "Get up in the rocks, Slim."

Blood was dripping off Slim's wrist and hand. Sweat stood out on his neck. But more than pain and sweat from the hot slicker inspired his hoarse reply. "He'll shoot if I try it!"

"So?" the girl said, and suddenly she was speaking in Spanish like a native. "Does it matter who shoots you now? Quick, before I do myself!"

The man took a hesitating step away from Rick's gun. Nothing happened, and he took a longer step. Then, with blood dripping off his fingers, he began to run up the rocky slope as if death already were at his heels. And Rick, with the strange prescience that greater dangers than his gun threatened the fellow, let him go.

"You see," the girl said behind his shoulder, "now there is nothing left. Must I shoot you?"

Rick shrugged and tossed the gun down beside the green carpetbag and the dead man.

The old stage driver had been using a pocket knife with furious haste on the harness of the dead horse. The knife was still in his hand as he turned back toward his stage seat, saw the outlaw running and Rick tossing down his gun.

"What'n hell?" the old man gasped.

"Take a look," Rick said with ironical bitterness. "And then get your stage out of here fast . . . if you can."

"But . . . but the lady! What's she . . . ?"

"She ain't a lady," Rick rasped.

He heard the girl chuckle under her breath and he held that against her, too. He was angry as only a strong man can be angry and she was laughing at him.

"You heard *Señor* Candleman," she told the driver.

The old man gave Rick a startled look. "Candleman?" He spat. His big mustache was quivering as he looked at the rocks where the gunmen were hidden, and then back at them. "I've done heard plenty," he said, and he spat again, and added: "An' seen more."

He climbed on the stage.

"Adiós," the girl said to Rick, and she was laughing again as she finished in Spanish: "It's better you return to the Río Tigre quickly."

"What the devil do you know about the Río Tigre?" Rick snapped back in Spanish.

She had stepped away from his back. When he turned, she was beyond reach, showing white teeth in a smile he would never like. The short-barreled gun she carried waved him to the stage step.

The driver had the reins and the whip. Rifles were waiting up there in the rocks. Rick glared at her and swung into the stage.

The long-lashed whip *cracked* like a pistol shot. The driver yanked the three remaining horses wide around the dead animal, swung the stage back into the road beyond, and they rolled toward Laguna.

Rick's hands were unsteady as he rolled and lighted a cigarette. Anger still ran hot and wild through his nerves. He paid no attention to the furtive, half-fearful looks the little drummer was giving him.

She had known his name—and that, perhaps, wasn't so puzzling, for he had the Candlemans' rangy build, high cheek bones, black hair, and dark eyes that old Ross Candleman had given to his three sons. But she couldn't have guessed about the Río Tigre Ranch, down there in the deep pampas of the Argentine. She had to know Candleman business to know that name. And once more Rick had the uneasy feeling that the Iron Hat range held bad luck for him.

II

Laguna had not changed in eight years. The same dun-colored hills and distant mountains brooded under the hot blue sky. The stamp of the border country was in the low, thick-walled adobe houses, hugging the earth that had spawned them. It was Saturday, and wagons and horses were thick at the hitch racks. The same saloons were doing the same brisk business that Rick remembered out of past Saturdays. The three-horse stage pulled up in front of the hotel and Rick looked for familiar faces in the crowd that quickly gathered.

The stage driver piled down, shouting: "Hold-up got the bank shipment! Might be a chance to git it back if a posse starts quick! Where's Dud Sloane?"

Rick saw the angular, familiar face of a young man about his own age and pushed through the crowd.

"Pat, you crop-eared maverick!"

It took an instant for a broad grin of recognition to flash on Pat Cody's face. His hand grabbed Rick's hand.

"I been lookin' for you, Rick! Your brother Dan told me he'd written you to come home."

For the third time Rick had that sharp uneasy sense of trouble waiting here for him. It wiped most of the smile off his face.

"I didn't get the letter, Pat. Must have left before it got there. Is Dan in town?"

"Haven't seen him."

"Why'd he want me to come home?"

"Figured he needed you, I guess."

"Trouble?"

"Always a little trouble one way or another, ain't there?" Pat Cody evaded. "Who jumped the stage?"

"Strangers . . . and a girl who rode from Mission Wells."

"Girl?" Pat said in amazement.

"A redhead. Pretty . . . and a hell-cat behind it. I've never seen one like her, and I've run across some wild ones since I left."

"A redhead?" Pat Cody repeated. He looked startled. His voice sharpened. "Didja see the men?"

"No."

Pat looked quickly around, as if scenting danger or trying to take in quickly what was happening. The crowd had grown. The sheriff had arrived, star pinned on his scuffed leather vest, worry on his broad face as he talked with the old stage driver, the little drummer, and the blocky cowman. And so quiet had the crowd gone around the spot that Rick heard the cowman's rasping words.

"She asked if he wasn't Rick Candleman an' he allowed he was. So what does he do but throw down my gun an' let the feller lope away. An' then he jabbered Mex with her an' climbed back in the stage! I dunno what the name Candleman means around here, but I got my ideas after what I seen. . . ."

Pat Cody's hand closed on Rick's arm, his voice low and urgent.

"Rick, I was headin' out to the ranch. Got a little spread of my own now, a swell wife an' a couple of kids. Come along an' stay with us tonight."

"Right now," said Rick grimly, "I'll drop my loop around that lying loud-mouth talking to the sheriff."

"Don't," Pat pleaded. "There comes Rufus Madden on that horse!"

"Dan wrote me the old trouble I had with Rufe was crossed

off by the law."

"What of it, Rick? Rufe's as ornery as he ever was. He's got a hand in the bank now, since his old man got heart trouble three, four years ago. Come on."

But Rick shook off Pat's restraining hand and pushed through the crowd.

Rufe Madden had dismounted behind the stage and shouldered to the sheriff. Rick reached them as Rufe was speaking angrily.

"There was twelve thousand dollars in the shipment! Maybe more! Sloane, why the devil don't you get after it?"

Rick stopped beside them, and it seemed to him the years rolled away. He felt the inner bristle that always had been there when he was around Rufe Madden since they were kids, meeting at the same little schoolhouse with Rufe's younger sister, Jean. And yet it was like meeting a stranger, too. Rufe had grown heavier, and it all was bad meat, soft and puffy. Rufe's loose mouth had taken on a thick, vindictive set. Dusty black pants were outside Rufe's boots; his dusty hat was pushed back on his curly black hair. His look slid off Rick and he jerked back with startled recognition. "What the devil are you doing here?" Rufe burst out.

Rick spoke to the sheriff. "I'm Rick Candleman. You've just heard one kind of talk about what happened out there on the road. Now I'll give you my say."

Sloane, the sheriff, had silver at his temples and his broad, slack, lazy face was beginning to look harassed.

"Tell it quick," he said without enthusiasm. "I got to get down the road after that money."

The sheriff's eyes were on Rufe Madden as he said it. He listened to Rick's terse story as if his mind were already on other things. Rufe Madden conferred hurriedly in undertones with other men as Rick faced the sheriff, and, as Rick finished,

Rufe's harsh accusation cut in.

"I just heard how Rick Candleman tied in with that hold-up! He's a damned thief and a killer, Sloane, like all the rest of his name. Why the devil don't you lock him up and get going?"

Rick thought as he turned that he might have known something like this would happen. He should have stayed clear from the Iron Hat country. He should never have come back. Then his hard fist smashed Rufe Madden's thick, vindictive mouth, and the fierce satisfaction that flooded him as Rufe went down was tempered by the knowledge that the years had closed up and again he had trouble on the Iron Hat range. Trouble once more with the Maddens. Wasted now were the memories of Jean Madden that had finally brought him back.

Rufe bounced up bellowing from a bloody mouth. Rick knocked him down again. This time Rufe stayed in the dust and the crowd surged back as Rufe snatched under his coat. Rick wasn't armed, and Rufe could see it. But that didn't matter to Rufe Madden. It was as if that furious night eight years back were repeating itself, action by action. Rick could have told them all what Rufe would try to do, and, because he knew, Rick moved fast and mercilessly. A jump brought his sharp-heeled boot and full weight down with paralyzing force on Rufe's elbow. Rufe yelled with pain and Rick caught the arm, heaved and slammed the heavy figure over on the ground.

Fury out of the past and of the present kept Rick from stopping there. Rufe's hat had fallen off. Rick grabbed the black curly hair and drove Rufe's puffy face hard into the dust again and again. He would have stopped after a moment and taken Rufe's gun away and let him up. But men caught him and hustled him back, holding his arms.

The red-faced sheriff jumped in front of Rick as Rufe Madden scrambled up. Rufe's face was smeared with blood and dirt and his eyes were half blinded by dust as he pawed under his coat.

"Don't try it, Rufe!" the sheriff yelled. "I'll have to lock you up, too! A mess like this ain't gettin' the bank's money back! Grab Rufe, men! He don't know what he's doin'!"

Rick smiled crookedly. Rufe knew exactly what he was doing. Nothing the matter with Rufe's calculating mind, ever. But then, even Rufe Madden couldn't shoot a man who was shielded by the sheriff and held by other men. Rufe pulled out a handkerchief instead of the gun and wiped eyes and face. A smile forced out on his bloody lips, already beginning to puff. He peered at Rick, then without a word he turned back to his horse, mounted, angled down the street and across to the bank, still wiping at his face.

"We'll settle all this after I git back," the sheriff told Rick angrily. "Come along now . . . I'm gonna lock you up."

Part of the crowd followed them to the jail. From a cell Rick heard the posse collecting out in front, heard the drumbeat of departing horses.

Rick rolled a cigarette, sucked in the smoke, and smiled crookedly at his bruised knuckles. All the trouble he could handle. The Maddens wouldn't let it rest at this. If there was any way of pinning that stage hold-up on him, they'd see that it was done. Rick's smile left when he got to that point. His mind switched hard to the hold-up and the red-headed girl. She'd known too much about him. The stage driver's manner had been peculiar when he heard the name Candleman. And Pat Cody's manner and words hadn't been any more reassuring. Rick looked up as a man stepped into the cells. It was Pat Cody, keys in hand, a grin on his angular face.

"Might as well move out while everybody's busy," Pat said as he unlocked the cell door.

"How come?" Rick demanded as he emerged.

"I deputied around for old man Sloane. He's a forgetful cuss," Pat said. "Likely to leave his keys anywhere. He hides an extra set in the bottom drawer of his desk, just in case. Thinks he's the only one that knows about it. He'll figure you found a mouse hole an' crawled through, an'll get drunk trying to puzzle it out. I got a horse for you out back with mine. We'll ride to my place, over on the north fork of the Sugarleaf, across the hills from your land."

No one noticed them as they kept off the main street, rode out of town, and put the horses into a lope.

"Let's have it," Rick said soberly. "What's wrong?"

"I figured you knew."

"Those two brothers of mine never were much on writing letters. If there was trouble, they'd be the last ones to bother me with it."

"Dan bothered you this time, Rick . . . only you didn't get it. I might as well tell you what everyone knows. Joe's gone bad. The Maddens claimed they caught him rustling. There was some shooting. Joe killed a man in the posse that tried to round him up and skipped across the border."

Rick's low whistle was amazed. "Joe rustling? He's only a kid."

"He growed up while you were gone," Pat said dryly. "Dan says Joe told him he wasn't rustling. But it was too late then to matter. Joe threw in with a hard bunch of border jumpers. Made no bones about it when he met the men across the line that he knew. They hole up over there under the wing of a half-breed named Sebastian Obrion, who cuts some ice as a politico in the Domingo section. And they raise plenty of hell on this side. Half the dirt that's done along this stretch of the border can be laid to the bunch."

"And Dan couldn't straighten Joe out?"

"Dan's had his hands full with his own troubles," Pat said

bluntly. "Word's been around for some time that Dan must have a tie-in with the Obrion riders. Don't matter that he's lost cattle like everyone else. Folks have got the idea those border jumpers are always welcome at Dan's place and Dan cuts in on some of their pickings."

"Anybody who knew Dan would know it was a dirty lie."

"A man gets to believing things he hears when he's being thieved out himself, Rick."

"It's because of Joe."

"Sure . . . but there it is. A man got a black eye just working for Dan. Three of his hands quit before he wrote you. Left him with old Cady Sowers. Dan'll be glad to see you, Rick."

Rick said slowly: "Not after the extra dust I've kicked up in coming here. Last letter I had from Dan almost a year ago didn't mention a thing." Rick rolled a cigarette and kept his eyes on it as he said casually: "Dan's letter said Jean Madden busted up with a fellow she was going to marry. She made the jump since?"

"Nope. It was Curt Hanna. Likely-looking fellow who bought out the Cross Bit spread after you left. Hanna's done well. He's a friend of Rufe Madden's and has bought into the bank. It looked like a good match. Nobody ever heard that Jean and Hanna had trouble. Surprised everyone when Jean busted it off at the last minute and never said why. She and Curt Hanna still seem to be friends, too. Just one of those things, I guess."

"That red-headed girl in the stagecoach meant something to you," Rick said abruptly.

"And to everybody else who heard a redhead had a hand in the business and faded off with the men," Pat admitted. "This Sebastian Obrion is a redhead and so is his sister, Maisa. Their father was a red-headed Irishman named O'Brien. They Mexed up the name and dug in over there. Talk has it that Obrion's red-headed sister and Joe are next thing to married . . . if they ain't married. Anyway, Joe's crazy about her . . . and, if the devil had red hair and skirts, he'd probably be her."

Rick nodded and rode in silence, thinking how bad it was. And when they crossed the deep, dry gash of the Arroyo Hondo, Rick nodded toward the brush-covered hills rising west of them.

"I'll cut off this way to the home place. I want to see Dan."

Pat nodded in understanding. "Dan'll feel the same way. I haven't seen him in better'n a week, but I guess he's waitin' for you. If there's anything I can do, ride over and name it."

That next hour's ride was the hardest Rick had ever made. There wasn't much left to think about. Joe, the slim straight kid brother with blue eyes and friendly grin, had taken his way and would have to cut his own tally.

Dan, the older, was messed up and tangled up. He might have a plan, but probably he didn't. Rick himself couldn't have arrived in worse circumstances. They both were tarred with the same black outlaw stick that Joe had brought home to the Candlemans. Rick's throat tightened a little when he passed the home fences and swung over to a solitary cow and read the familiar CA brand on hip and shoulder. He rode faster toward the meeting with Dan. And when he reached the trickle of water in Gunshot Creek, Rick pulled up short, staring.

Gunshot Creek's sands were white and dry as usual. On the other side, upstream, the tall cottonwoods thrust into the late sunlight as Rick had remembered through the years. The old thick-walled adobe house was there, too. But it was different. Windows and doors were gaping. Faint blue curls of smoke drifted lazily from where the roof should be. Buzzards were wheeling in the blue sky and the challenging nicker of a horse at the back corner of the house was the only life Rick could make out as he slashed his own horse into a gallop.

The creekbed hid him for a moment, and, when he rode up under the cottonwoods, the strange horse and a rider were poised to leave. The man had jerked a rifle from the saddle scabbard and held it ready. The place had been burned out. And the wheeling buzzards signaled death.

"What happened here?" Rick called roughly, and a second later saw the rider was a girl. Then he recognized the girl and a stifled gladness held him wordless as he rode to her.

"Rick!"

He nodded, seeing her for an instant in short dresses at school, and later slim and eager in the year they had drawn close before he went away. She was older now, lovelier in her mid twenties, and uneasily he noticed that her eyes were tearful.

"Dan said you were coming, Rick."

"Where's Dan?"

"There," Jean said huskily, pointing to the back of the house. "And Cady Sowers, too. Inside. I . . . I had to make sure before I left. Oh, Rick!"

III

The air reeked of charred wood and dying fire as Rick saw Dan Candleman lying in the back doorway. Sowers, inside the building, had not been so fortunate. The heavy log *vigas* of the burning building had crashed in on Sowers. His body was half buried in the roof wreckage. But Sowers had been dead from a head wound before the roof fell. Haystacks, the old bunkhouse, saddle shed, and store house, all had been burned.

Jean was with the two horses, wiping her eyes, when Rick came back to her with a stony face.

"Any idea what happened, Jean?"

She shook her head. "I rode over to ask Dan again when you were coming. Rick . . . Dan didn't expect anything like this! He was worried, but not about *this!*"

Bitterly Rick told her: "Dan never could figure that men can be as dirty as they are." And with the same bitterness: "I tangled with Rufe again as soon as I got in Laguna."

"Was it necessary?"

"Maybe not. I could have agreed with Rufe." He told her what had happened. "Jean, you know Candlemans and Maddens never got along. I didn't help my family any when I tangled with Rufe eight years ago and rode away from here."

"Rufe said the trouble was over me, Rick. I've always felt I was to blame."

Rick shrugged. "If it hadn't been you, it would have been something else. Joe hit the Candlemans harder when he went bad. This stage hold-up today makes it worse. Joe might have been back there in the rocks himself, sighting a gun on the stage. Chances were he was, if that redhead was his girl. Maybe that's why I didn't get shot when I jumped out and took a hand."

Jean stayed pale and silent, and Rick turned to the ruin behind them. "The Candlemans didn't do *this.* It was done before the stage hold-up. Dan and the old man in there couldn't have had much chance. Neither one has got a gun that I can see. They weren't looking for trouble. Dan opened the door and got shot down like a dog. And then Sowers got it and the place was fired over their bodies. It was murder, Jean . . . murder, to get the last Candleman out of the way around here. Who'd do that?"

Jean was pale. "I don't know, Rick."

He seemed to have forgotten her for the moment. "I didn't see much beef inside Dan's fences. Looks like the place is cleaned out. Joe wouldn't have done that to his brother. I wonder who knew I was coming home."

"I don't know," Jean said huskily. But her pallor was intense; something like fright was in her look.

Rick eyed her without comment. It was impossible to guess what was in his mind. "It's late. Better start home," he said.

"I . . . I can ride to Laguna and let them know."

"Laguna didn't help Dan while he was alive," Rick answered her shortly. "I'll do what's needed here . . . alone."

Jean rode away without looking back.

Rick finished by firelight. The graves were under the cottonwoods beside the creek. No coffins, no shrouds. He'd been lucky to find an unburned shovel. Dan would stay here as he had lived, the last Candleman on the place. But not the last Candleman.

It was late when he reached Pat Cody's. Barking dogs brought Pat out.

"Trouble, Rick?" Pat guessed.

"A little." Rick got stiffly out of the saddle and tersely told his story. "Everybody around here knew I was coming back," he guessed.

"Dan told me he'd written you to come. Said he'd told Jean Madden, too. That's all I know of."

"That's good enough. Got a fresh horse, a rifle, and a gun?"

"Sleep on it, tonight," Pat urged. "If the men who killed Dan are around these parts, you'll be jumping right under their sights. The law's after you anyway. They'll have you where they want you."

"I'm riding south after Joe," Rick said.

"I'll get your outfit," Pat yielded. And when the fresh horse was saddled, sandwiches stuffed in the saddle pockets, rifle in the saddle boot, belt gun and cartridges strapped on Rick, they had a final smoke out under the stars.

"I hate to see you riding for trouble, Rick."

"I ran away once," Rick said slowly. "I thought I was staying down there in the Argentine because I was making money and liking it. But mostly I guess I was staying away from trouble. I knew, if I came back, there'd be Candlemans tangling with Maddens again. It's been that way ever since Ross Candleman and Cory Madden settled in these parts and had their trouble over water rights in the year of the big drive."

"I know," Pat agreed. "But it don't have to keep up."

"I'll see you before I start back south," Rick said.

Two days later he was in the Domingo country south of the border. From a cactus-studded rise he saw, far off, the blood-red sheen of the setting sun on water that would be the Laguna de Domingo. The blot of low adobe houses and trees on the west shore of the lagoon was Domingo, crossroads for open and furtive trails a hundred miles in any direction. He had been there once as a boy, with his father. He had thought Domingo pretty then, the three-sided little plaza opening on the placid lagoon, the sandy winding streets vanishing back among the low sprawling adobe houses and corrals. But big Ross Candleman had carefully barred the door of the low patio room behind a *cantina* where they had spent the night, and had slept with loaded gun under his pillow.

Years afterward Rick remembered the noisy music, loud talk, yells, and singing of the night. Gunshots, too, and in the middle of the night a man's cry outside their door. In the morning he had seen drying blood on the patio flagstones, and understood with hot excitement that death had stopped outside their door in the night. Now once more in the town, Rick again had the feeling of death as he stepped inside the *cantina* where he had slept as a boy.

Massive ceiling beams were dark with age. Dull brass lamps threw heat into the smoky reek. Mexicans and *Americanos* were in the place, girls from both sides of the border. A drunken peon in rags snored in a dark corner. Men were arguing at the end of the bar. A few couples were dancing. Later there would probably be more dancers and the night would become wilder. Men looked him over as he drank at the bar. Strangers were under suspicion in a town like this until their business was known.

A Mexican barman with drooping black mustache and beady eyes shook his head when Rick asked where Joe would be. A man who had stepped in at Rick's shoulder said: "You looking for Joe Candleman, too, stranger?"

The speaker was as tall as Rick, broader and a few years older. He was American, dressed in dusty gray broadcloth, a silver-mounted gun visible under his coat. Teeth flashed in his heavy handsome face and his eyes crinkled.

"I'm Pete Jones."

"I'm Pete Smith," Rick said briefly.

"Drink?"

"Another'll hold down the first one." Rick grinned.

They were smiling as they drank. Jones looked like a prosperous cattleman. "They say Joe Candleman ought to be back tonight sometime. He'll stop in here."

"Who says so?"

"Sebastian Obrion, his brother-in-law." Jones twisted his glass between strong white fingers and grinned, but his eyes were thoughtful. "You remind me some of Joe Candleman. Same build . . . something about your faces. Joe Candleman's a great boy."

"I haven't seen him lately," Rick said briefly. "Maybe you can tell me where his brother-in-law lives."

"Right now," said Jones, "he's back there at the corner table."

"Thanks," said Rick. "Thanks for the drink, too." He wondered as he left the bar how crooked the American was. He looked like a prosperous cattleman who had crossed the border to turn a shady deal in beef.

Then the man at the corner table took all Rick's attention. He was built in the shoulders like a bull. The hat pushed back on his head showed challenging red hair. Seeing the brother, you would know the girl who had ridden in the Laguna stage.

"I'm Joe Candleman's brother," Rick said bluntly. "Where's Joe?"

Obrion drained his beer glass. He could pass for either American or Mexican, but his smile was Latin. "So? Dan Candleman?"

"I'm Rick Candleman."

"Ah . . . the one from South America?" Obrion stood up, chuckling as he dropped a heavy arm on Rick's shoulder. "José is a brother to me. *Señor* Rick, you are of the family. Command me."

South of the equator you lived with such courtesy. Rick stayed blunt. "Where's Joe?"

"*¿Quién sabe?*" Obrion said expansively. "He will be here."

"A sign on the backbar says they've got rooms here. I'll put up my horse and catch some rest," Rick decided.

Sebastian Obrion rapped on the table with an empty beer bottle. The man who hurried to them was short, bloated, and swarthy.

"A room, hot water, and a razor, anything my friend wants. And his horse will be put in my corral," Obrion ordered expansively.

It was done so hurriedly that a stranger could not doubt Obrion's power in these parts. In a patio room Rick washed, shaved in hot water brought in a bucket, and dropped on the bed and closed his eyes for half an hour.

He felt better when he got up. He dressed, blew out the lamp, and stepped out to see about Joe. Furtive movement in the darkness at the left of the door made him lunge suddenly that way.

He caught an arm—and, because he remembered this patio from past years, Rick was fast and rough in grabbing the stranger's throat and slamming him against the wall. The match he thumbed into flame showed a dapper little Mexican with fear-popping eyes and purpling face.

"Crawled out of a rat-hole to snoop on me, eh?" Rick snapped in Spanish.

"*Madre mía,* I was but looking for my room."

"You found it. *¡Vamos!*" Rick sent the man stumbling across the dark patio.

A low-vaulted passage led to a door in the end of the big barroom where music and noise were louder now. Rick was halfway through the doorway when he caught sight of the red-headed girl of the Laguna stage—Joe's wife. He had expected to meet her here, had guessed Joe had been with her across the border. But Joe's wife here in the *cantina* was not what stopped Rick in mid-stride. Sebastian Obrion's sister was the type who would go where she pleased in Domingo. No, it was the sight of Jean Madden at the same table, smiling at the man who called himself Jones, that wrung a stifled oath from Rick.

He could see Jean had ridden hard and long. She looked tired. She must have started south quickly after leaving Dan's body and the smoldering ranch house. Her friendliness with the lot of them at the table turned Rick cold and bleak. But Joe wasn't there. While Rick looked over the crowd for him, the dapper little Mexican Rick had shoved into the dark wall sidled to Sebastian Obrion's ear with a message.

Obrion had put a watch on Joe's brother and was getting his report. Rick turned back to his room, got his rifle, locked the door, and tossed the key out in the dark patio. Years ago there had been another vaulted passage at the back of the patio and a barred door leading outside. The door was still there.

He had seen his horse being led to Obrion's corral. He went there now. The two peons in charge squatted beside a tiny fire at one corner of the shed. The men showed no surprise. Strangers evidently came and went from Sebastian Obrion's corral at all hours of the day and night. Because Obrion's orders had covered everything he might want, Rick tried for a fresh horse.

"Sí, señor," he was told readily.

The fire flared as the other man dropped on a twist of hay. Rick peered at the uneasy horses. "That big bay ought to do."

"Another one, *señor.* That is the horse of *Don* José Candleman."

"So, he's back, is he?"

"*Don* José is in the bed with a lame foot, *señor.*"

"Where's his house?"

"Where but the house of *Don* Sebastian?"

"I'll take that black horse," Rick said quickly, and, when he rode from the corral, he had directions for finding Obrion's house.

A block beyond the plaza, facing the downslope to the lagoon, Obrion's house looked big and massive for all of being one story high. Iron bars covered the windows. The single narrow entrance through a roofed passage to the patio was closed by an iron grillwork gate. The gate was locked. But a shadowy, blanket-wrapped figure rose up from the passage floor.

"I will see *Don* José," Rick said in Spanish, and it hardly seemed he could be talking about his kid brother.

"Don José is asleep, *señor.*"

"Wake him up."

"*Don* José will not see anyone," was the surly answer.

Rick grabbed through the gate bars, got the blanket, the shoulder under it, yanked the figure close against the gate. His gun jabbing through the bars stopped a warning cry.

"Open up!" Rick said viciously.

The place was bigger than he had suspected. There was a back wing and a back patio, and in a corner of that back wing the gateman knocked on the door of a lighted room. A lusty bellow of Spanish answered.

Rick pushed the gateman into the room and followed. Joe Candleman was in a chair by a table with his bandaged left foot propped on another chair. Joe had been oiling a gold-mounted six-gun. He stared and lurched up with a delighted yell.

"Rick! My God, what're *you* doing here?"

It was hard to find the kid brother in this tall, muscular young fellow with a lean, reckless face. Joe was a man now. But he was more. Joe was hard. Even while he laughed delightedly and pumped Rick's hand, his eyes were gray slate and there were lines on Joe's face that should not be there at his age.

"Can this *pelado* speak English?" Rick asked.

"Only a few words," Joe said. "What's the idea of bringing him in here this way?"

"He tried to keep me out. Said you weren't seeing anybody. Your brother-in-law told me over at the *cantina* that you were out of town. He got me a room at the *cantina,* and then put a man watching me."

"So?" said Joe. He was smiling as he took a limping step, slapped the peon, and demanded why the house was barred against this visitor. He had to slap the man again before he got the whimpered answer that *Don* Sebastian's orders had been followed.

Joe cursed him, shoved him to a corner, and sat down. "I don't know what this means, Rick. I'll find out when Sebastian comes in. Horse pitched me off the other day and sprained my ankle."

"He should have broken your neck," Rick said in a level voice.

Joe went sulky as he looked up. "Never mind saying it. This is the way it turned out. It's my hard luck and my business."

It was like speaking to a stranger. Joe's gray eyes were slate-hard now, but Rick was hard, too. "It's my business when I find the name Candleman means something low-down and no-good. It was Dan's business, too."

"Dan gets along."

"He will now," Rick agreed. "He's dead . . . murdered. And the house burned down over him. I buried Dan myself before I started south."

Joe's mouth opened. He suddenly looked older, stricken. "Tell me about it," he said thickly.

Rick told him with cold, edged words.

The handsome recklessness was gone from Joe's face as he stood up. He talked jerkily as he limped around the room.

"Last time I saw Dan was a couple of months ago. He was worried about money to make a payment to the Laguna bank. But he wouldn't take my money. Said it was blood money."

"Wasn't it?"

"Hell, don't rub it in, Rick. I told Dan the Laguna bank wasn't any better. A man named Curt Hanna who bought into the bank after you left had been working with Sebastian Obrion since before I had my trouble and jumped the border. Sebastian got drunk and let it out just before I saw Dan. That's how Sebastian always has luck when he sends men across the border."

"That's all I need," Rick said. "It was worth riding here to get it. Dan was the kind to threaten this Curt Hanna and the bank that he was going to make trouble. I guess that's when he wrote me to come help."

"Funny, ain't it?" Joe said, grinning crookedly. "Me an outlaw here across the border . . . and the Madden bank back there in Laguna riding high and holy?"

"Funny," Rick agreed. "The Maddens got as low-down as you made the Candlemans . . . only they stayed smarter. Good bye, Joe."

Joe had tied a rope-soled sandal on his bad foot, had put on gun belt and coat. Now he caught a sombrero off a wall peg. "Let's go, Rick."

Behind Rick in the doorway a woman said: "*Querido mío,*

where do you go?"

Joe's red-headed wife had returned in riding clothes. A braided quirt still dangled from her wrist. She was, Rick thought, something half wild and dangerously lovely as she smiled at Joe.

"Rick says he met you on the stage," Joe said. "We're riding, Maisa."

She was not surprised at Rick's presence. Obrion had evidently told her he was here in Domingo, but she begged Joe quickly: "I'm just back . . . and you're leaving me?"

"I told you to let that stage alone, Maisa."

"But it was fun. Please, Josito . . . don't leave me tonight."

Joe answered her deliberately. "Maisa, you're like fire in the night near gunpowder . . . pretty as hell, but a man never knows what'll happen. I'm tired of wondering and not liking most of the things that happen. I hate to say it in front of my own brother . . . but, when they cut hang ropes for all of us, they'll need one for you, too. Now go to bed or figure out some dirt with your brother. I'm riding with Rick."

The wild, stormy side of her blazed at him then. "Joe, you fool! You can't go with him! Suppose your brother Dan is dead? You can't help him! You belong here with us! You've got to take what happens along with all of us!"

Joe took a step and caught her wrist. "What do you know about Dan? Did you and Slim and the boys kill Dan while you were over there taking that stage?"

"No, Joe! I didn't know about it until I got back! Sebastian told. . . ."

She stopped abruptly, frightened by the look on Joe's face.

IV

Only that look on Joe's face kept Rick quiet, coldly waiting for what Joe would do. And Joe, even a stranger could have seen, was meeting his own hell as he looked at his red-headed wife. The hell wrenched out in Joe's voice.

"So Sebastian had my brother killed?"

She was suddenly like a lovely trapped cat, too frightened now to flare and fight with her temper and willfulness. Joe was not hurting her arm, but a low moan of denial came from her.

"Not Sebastian, Joe. He didn't have anything to do with it. But he knows about it. Just today he knows, I think. And he's angry. He told me that your brother Dan was going to make trouble for Curt Hanna and his partner in Laguna. Dan warned Hanna there would be trouble. Curt Hanna's here in Domingo now."

"Why?" Joe asked through tight lips.

"For his share of the bank's money we brought back. Sebastian is with him at the *cantina.*"

Rick spoke to her quietly. "Curt Hanna is the big fellow who was talking to Jean Madden at your table?"

"Jean Madden?" Joe blurted.

Maisa said: "We found her on the trail with a lame horse. She was riding here to meet her brother."

"Why does she have to meet her brother here across the border?"

Rick answered Joe's question with rough bitterness that had seethed since his sight of Jean at the *cantina* table. "She followed Rufe here to warn him trouble's coming fast about Dan. She's a Madden. I used to think different . . . but there it is. Rufe must have started this way after I tangled with him in Laguna."

Joe glared at his wife. "Is Rufe Madden here, too?"

She swallowed, nodded. "He came in the *cantina* just before I left."

Joe let go of her wrist. His voice was deadly. "Maisa, you got into my blood like a fever I couldn't shake off. I stood a lot.

This is the end. Don't leave this room or let Gregorio out until I tell you to."

"Joe, don't go! You'll get into trouble!"

"You heard me," Joe said, turning to the door.

Rick wouldn't have believed until this moment that tears would ever soften terror in her eyes as they did now.

"Josito," she pleaded, "Sebastian needs those men from the Laguna bank. You know Sebastian. He thinks only of himself."

"I know Sebastian," Joe said, and hobbled out behind Rick.

"Robbing that Laguna stage was kinda snapping at the hand that fed him, wasn't it?" Rick said.

"Not the way the Laguna bank is run," Joe grunted. "They'll claim they lost twice as much as Maisa and the boys got. It'll cover a lot that's already been taken out of the bank. Hanna'll get some gold from this end, too, as his cut. Everybody wins but the other stockholders in the bank. That's the way Hanna and Rufe Madden do business."

They fell into silence as they crossed the dark back patio. And the silence was a bond from the past. . . .

In the front patio Rick's hand dropped to his gun as they unexpectedly met Sebastian Obrion hurrying back toward Joe's room.

"José?" Obrion called, stopping.

"It's Joe tonight," was the short answer. "Joe Candleman and Rick Candleman. What the devil's the idea of having Rick kept out of the house?"

"So?" Obrion said. He chuckled. "Have you seen Maisa?"

"Yes."

"Then you know my friend Hanna is here from Laguna. And he's angry, Joe, because your brother Dan promised him trouble for the bank. *Dios* . . . what can I do? I told Hanna you were away from Domingo. It is better that you don't go to the *cantina* now, eh?"

"Sebastian, you're damned careful of me all of a sudden," Joe snapped.

Sebastian Obrion chuckled. "OK, Joe. You're going to the *cantina,* no? But I told you."

"Yeah," Joe said. "I'll remember it. Is the Madden girl there with her brother and Hanna?"

"So now you ask me," Obrion said, shrugging his big shoulders. "At the *cantina,* Joe, if you got to know."

"Fine," Joe said. "Come along."

"Later. First I will see Maisa."

"I told you not to make a mistake about me tonight," Joe said in sudden warning. "Watch him, Rick, while I see why there's a light in that room over there where guests are always put."

"*Por Dios,* Joe!"

But Joe had already faded across the dark patio, limping toward a thin thread of light at a curtained window.

Obrion swore angrily under his breath. "I wash my hands of it. Good night."

"Hold it," Risk said, hand on his gun. "Joe knows what he's doing."

The door opened to Joe's knock, letting out yellow light. The murmur of voices came to them. Obrion again swore angrily.

Then the door closed. Joe started limping back to them. And Sebastian Obrion gave a shrill piercing whistle and jumped back.

Rick drew fast. He could have shot the man. But he was not here to kill Sebastian Obrion in his own house. The black shadows to the front of the patio swallowed Obrion's plunging form.

"Who whistled?" Joe called.

"Obrion. He's running out the front!"

Joe cursed. "I knew he was pulling a ranny on us! Come on!"

They bolted through the passage together, Joe moving as

quickly as he could, his face taut in a grimace. But when they got outside, a running horse was fading off into the night, and Rick's horse was gone.

"We need horses first," Joe panted. "This place is full of gunnies who cut wood when Obrion yells whittle. Let's get to the corral. Sebastian was lying, Rick. Jean Madden was in that room. He knew she was there all the time. Keep your gun handy."

As they moved side-by-side through the night, Rick held his pace in rein with Joe's. His brother muttered: "No use wondering who Sebastian's siding with. I could have told you. He's for anything that makes him money."

Joe was gasping for breath from the strain as they ran down the alley that sided the Obrion pole corral. The tiny fire was burning at the corner of the saddle shed. The two peon hostlers were squatting beside it, smoking, as Rick emerged from the shadows, Joe directly behind him.

"Two horses saddled quick!" Joe called in Spanish. "My El Rey and another."

One of the hostlers threw an armful of hay on the fire as Joe started clumsily toward the saddle shed. As the flaming hay blazed light over the corral, Rick yelled: "Down, Joe!"

Rick's gun fired at the corner of the saddle shed where a man had appeared with a rifle sighted at Joe. The licking flame above the dry hay made the target clear. The rifle bullet tore into Joe as Rick's gun fired.

The men dodged back into the shed, and Joe went spinning, staggering off to the right, hit badly, helpless, without even a chance to draw his own gun as he plunged to the ground.

Rick felt a cold shock in his left leg, heard the rifle shot back across the corral. His first hunch on the Laguna stage had been right. The Iron Hat range was poison for him. First, Dan dead in the burned ranch house. Then Jean Madden to mock the memories that had brought him on the long journey back. Then Joe, outlawed and gone bad. And when he had Joe back at his side, as a brother once more for a night, this ambush had dropped Joe with a treacherous shot. And here death was spitting across the corral at him.

But he could still move, still keep his feet—and Rick ran, now limping himself, to the fire. He heard a second rifle shot behind him. It missed him or hit Joe, crawling torturously on the ground. Rick ran through the fire, kicking hard, scattering blazing hay and wood embers in a shower of sparks, flame, and smoke. And in the flare of light it made, Rick dived to the ground at the end of the saddle shed.

The peons had vanished. Frightened horses were whinnying and raising dust as they bolted around the corral. The scattered fire died to a duller glow.

The long gun's thin report came again across the corral. The bullet screamed away into the night. And from behind the gun a voice shouted: "He's there at the end of the shed, Curt! I hit him! Go out an' get him!"

But Curt Hanna was swearing, groaning inside the adobe end wall of the shed, and he did not answer. Another rifle bullet drove dirt particles from the adobe wall into Rick's face.

"Curt, are you gonna get him?"

Rick answered with bitter fury out of the past years. "Try it yourself, Rufe! Or aren't you man enough?"

"I'm man enough!" Rufe's shout came back through the rising dust that was hampering his shooting. "I was man enough to get that damn' brother Dan of yours! You'll be the last one, Rick Candleman! We got Dan first before you could get back. And soon as I found out you'd skipped jail, I started across the border to catch you with Joe, if Hanna hadn't killed Joe first as he started out to do. I knew you'd head this way to hook up with him. We're sending the last of the Candlemans to hell tonight! And Sebastian Obrion's bringing his men to help. Come out and get it before some of Obrion's men drag you out!"

Dust was drifting thicker over the dying fire glow as Rick came out, his hands reaching for the top pole of the corral. He went over fast, falling on the dirt outside, and there was no shot from Rufe Madden's gun. The milling horses, the dust, the dying fire light might have kept Rufe from seeing him.

Half a dozen freight wagons stood outside the back of the corral. When Rick passed them and turned the next corner of the corral, he heard the obscene taunts of Rufe Madden ahead. He saw Rufe's dark bulk crouching, sighting a rifle through the corral poles.

"Come get the last Candleman, Rufe!"

Rufe Madden whirled, snatching the rifle back from the corral bars. It was too dark to see Rufe's thick, vindictive face, but he was caught by surprise. His hasty shot missed.

Rick ran at him, shooting. The first one missed. Rufe had time to lever in another cartridge and start to snap shoot. He never pulled the trigger. Rick's lead smashed him on down to the ground.

Rick stopped for an instant to make sure it was done, and kept going to the corral gate, which he jerked wide. Joe was flat on the ground in that dangerous mill of frightened horses.

A running figure reached the gate as Rick started in. He almost drove a bullet before he recognized Maisa Candleman.

"Where's Joe?" she cried at him. "I heard shooting!"

"Joe's down here under the horses," Rick snarled at her. "Rufe Madden did it . . . but your damned brother's in on it! Going to wipe out all the Candlemans tonight. Get outta here before I forget you're a woman!"

But she darted into the corral. Rick followed her. And the nearest horses instantly found the open gate and went out in a thundering, frightened stampede.

A gun blasted loudly in the middle of the corral, and, when Rick plunged through the settling dust, he found Joe sprawled on his face, six-gun still in his hand. Beyond Joe, near a smoldering brand from the fire, lay big handsome Curt Hanna with his face to the stars and the ugly smashed hole of a .45 bullet in his right cheek. Joe had done that and collapsed again.

When Rick turned back, he found Maisa Candleman down in the dirt and dust, holding Joe's head, crooning and crying to him.

"Joe, speak to me! My dear! My dearest *querido!* My big, brave *niño!* Joe, if you die, your Maisa dies, too."

"You're wastin' your breath," Rick said harshly. "Here comes your brother and a bunch of his hardcases to finish it off. Get outta the way. Lemme drag Joe in the shed and make a fight of it."

Maisa gave him no answer. He might not have been there as she caught the big .45 from Joe's hand and whirled up, facing the corral. Some light still came from the last embers of the fire. Enough to show the wild frantic passion on the red-headed girl's features as she stood over Joe and faced the gate with the gun cocked.

Rick had heard the shouts of running men, had guessed correctly. Sebastian Obrion had gone to the plaza for help. Now Rick knew what was coming; his crawling nerves cried to get under cover in the saddle shed. And yet he could not leave Joe out here in the open with his wife. Rick crouched, gun ready, waiting for the shot that would start the end of the Candlemans.

But the shadowy forms that ran to the outside of the corral stopped there uncertainly as they saw the girl facing them. Then Sebastian Obrion's angry shout came from among them.

"Come out, Maisa! Get back to the house!"

"Not until he's dead!" she cried wildly back at her brother. "And when he dies, then I come to kill you, Sebastian! I swear it on our mother's grave! Tonight I promise you, Sebastian Obrion, I kill you for this thing you have done to my Joe! Shoot me now! If he dies, then I die, too, anyway! And now I shoot the first one who comes near my Joe!"

In the silence that followed, a rough amazed comment from one of the gunmen burst out: "Does she *mean* it? Sebastian, she's your sister! It's up to you!"

Sebastian Obrion's reply through the corral bars was injured. "Maisa, this is not my work! Hanna and Madden came here to do this!"

She cried back: "What do I care about them now? They're dead! You are the one who can hurt Joe! Come here, Sebastian, like a man, and face me over my Joe!"

"I don't think I can do that now," Sebastian Obrion refused out of the night. "But if Madden and Hanna are dead, Maisa, what have I to do with this? I didn't come across the border to kill your Joe."

"You lie, Sebastian!"

"I swear it," said Sebastian reasonably. "If Hanna and Madden are dead, what do we gain by hurting my sister? Put up the gun so we can help Joe."

"I think he means it," Rick said.

"Where there is no money to make, he means it," she choked, and lowered the gun and dropped to her knees beside Joe again.

Joe was stirring, speaking Rick's name painfully. Rick went to a knee quickly. Joe's dirt-crusted face worked in a painful grin.

"I heard most of it, Rick. Ain't she somethin' to love? I told her she was in my blood like a fever, an' she was, an' always will be."

"I don't blame you, kid," Rick said with a lump in his throat. "How bad you shot?"

"Can't tell. It's up under my shoulder. Kinda numbs me but there ain't any blood in my mouth yet. Rick, listening to Maisa made me think of something I almost forgot, the way things happened so quick. That Jean Madden was all tore up about you when I talked to her in the doorway. She came across the border lookin' for you. Said Pat Cody told her you was headin' this way. Her brother Rufe had come home, questioned her sharp about you, and saddled for a trip. She figured Rufe was coming after you an' she outrode him to get here ahead of him and warn you he was coming. Said she told Maisa and the others she was lookin' for Rufe, so they wouldn't stop her getting to you when you showed up. Rick, she was near crying for worry about you."

"Joe," said Rick in a shaking voice, "you aren't lying to me?"

"Would I lie, Rick, when I'm this close to heaven and with Maisa to think about for myself?" Joe denied weakly. "Seems like you ought to do something about Jean Madden, Rick."

"I came back from the Argentine to do it," Rick confessed. "Joe, they're going to take you to the house. I'll see you there."

Joe was grinning knowingly as Rick stood up and Obrion's men swarmed around the spot. They were used to bullet wounds. They'd take care of Joe as well as anyone.

But Rick turned back, pushed through the men, and knelt again by Joe.

"Joe, I'm going back to the Argentine quick now. There's plenty of place for you and your wife down there . . . and nobody worries about what's happened in the past up in this part of the world. It'll be a home and a chance again."

Joe was still smiling faintly up at the dark sky, his face pale in the moonlight, when Rick suddenly realized that he and Maisa were alone, and turned blindly away. Maisa let out a scream and yanked Joe's body to her.

Rick rose then and passed silently among the Mexicans who

had gathered around Joe in the corral, not seeing them. He vanished in the shadows of the night, but he had been walking in the direction of the room Obrion reserved for guests.

★ ★ ★ ★ ★

Shafter Range

★ ★ ★ ★ ★

I

The slash of brilliant lightning in the night sky above Azul gave Shafter first warning. He was leaving a feed corral's arched gateway west of the Azul plaza, carrying saddlebags and carbine, whistling by habit, when the livid glare filled the dusty street. A waiting buggy loomed for an instant off to the right, and Shafter had the quick, alerting sense of danger that was to stay with him. The gray horse and the dun horse in the buggy harness had passed him in the noisy plaza short minutes ago as he rode through, seeking a livery barn or corral. A strange buggy had followed a man who had not entered this town of Azul in twenty years—since a boy of nine, and then only one night.

Shafter was achingly tired after grinding days of riding south out of western Colorado. He was ravenously hungry. But as blackness returned and thunder growled across the rooftops, his impulse was to settle the mystery quickly. Hot-headed impulses, Shafter long ago had learned, were treacherous indulgence. Still whistling, he turned toward the plaza, walking with long, tired strides. The buggy, he hoped, would follow; his thoughts, meanwhile, jumped to the completely fantastic letter from old Johnny Carr that had caused this hurried trip to Azul.

Old Johnny had written the stuff of which dreams were made—and men killed—and Shafter believed not a word of it.

Michael, my boy—hear the corks? The champagne corks? We're rich. We can't lose unless we're killed. Meet me in Azul about the 21st. Don't fail me, Michael.

Yrs., John Randolph Carr

Shafter's smile came wryly. Champagne again for old Johnny, who had known champagne well—and all that went with it. Unless we're killed. . . . The threat to Johnny, whatever Johnny's folly now, had started Shafter out of Colorado. No one but Johnny Carr could suspect that Michael Shafter would ride into Azul tonight. But someone must have suspected; the buggy had passed him in the plaza, followed him, and waited near the feed corral gate. Vaguely Shafter remembered the shadowy bulk of a man holding the reins, a young woman beside him. He wondered what was being said now back there on the dark buggy seat.

The girl spoke first in the murk under the buggy top. Her name was Joan Wolcott and she was not greatly interested. "Is he the one you followed?"

The massive man beside her hunched on the seat, peering after the young stranger whose idle whistling drifted back. He grunted assent; he seemed held by emotions unusual in him.

Joan waited silently. This bull-built Con McCloud was only another unpleasant part of the rather fabulous, lonely existence given her in careless charity years ago. Now she was twenty-one and aware that no one really cared whether she existed or not. It was the worst kind of loneliness. Increasingly Joan met it by doing what she pleased when she pleased.

McCloud's breath exhaled softly. He muttered: "Bound to be."

"Who is he?"

"Trouble."

"What trouble?"

"Ain't anything you know about." McCloud straightened, thick shoulders bulging the black suit he seldom wore, which made him seem ungainly, awkward. "Go after him . . . stop him five minutes, ten if you can."

Joan had feared Con McCloud at times, as many others did. But not even when she was fifteen, sickened as McCloud's awesome fury beat down a strong man, had she let him suspect her fear. And now a tall young stranger in a shabby buckskin jacket, whistling jauntily, had unsettled Con McCloud himself.

"Stop a strange man on a dark night like this?" Joan was coolly disdainful. "I'm not a saloon girl."

"Act like one if that's what it takes." McCloud slapped the reins into her hands. "You been ridin' high for years. Now you're needed. Do what I tell you."

His burly figure left the buggy with the heaviness that could be so deceptive. An ungainly, hurrying shadow, McCloud vanished into the black mouth of an alley just ahead.

Lightning flared again from inky thunderheads as Joan moved over on the seat. The street ahead was empty now. Suddenly, illogically she resented the stranger because he had loosed McCloud's contempt for the situation in which she lived. Joan reached in temper for the buggy whip. She had thought of something that would stop any young man.

This wide plaza of Azul, Shafter was thinking, had changed less than himself. Twenty years ago he had been a small, bewildered boy, leaving the territory with his newly widowed mother. Tonight the same low adobe buildings spilled yellow light, shrill singing, bored chants of monte dealers, loud laughter, and talk. Strangers still jostled along the dusty walks. From St. Louis and St. Jo, California, old Mexico, and far north, the long roads and trails pointed to Azul. Traders and settlers, outlaws and soldiers, miners, cowmen, gamblers were always here.

Out in the plaza bearded teamsters were lashing stained wagon sheets to the bows of huge freight wagons against the coming storm. A new sound reached Shafter; somewhere behind him horses were coming in a smart run, a team by the rhythm, a buggy by the lack of clatter. He was turning when a splintering *crash* filled the night; a second loud smash came as Shafter ducked past the heads of a startled wagon team waiting by the walk.

The front wheel of the buggy had hooked into the rear wheel of this wagon and had collapsed. The reeling buggy had slammed its back wheel into the same spot, and the back wheel had caved in. As the buggy pitched over on axle ends, the team—a gray horse and a dun horse—swerved out toward the big freight wagons.

The teamsters shouted, waved arms. The dragging mess of the buggy, seat empty, skidded past Shafter in a boil of dirt and dust as he ran to the girl who lay motionless in the plaza dirt. She looked small and abandoned. A gay little hat was askew on black hair. Cheek bones on the high side gave her smudged face rebellious strength, even now, as Shafter dropped saddlebags and carbine and knelt by her.

Another man hauled up, blurting through a scraggly beard: "Busted smack into my wagon! Wasn't no sense drivin' so clos't!"

Other men were arriving.

"Anyone know this girl?" Shafter called.

A voice behind him said: "Seen 'er at the hotel, seems like."

A cool gust swept dust across the plaza; a raindrop patted Shafter's cheek. He looked up at the faces crowding around. Who knew anyone else in this plaza of Azul?

"I'll carry her to the hotel," Shafter declared. "When I lift her, put the saddlebags on my shoulder and the gun in my hand."

As he turned toward the hotel with his burden, another large drop struck his face—another—another. A colder gust slatted wagon sheets and lifted more dust. Shafter broke into a run. *Where was the man,* he wondered, *who had been in the buggy with this girl?*

The weathered adobe front of the old hotel lifted beyond the plaza corner. He was panting as he fumbled for the iron latch of the hotel door—and the storm caught him there. A driving wall of cold wind wrapped him in thick dust and pushed him into the lamplit lobby. Behind him a great sheet of blue-white lightning tore the night apart. Women cried out in the lobby. A shattering thunder crash shook the building as Shafter forced the door shut against a wind-driven deluge of rain.

As he paused, breathing in near gasps, memory flooded back. Here, inside this same door, the small boy had stopped twenty years ago, blinking at the bright lamps and strange faces. Dust drifted about the lobby. Startled faces stared at the stranger in an old buckskin jacket, saddlebags on a shoulder, carbine in hand, dirt-covered limp body in his arms.

"Who knows this girl?"

The women in sight were all mature, thoroughly respectable. Two cavalry officers, obviously with their wives, gazed without recognition. The large woman who replied was rising from one of the bull-hide chairs.

"You got both arms full of Joanie Wolcott, from Grenada," she announced in booming humor. "It take that rifle, young man, to bag Joanie?"

Shafter panted—"From Grenada?"—and was not too surprised. From Grenada, south of Azul, Johnny Carr had mailed his improbable letter. "She was thrown from her buggy," Shafter said as the big woman came to him.

Her broad face, scoured to healthy roughness by sun and wind, was shrewd and amused as she regarded his burden. "I'm Lyd Adams, from Grenada." A red ribbon end flaunted jauntily from her faded green hat. Gray threaded her carroty hair; vigor and zest radiated from her.

"She's hurt," Shafter said.

"Don't let that kitten bump on Joanie's forehead foozle you," Lyd Adams said genially. "She's had worse. Any bones busted?"

"I haven't examined her bones, ma'am."

"Always look afore you snatch up a young lady," the big woman said cheerfully. "Joanie seems to be hangin' together as usual."

Other women were gathering around them with delayed sympathy. "That bruise on her forehead. . . ." "The poor dear. . . ."

"Joanie Wolcott ain't exactly poor," Lyd Adams's booming humor informed them. "She could probably get money to buy you ladies in a chunk an' throw you out . . . an' likely she'd throw you. Hey, Jackson, where's Con McCloud?"

Jackson was the clerk pushing through to them. Again Shafter had the feeling time had turned back. Jackson was the clerk of twenty years ago, hair gray now, middle comfortably plump.

"She went out with McCloud," Jackson said uncertainly. "He ain't been back."

Impatiently Shafter reminded: "This girl needs a doctor, and a woman with her."

"A species Joanie ain't too fond of," Lyd Adams said offhandedly. "I'll take your gun and saddlebags, young man. Jackson, get her room key. Ladies, you're in the way. Vamoose!"

Shafter smiled as he followed the jaunty red hat ribbon. The woman's blunt humor swung like a club. She knew this girl from Grenada; she might know why Mike Shafter had been followed tonight.

Over a shoulder Lyd Adams asked briskly: "Where'd it happen?"

"In the plaza."

"Joanie drivin' alone?"

"Yes."

"McCloud'll throw a grizzly tizzy." She seemed amiably amused by anything that would irritate the man.

In a dim passage where cotton cloth was tacked shoulder high on lime-washed walls to keep the lime off passing clothes, Jackson unlocked a room door. His match flared inside; a lamp bloomed with light, and Shafter carried the girl in. Age-darkened logs held up the low ceiling. An iron bed, two plain chairs with hide seats, a pine washstand, and a low chest of drawers were the furnishings. The girl moaned softly as Shafter lowered her carefully to the bed. Overhead the howling sweep of the storm sounded muted, distant.

Lyd Adams put the carbine and saddlebags by the door and came to the bed. "Wet a towel," she directed briskly. "Jackson, get Doc Seaton."

"In this storm?"

"Like a duck, less'n you tell Con McCloud you won't fetch help for Rufe Wolcott's kin."

"I didn't say so," Jackson said sulkily. He hurried out.

Shafter twisted a wet towel until it was damp over the washbowl, took it to Lyd Adams, and watched her wipe dirt off the girl's face.

"If I'd had Joanie's figger an' face when I was her age. . . ." The big woman chuckled without looking around. "Never mind thinkin' it. I got a mirror. What happened to Joanie's buggy?"

"The front wheel struck a wagon standing by the walk."

Lyd Adams shook her head, puzzled. "Joanie can drive better'n most men. I've seen her haze a jerk line team down a squirrel grade."

Evenly Shafter asked: "Who is Con McCloud?"

"Him? Con's the big bull who paws dirt, bellers, an' bull-butts trouble for Rufe Wolcott who owns the corral . . . an' owns McCloud, ear crops, hip brand, an' nose ring," finished

Lyd Adams dryly.

"That's considerable owning. Who is Rufe Wolcott?"

"He owns a hog-size chunk of Grenada and everything around. You a stranger, young man?"

"I rode in tonight."

"Explains the saddlebags, anyway." Her shrewd gaze considered him. "But not that bullet hole an' dried blood in your left sleeve."

"A Jicarilla Apache tried for my horse and outfit."

"Them Jicarillas get drooly over a good horse or gun. You was ridin' through rough, empty country. Got a name?"

"Shafter . . . Michael Shafter."

"Well, Shafter, I'll give you thanks, which I ain't likely to get back from the Wolcotts. Leave us alone now. I'll see to Joanie."

Shafter looked back from the doorway. "She's related to a sizable part of Grenada and the country around?"

"Joanie is Rufe Wolcott's niece. He never married. G' bye, Shafter."

Joan Wolcott heard the last few words, then at the bedside Lyd Adams said: "You can open them big eyes now, chicken, an' scratch." Joan tried to sit up; she sank back on the pillow, groaning. Lyd Adams regarded her with grim humor. "He never suspicioned but what you was beauty at death's door."

Joan touched the bruise on her forehead and winced. "Was this man Shafter carrying saddlebags?"

"Why, I think so?" returned Lyd Adams with blunt shrewdness. "Seeing as you was laid out cold all the time."

"I saw a young man on the walk, carrying saddlebags, just before it happened," Joan said truthfully.

"Explains a lot," Lyd Adams said dryly. "Watchin' a tall, good-lookin' stranger instead of your drivin'. I've heard of girls losin' their heads over men, but not one losin' her buggy. You rest whilst I see what Jackson's doin' about the doctor."

Alone, Joan closed her eyes; her head hurt, her body ached from the reckless, dangerous thing she had done in temper. In that miserable mood, she heard heavy steps enter the room. When she looked, Con McCloud was scowling down at her.

"I heard you broke up the buggy."

"I stopped him," Joan said weakly, coldly. "His name is Shafter. Who is he?"

"Shafter?" It broke from McCloud in a slapping rasp. For an instant his thick-muscled figure looked at bay against some threat. The muscular features hardened. McCloud's gaze took on calculation as he looked down at her. "Be easy now to get friendly with him."

"Get out, McCloud!"

"When I'm minded."

He was a massive, threatening bulk poised over her. In her weak, aching state, Joan knew that she did fear this man. He had an implacable, destructive force when needed, ignoring right and wrong. All that McCloud ever considered was what Rufe Wolcott wanted—or what McCloud thought was needed.

"All you ever did was take from Rufe," McCloud said with brutal bluntness. "Time now to do what you're told."

"I did tonight," Joan reminded thinly. "It was the last time. And whatever made you think I had gratitude for anything?"

He was glowering down at her when Lyd Adams returned, loudly cheerful. "Here's Doc Seaton, half drowned but willin'."

Joan gratefully closed her eyes and lay thinking about the young stranger named Shafter. What threat had he brought to Azul, to Con McCloud?

Shafter was thoughtful as he carried the carbine and saddlebags back to the bright lamps and waiting strangers in the lobby. He knew a little more now, most of it puzzling. Jackson was behind his counter again, wattled cheeks still damp and storm-whipped.

"Does John Carr have a room here?" Shafter inquired.

"Room nine, east patio."

"I want the room next to Carr, if possible."

"Ain't a room next to anything. Gully-buster rains like this one have flooded arroyos an' washes," Jackson said indifferently. "Stagecoaches are stopped, which is why these folks are waiting like they aren't going anywhere."

"Where is Carr?"

"Likely in his room."

Twenty years ago a spotted dog had trotted across the east patio and nuzzled a small boy's hand, bringing a moment of warmth to the boy's loneliness. Tonight the storm whipped furiously into the open patio. A guttering lantern swung erratically in the roofed walkway around the patio and gave no useful light at all. Stabs of vivid lightning glared through the driving slants of rain. Wooden spouts in the low roof parapets were cascading gouts of white water. The lightning brought out room numbers on doors facing the patio. Number 9 had a curtained window that was dark.

Shafter tried the door and stepped inside, smiling over the whoop of welcome he expected Johnny Carr would give at finding him here. No sound. He closed the door and groped for a match. He was still smiling when a hand out of the dark found his arm.

The instinctive smash of his fist barely halted as a woman said: "He's dying, I think."

His hand slapped down to her wrist. "Who's dying?"

She gasped and pulled frantically away as wind blew the door open and the tumult of the storm swept in around them. Lightning glared again; in the blue, eerie glow Shafter saw the girl whose wrist he held. Young, eyes enormous—her other hand bringing a thin little blade out of the neck of her dress.

Blackness dropped again as Shafter released her wrist and

jumped back. "I'm Johnny's friend!" Thunder drowned most of it; he went back another step. The absurdity of it struck him—cornered by a frightened young girl in Johnny Carr's room. The storm covered any movements she made. Shafter retreated another step, holding the carbine out between them in the blackness. Lightning flared again—and she was gone, outside, obviously.

The breath Shafter drew was rueful. She could vanish quickly into some nearby room or in the shadowy passageways of the old hotel. He did not try to follow; his match sputtered alight on the rough leather of a saddlebag.

The lamp on a pine bureau at his left felt slightly warm when he lifted the chimney. Light spread through the room. His glance stopped on the bed.

"Johnny?" Shafter said sharply.

Whatever was under the blanket did not move. And now Shafter knew who had been dying; why panic had seized the girl when her wrist had been caught by a stranger. She had a knife, Shafter remembered as he reached the bed and lifted the blanket.

Old Johnny lay peacefully, thinner and frailer than a year ago. His white shirt was immaculate, as always; white hair straggled over his forehead. He might have been asleep. What man had the girl been expecting as she waited in the dark room, with Johnny under the blanket?. The slightest bruise was visible on Johnny's left cheek bone when Shafter bent close.

He found a fainter discoloration on Johnny's neck, and, as he turned from the bed, his reflection jumped at him from the mirror above the washstand—tired lines grimed with dust under rough stubble, wide mouth set in a tight line as he thought of Johnny's exuberant letter. *We're rich, Michael . . . unless we're killed.* Johnny had believed; Johnny was dead. Dismal reproach came to Shafter as he searched the room. If the wrecked buggy had not delayed him, if he had not wasted time carrying the girl to her room. . . .

The scanty contents of Johnny's worn carpetbag were tumbled in confusion from a hasty search. Shafter looked back at the bed, thinking of all he owed Johnny Carr. His own life for one thing, some years ago. A sense of real loss, of having failed Johnny went with him as he left the room. And back of that the Wolcott girl—a better driver than most men—following him, wrecking her buggy almost beside him, delaying. . . .

The lobby was placid, the clerk not interested when Shafter inquired: "Has anyone else asked for Carr?"

"Nope. Wasn't he in his room?"

Shafter looked around as the lobby door burst open. Three sodden strangers bolted in out of the storm. To the clerk Shafter said evenly: "I want a doctor to examine Carr. He's dead."

"Doc Seaton's in Miss Wolcott's room. . . . Dead?"

"I'll get the doctor," Shafter said, turning away.

Lyd Adams opened the girl's door when he knocked.

"Joanie is restin' easy with a hung-over head," she said genially. "Your interest an' sympathy, young man, does you credit. Ain't a blessed thing you can do. G' bye again."

"A man is dead in room Nine," Shafter said shortly. "I want the doctor."

She was startled; she stepped out in sobering concern and closed the door.

"Trouble," she said grimly, "draws to you like a mad stone, don't it, Shafter? That's Carr's room . . . old John Carr. He dead?"

"You knew Carr?" Shafter asked.

"Wasn't a nicer old man. Friendly-like to everyone. He kep' books at my coal mine near Grenada. You sure it's him?"

"I knew him, too." Bookkeeper at a coal mine . . . ? Shafter thought of all that Johnny Carr had once been. Coal mine ledgers. How did they fit with Johnny's fantastic conviction that wealth was close again?

A peremptory voice lifting at the end of the long, dim passage brought his head around. "McCloud in Joanie's room?" the voice called.

The three dripping strangers who had bolted in out of the storm were hurrying toward them.

"That first 'n'," Lyd Adams said, "is Vince Wolcott, Rufe's nephew."

"And the other two?"

"One in the slicker is Curly Ames, works on Rufe's ranch. Last one is Jess Parker. He don't work. A tinhorn Vince spends most of his time with."

Shafter weighed this new Wolcott approaching in muddy, squishing shoes. A wiry young man, gray suit soggy wet. Hurrying, face flushed, excited. He jostled Shafter's shoulder when he reached them. It was deliberate, Shafter guessed, a show of arrogant confidence.

Lyd Adams stood solidly blocking the doorway. "Joanie had an accident. McCloud'll come to the lobby."

Vince Wolcott caught her arm; the driving excitement was in him like whiskey, Shafter thought, arrogant and urgent, spilling at the big woman in an irritable order. "Get away from the door! I'll see McCloud and Joanie when I like!"

Shafter remembered hot-headed impulses—a treacherous luxury. He had his own tensions, not helped by being jostled, and his hand clamped on the wet, gray coat sleeve.

"Next time, sonny, don't bump me. You heard the lady."

"Jess!" Vince said sharply, without turning his head.

Lyd Adams blurted a warning: "Behind you, Shafter!" Too late.

The back of his head seemed to explode; vision whirled and went black as he reeled against the cloth-covered wall. Rubbery legs were letting him down to a knee as blurred sight returned. Shoulder against the wall, Shafter looked up—and the sallow face of the man named Jess Parker was grinning at him. Parker had struck from behind with the barrel of the gun he was holding.

"They get strangers this way," Lyd Adams was saying in angry indignation. "One in front, t' other behind. A fast man'll kill 'em both for it one day!"

Shafter struggled up and had to lean against the wall again. *When will you learn?* Both men were enjoying it. Another Wolcott ran through Shafter's thoughts. He saw attention leave him as the room door opened. The bull-shouldered figure in a black suit completed it. Con McCloud, Shafter knew, the same massive figure that had been driving the buggy when it had passed him in the plaza the first time, following him.

The man's voice was harsh with irritation. "What's wrong here?"

"Fish for you to fry, McCloud!" Lyd Adams said scathingly. "Shafter here's the one who carried Joanie in. Parker buffaloed him from behind."

McCloud's—"Shafter?"—seemed startled, then the harshness was directed at Parker. "I've had enough of you. Don't show back in Grenada."

"Tell him, Vince." Parker's malice was unmistakable.

The driving excitement spilled from Vince Wolcott: "Curly Ames half killed his horse bringing word. Uncle Rufe's had another spell . . . worst ever."

Something odd happened to all of them. Even to Lyd Adams. Anger left them; suddenly they were thinking of something beyond Shafter's knowledge.

"How bad is Rufe?" McCloud's demand was thick.

Deliberately, it seemed, Vince waited a moment. "He may be dead." Only a keen ear, a stranger's ear, weighing them intently would have caught the exultant note that Shafter did. Then he knew that Lyd Adams had caught it, or guessed it.

"Rufe has had spells before." Her scorn had a bite. "Likely it'll be a long wait for you an' Parker to start spendin' that million an' a half the Boston syndicate is offering for Rufe's holdings."

Vince challenged angrily: "What do you know about that offer?"

"I ain't a clabber head like you think . . . an' you ain't half as clever as you think." She was caustic. "More's the pity, you never will be."

Shafter's pulses had jumped. Had Johnny Carr known about this? Over a million cash being discussed at Grenada? He was looking at the floor, at McCloud's scuffed black boots, suddenly staring at the boots in fascination. Boots and shoes of the men who had bolted in out of the storm were wet, muddy. But McCloud's boots were dry; the black pants were dry to the last bottom inch. The chill fingers of danger tapped across Shafter's back as he looked up at the heavy, muscular face. It was a wide face, with hard meaty cheeks, with thick brows over flinty eyes. A man sure of himself, of his strength, power, the kind of man who destroyed rather than argue.

McCloud's harsh tone reached at young Curly Ames: "Did you see Rufe?"

The wet slicker rustled as Curly pulled off his soaked hat. His damp young face was worried.

"He was kinda reachin' for words, weak-like. 'Tell McCloud I want Joanie back from Azul quick,' was all he said."

"You didn't tell me that," Vince said angrily.

"Wasn't sent to you," Curly said uncomfortably.

"But you looked in the saloons for these two before you got me," McCloud's cold rasp accused.

"No, sir . . . I come straight here to the hotel," Curly said defensively. "You wasn't around, so I went lookin', an' met them."

"Tell anyone else?"

"No, sir."

"Wait in the lobby." Curly left with a look of relief, and McCloud's thick thumb jerked at the door. "I'll talk to you in there, Vince."

Vince shrugged and obeyed. McCloud's unwinking appraisal was on Shafter when Lyd Adams spoke with grim soberness: "Shafter came for Doc Seaton. Old John Carr is dead."

"Where?" The flinty eyes were still on Shafter.

"In his room," Shafter said. He was standing steadily now, and he had never been, he suspected, in greater peril.

"You a friend of Carr's?"

"I am." Shafter touched the back of his head and red came away on his fingertips, where Parker's revolver barrel had cut the scalp.

"Where you from?" McCloud demanded.

Shafter was a full inch the taller, but when he looked at the solid bulk of the man, he had a sense of smallness. McCloud's stare had a dark shine, estimating him. Shafter thought of Johnny's frail figure on the bed; he looked at McCloud's dry suit, and a completely murderous impulse hardened in him. A shadow of it must have touched his face; McCloud seemed to tighten watchfully.

"None of your business, whoever you are," Shafter said softly.

He turned away, ignoring avid curiosity on Jess Parker's sallow face. His neck felt bristly in back as he sensed McCloud's stare following him. *Dry shoes, dry suit.* McCloud had gone out with Joan Wolcott and had not been seen afterward, but his shoes and pants were proof he had been in the hotel before the storm broke—about the time Johnny Carr had died.

★ ★ ★ ★ ★

The first wild fury of the storm had moved on when Shafter returned to Johnny's room. Thunder was receding; the rain was easing. In the sparsely furnished room, where a small glass lamp glowed silently, Shafter pulled his rolled cartridge belt and gun from a dusty saddlebag. At the bed, where Johnny's body lay under the blanket, he buckled on the belt, rolled a smoke, and thought of what he knew and did not know. The young girl, for instance, who he had caught in here—if she would talk—if Joan Wolcott would talk.

The door opened and Shafter turned warily. A ruddy, calm man walked in, damp slicker over an arm, sagging wet hat on his head, small leather bag in his hand.

"Doctor Seaton," the intruder said. "Shafter?"

"Yes."

Seaton tossed slicker and hat on a chair, dropped the bag by the bed, and drew the blanket down. "You found him like this?"

"Yes."

If the doctor saw the almost invisible bruises on Johnny's cheek and neck, he withheld comment.

"Old age," was his regretful conclusion after some moments. "He had symptoms. I warned him last month not to exert himself." The clerk stepped into the room, and the doctor said briskly: "You can move him." He nodded to Shafter and left.

Jackson looked glumly at the bed. "Here's a room for you, mister."

Shafter nodded. "Can I get a steak in your dining room?"

"Eatin' is finished, but there's deer, bear, or beef."

"Beef. And I'm looking for a young native girl. She's wearing a dress with small flower prints."

"Sounds like the Griegos girl, works for the Wolcotts in Grenada. She don't take up with strange men," Jackson said shortly as he started out.

When Shafter had sighted the yellow, pinpoint lights of Azul tonight, he had wanted only a hot bath, shave, a steak—thick and crusty-charred—and a talk with Johnny Carr. Now Johnny was dead. Still unbathed, unshaved, he had the steak in the deserted hotel dining room. Little flicks of hot pain came and went in his head as he weighed all that had happened in one short hour.

Johnny had left a witch's tangle of mystery. The bull-built Con McCloud, Joanie Wolcott, the lush young Griegos girl were part of the mystery. And behind it all must lurk Johnny's illusions of wealth for himself and Mike Shafter. He was lifting the chipped white coffee cup when vigorous steps entered the quiet dining room. Shafter got to his feet.

"Set an' eat!" Lyd Adams's amiable voice boomed across the vacant tables. She added: "If you got any appetite left." She sat solidly opposite. "Joanie Wolcott has took off sudden for Grenada, floutin' doctor's orders to rest quiet tonight."

Shafter cut a bite of steak, reminding himself that this big woman must have answers he needed. "She was sent for, wasn't she?"

"Vince like to choked on that."

"Why?"

"Maybe you ought to know more." Pans *rattled* in the kitchen and Lyd Adams lowered her vigorous tones. "Take Rufe Wolcott. He grabbed everything he could get his hands on. It was in his blood. Kinfolks was his weak spot. When a brother died, Rufe took in Vince, real young. Another brother died an' Rufe took in Joanie."

"A man could do worse."

"Rufe could've done better. He took in Joanie like he'd throw a maverick in the herd and forget it."

"Some maverick," Shafter murmured.

"Your eyes are workin', at least, Shafter. Joanie was a skinny little thing, scared an' lonesome. Rufe paid her no mind. Vince was jealous an' bullied her. Even then it was sorta understood Vince might get what Rufe left. Vince didn't want a girl cousin around sharin'."

Shafter picked up the coffee cup. He was thoughtful across it. "Is this Rufe Wolcott really worth over a million?"

"Closer t' two, I'd guess."

"How did he get it?"

"Grabbin'. A silver-gold mine Rufe opened near Grenada held high-grade. Money rolled in. Rufe built a smelter an' made his XR Ranch largest in this part of the territory. Grenada growed fast. Rufe grabbed in town, too."

"You kept your coal mine."

She chuckled. "Rufe needed coal for his smelter. Any grabbin' at me, I'd have skunked his smeltin'. It pained Rufe, but kep' him real friendly."

"And now a syndicate in Boston wants to buy?"

"Everything Rufe owns, to get his two mines an' smelter, which handles ore from a hundred miles out."

"Nearly two million. . . ." Shafter cut slowly into the steak again. "Men have been killed for less."

"Women killed, too." The new note in Lyd Adams's voice was grim.

Shafter looked across the table at her. "Joanie Wolcott, for instance?"

"I didn't say so."

"As a relative, she has certain legal rights, unless cut off in a will, doesn't she?"

"I ain't a lawyer."

"Don't have to be." After a moment Shafter asked briefly: "Where's McCloud? Where's Vince Wolcott?"

"Con McCloud lit out for Grenada, to see how bad off Rufe is. Vince didn't say what he meant to do."

"And I'm supposed to be interested in the girl hurrying to Grenada?"

"Joanie," said Lyd Adams earnestly, "oughtn't to be alone on the Grenada road tonight. Curly Ames had to ford the Palomas Wash a mile below the road. The water was that deep then. This storm'll make it deeper. And Joanie will try to cross, regardless. She's like that. Ain't no one in Azul I can turn to. I drawed a blind card comin' in here to you."

Shafter drank the last of his coffee, regretfully eyed the remainder of his steak as he stood up. Relief lighted Lyd Adams's wide face as she stood up, also.

"Wouldn't take much more to make me partial to you, Shafter."

His laugh came then, for the first time since reaching Azul tonight. "I seem to have reached that point with you already, ma'am."

The storm had moved into the southeast when he rode out of Azul on a fresh horse, rented from a livery barn behind the hotel, where Lyd Adams had left her buggy. Stars glinted in patches of opening sky. The muddy road held glistening water through which the bay gelding splashed in a steady road run. Lyd Adams was following in her buggy as far as the Palomas Wash.

Stabs of pain in the back of Shafter's head kept his temper raw as he forded small arroyos filled with muddy, rushing water. Finally, when the road pitched down a brush-bordered descent, and he halted the gelding for a blow, he heard the deep tumult of water growling close ahead in the night. That would be the Palomas Wash, and, when he thought of Joanie Wolcott trying to cross water like that, his first real concern for her safety set in.

When Joan had heard the angry Palomas torrent, she had sensed the danger in crossing. In dry weather, the Palomas Wash was an empty channel snaking out of the foothills, white gravels and sands hot and harmless as they thrust and twisted between steep slopes. Heavy rains brought the Palomas alive, brutal, boiling and soupy with mud and sand. Its rushing force out of the high hills was sometimes unbelievable. High banks were torn away; huge boulders ground audibly along the bed. Heavy wagons had been swept downstream; men, animals had died when the Palomas was running. And she had to cross.

Joan had no illusions as to why she was making this night ride against the doctor's orders. It was her conscience. In her room back at the hotel, watching Vince standing wet, scowling, excited and suspicious by her bed, a flash of guilty insight had come. In Vince, at that moment, Joan had seen too much of herself. All that Vince had ever thought of had been himself. And she had been little better; she had taken much, given little. The very clothes she wore had been given to her. And now that remote old man who had done so much for them both was suddenly ill and helpless and had sent for her. The least she could do was reach Grenada tonight and tell him she did have gratitude, tell him what it had meant to a small, frightened girl to have someone want her enough to offer a home. If he snorted and brushed it aside, that would be his way, but he would know.

A final, level reach of the road pitched abruptly into the wash. And there, ahead of her, the shadowy bulk of a rider swung his waiting horse.

"How deep?" Joan called.

"Deep enough."

She frowned. Jess Parker had ridden this way ahead of her.

Sly amusement filled Parker's comment as she neared him. "Vince said the doctor wouldn't let you out tonight."

"Is Vince here?" Joan asked coolly.

"He headed for Grenada, too." The malice increased. "The lot of you running to the old man as soon as he's sick . . . so he'll know how much you like him."

"What better time?" Joan reined off the road, following shallow wagon ruts downstream that paralleled the wash. Jess Parker followed her, riding in close. Coldly Joan reminded: "I heard McCloud tell you to stay out of Grenada, in case you're following Vince."

"When Vince takes over, he'll run McCloud out of the country. Vince is waiting."

McCloud gone? Joan tried to visualize it. "Vince couldn't do without him," she said levelly.

"No? Why not? Vince would sell out."

"Yes . . . Vince would do that." Joan thought: *It would be the end of McCloud . . . inside. Part of McCloud is in everything Uncle Rufe owns. It's all McCloud lives for.*

Jess Parker's cynical comment stayed with her. "A man like that is dangerous to keep around. He'd hate anyone who got what he'd helped to build."

Joan rode in silence. The man had spoken her own feelings about McCloud. She had never liked this sallow Jess Parker. He lived by his shady wits, was reputedly cold-blooded with the gun he wore in a shoulder holster under his coat. Increasingly he influenced Vince, and none of it was good. But tonight, close to the growling rush of the Palomas, Jess Parker's company was oddly welcome.

His presence was reassuring when she looked off to the left through the wan starlight in the clearing sky and caught glimpses of the dark, rushing water she intended to ford. This was empty, lonely country, and tonight the Palomas had never been more dangerous. The wagon ruts dipped down to fairly level ground. Along here the channel of the wash widened out and the current slowed somewhat and ran more shallowly. They halted at the bank edge and gazed out over the black torrent.

Blotches of brush and débris shot swiftly into sight, raced

past, vanished downstream. Froth-topped currents eddied between the shallow bank, where their horses moved restlessly, and a tangle of flooded *chamisa* farther out. In the pale starlight, the opposite bank looked far away.

Jess Parker was casual. "Can you swim?"

"No, this isn't swimming country."

"McCloud crossed. Vince crossed." He was encouraging her. "Looks deeper than it is."

Out there the storm was hurtling from the high hills. The sky was clearing; the howling, thunderous deluge had passed on to beat and scour the sheer cliffs and conifer stands of the mountains to the east. But the storm had not died, really; it had passed from the sky to the ground, scattered, but running swiftly together again, gathering its mighty force in the channel of the Palomas. The look of the storm had changed; its savagery still lived. Joan tried not to think of it; she thought of the sick old man in Grenada who had sent for her.

"If Vince made it, I can." She was calm, forcing the calm even inside. But now she wished for a man's solid saddle as she braced on the side-saddle and urged her horse out into the first eddies.

Jess Parker rode in beside her.

"If your horse loses footing," he called over, "I'll be close!"

He sounded a little tight, strained, now, but Joan was taut herself as she balanced on the insecure side-saddle and headed out into the dangerous crossing.

II

Shafter found the shallow wagon ruts to the Palomas ford where Lyd Adams had said they would be. The sucking growl of the torrent was close on his left as he rode toward the ford. Had the Wolcott girl really tried to cross that? She was still ahead of him; she must have tried.

In the saddle like this, riding alone at night, there was time to think. Long ago, Shafter recalled, there had been one sun-drenched day when the small boy named Mike Shafter had ridden beside his father on the sheer bank of a wash like this. The sandbars below them had been white and dry in the brilliant light—and his father had spoken soberly. "A friend of mine, Son, was drowned in this wash."

"Couldn't he swim out? Heck, I would!"

"Carried him downstream between high banks like these. He didn't have a chance."

"Gee!"

"Don't ever trust a wash like this, Son, when it's running deep. Remember. never take a chance on it. Race you down the channel now . . . last man washes dishes for Mother tonight . . . *eeeeh-yoow wwwww!*"

That kind of a father, tall and laughing, ambushed and shot within a year, and an emptiness had come into the boy's life. His mother's life, also. In weeks she had sold out and left the territory, in grieving flight, Shafter knew now, from her memories. Quickly this immense, lonely Grenada country had faded, become unreal. Now it was real again; only the boy had changed. Shafter was musing as he rode down a short slope and sighted figures in the starlight ahead—two riders heading out into the black torrent of the Palomas. One rider unmistakably sat a side-saddle.

The man was on the upstream side; he should be downstream from the girl. Shafter wondered who the fellow was as he put the bay gelding into the water, running out from a line of flooded *chamisa* brush. The two riders ahead did not look back. Water was boiling stirrup high against their horses as his own gelding began to fight the increasing power of the current.

He kept the gelding's head high with a tight rein, alert for floundering in quicksand. One stagger off balance, footing gone, and the water would sweep them over and under. Horse and rider would be sucked, tumbled, buffeted downstream into even swifter, deeper water plunging between higher banks. And still the two riders ahead did not look back. A dead tree came fast on the roiling surface; jagged limbs were grotesque claws reaching, seeking—Shafter's warning shout died unuttered when he saw the tree would barely miss them. The gelding under him lunged, snorted as a soggy mass of tumbleweeds piled against his front leg. Shafter's voice was reassuring; the weeds held there for a moment, then scraped around and whirled on.

Water was piling around his own stirrup irons when he saw disaster ahead. The man's horse staggered—or was the horse yanked around? It happened too fast; the starlight was too dim. He watched the current drive the reeling horse into the girl's horse. He spurred hard then.

The gelding was plunging ahead as Joan Wolcott's horse floundered off balance, lost footing, and went down into the full grip of the current—down out of sight. Joan's arms were wildly catching at the water as she disappeared. Again Shafter spurred, hard and savagely this time. Her arm, her shoulder broke the black surface; he wrenched the gelding's head violently, leaned far out and down. His straining hand touched wet cloth; his fingers dug through, clamping into the flesh beneath as her struggling figure swept helplessly against the plunging gelding's front leg. A few feet away her horse lunged up and was swept under again.

Bracing in the stirrups, Shafter hauled her head above water. She was choking in high, thin spasms as he dragged her to the stirrup. Black hair covered her face as she caught frantically at his leg. He yanked the gelding's head upstream; Joan was coughing, strangling as he dropped reins on the saddle horn and reached down with the other hand.

Grunting with the effort, he dragged her up and dropped her

streaming body, face down, across the saddle. Holding her there, he drove the gelding on across in a floundering rush. She choked, coughed, but hung soddenly, face down, not struggling. Later, Shafter remembered that—helpless, undoubtedly still gripped with panic, she stayed like that as she fought for breath.

The water, suddenly, was less deep; more flooded *chamisa* loomed darkly ahead. They broke through, splashed shallowing water, and came out on firm earth. The gelding halted, trembling, blowing. Shafter sucked a long breath of relief.

"Can you stand now?"

"Of course," her weak voice answered.

He lifted her like a dripping sack and lowered her to the ground. She held to the stirrup leather for a moment, and then stepped back unsteadily. Behind them another blowing horse splashed to the bank. Shafter reined hard around.

"What happened out there?" His demand was uncompromising.

He saw peering suspicion and recognized the man. His spur raked as Jess Parker's hand grabbed toward the shoulder holster inside his coat. The man was tearing at the buttoned coat as Shafter's gun cleared the holster. Leaning out, he slammed the heavy barrel to Parker's head as the lunging gelding scraped by. When he spun the gelding back, Parker was wilting.

Joan Wolcott caught the bit of Parker's startled horse as the man slid limply to the ground and lay there. Her stifled question wrenched out. "Why did you do that?"

Shafter was curt as he dismounted. "Felt like it." He rolled Parker face up, reached inside the coat for the shoulder gun, and threw it far out into the Palomas current.

"You're the man who carried me in from the plaza . . . you're Shafter." She followed it with a strange remark, brushed with unreasonable hostility. "You do bring trouble."

"I find trouble." He held his own hostility back as he

remembered her wrecked buggy that had kept him away from Johnny Carr. Her hands were fumbling at her hair, pinning wet coils back off her forehead. Dripping jacket and skirt were clinging close. She was slender but firm-muscled; limp in his arms in the Azul plaza she had felt as she looked now. She shivered in the edged night air and Shafter pulled off his old buckskin jacket.

"Get into this." He was not particularly solicitous; she needed the jacket.

It fell about her in loose folds; she hugged them close and regarded him in frowning uncertainty.

"You weren't there when we started across. How . . . where . . . ?"

There was some humor, barbed and backed with the hostility he felt in the moment. "You came out like a drowned gopher. Squeaked like one." But when she shivered again inside the jacket, Shafter said formally: "I'll start a fire."

"No . . . I was thinking of . . . of the water out there. The stage relay station is only a few miles." Looking out over the boiling race of the Palomas, Joan said: "I wonder if my horse. . . ."

"He had a chance," was the best Shafter could offer. Jess Parker groaned. Shafter bent over the man again. "Can you hear me?" Parker's eyes opened. "We'll leave your horse at the relay station," Shafter said evenly. "Miss Wolcott's horse may be out on this side. Hunt for him or walk in."

"I don't want his horse!" Joan protested.

"No one asked you." Shafter was deliberate. "I think he tried to knock your horse under. Ride his horse or drop on my lap. I won't leave you here with him."

"No one tells me what to do!" She did have temper, flashing.

His own dark mood eased as he looked at her. His thin smile came from humor without friendliness. "Get up or get hoisted up, young lady. You're wasting breath."

It would be *hoist,* he thought for a moment as she glared. Then her hand lifted her sodden skirt and she caught the reins of Parker's horse.

"Look the other way," Joan said coldly.

The wet skirt rustled; when he looked back, she was astride the horse, man style, smoothing the skirt down as far as possible. Shafter topped his saddle as Parker sat up, groaning through clenched teeth, bracing weakly with an unsteady palm on the earth. There was justice in the sight as Shafter remembered his own rubbery legs and spinning senses back in the hotel. He laughed at the man without pity. "Fun, isn't it?" he said. "You can laugh about it while you walk in." And then in cold brusqueness he gave Parker his choice. "I'll call it even if you'll take it that way."

Parker looked up in baleful silence. Not *even,* ever, with him. At least now he had warning, Shafter reflected, but, another one to watch. . . .

Two gunshots breached the night with dull drifting echoes on the far bank of the wash. Shafter rode to the water's edge. Over there, far over there beyond the black race of churning water, a faintly visible blotch on the low bank must be Lyd Adams's buggy. He fired three answering shots—and a single shot replied.

"What was that?" Joan was suspicious as they rode up the sloping bank.

"Lyd Adams, asking about you."

"Lyd . . . out here from Azul?" She was startled. "Why?"

The humor came back, without kindliness toward her. "Lyd Adams was worried . . . a rattle-headed girl ignoring her doctor and trying to cross this wash tonight."

"It sounds like Lyd." Her temper had not taken the bait; she was mystified, looking searchingly at him. "You rode ahead of Lyd . . . a stranger . . . ?"

"Not a stranger to bringing you in from idiotic messes." That should hold her. Joan bit her lip visibly in the starlight. His brief grin was his reward.

More wagon ruts were taking them over undulating, brush-cluttered ground to the road. Joan finally broke the silence. "You knew John Carr?"

"He was my friend."

"I liked him."

He had a violent moment of wanting to remind her of the young Griegos girl who he had caught in Johnny's room, to remind her of McCloud's dry suit, dry boots—and her own buggy following him in Azul tonight. But she knew all that and had no idea that he knew. The less any of them suspected Mike Shafter's knowledge the better.

"Johnny," he said calmly, "was a fine old gentleman." No more passed between them until they were on the muddy road and small campfires in the distance ahead winked invitingly. There were questions to ask while still alone with her.

"You people from Grenada seemed everywhere in Azul tonight," Shafter said with idle disinterest.

"I drove over to buy some things," Joan said absently. "Vince stays in Azul much of the time these days."

"Drove over alone?"

She seemed to sense purpose in his casual questions. Again her head turned, watching him. "Marina Griegos came with me to visit her cousin in Azul. She works for us." Cool and precise, Joan continued: "Con McCloud is always riding to Azul on business. I can't speak for Lyd Adams or John Carr. . . . Now, Shafter, why were you in Azul tonight?"

"To meet Carr." That much they knew; a little more did not matter now. "I rode in from Colorado."

"You live in Colorado?"

"I own a small stageline there, which may be a big line

someday. I have a small mine that works three men, and may work three hundred with luck." She was watching him closely, listening intently. Hostility ebbed for the moment as he talked more than he had intended, his humor toward her, also. "Each month I'm broke and can't make it through another month, but I do. Scratching and scrabbling, all fingers crossed."

"Why, it sounds like fun." Rich warmth in her interest surprised him. "It is fun, isn't it?"

"Being broke?"

"Of course not. Well, yes, broke and full of hopes and plans. Trying to build something you believe in."

"There's no champagne in it." Thank Johnny's letter for the unthinking, dry comment.

"Oh, I'd imagine so." Her warmth lasted a moment more. "All champagne doesn't come in a bottle." They were nearing the small, glowing campfires and the moment broke, receded. "Wagons waiting at the stage station for the Palomas to go down," Joan said coolly.

The bulky, white-topped wagons waited on flat ground by the station. Joan reined up at the first wagon. "I'll get down here." He looked away, heard her drop lightly to the ground. She came to his stirrup. "You helped me," Joan said in the same cool tone, handing up his jacket. "Now I'll help you. Grenada won't be friendly to you. Don't go there."

"Advice . . . or warning?"

"Both." Joan hesitated, looking up at his shadowed face. "Do you really think Jess Parker tried to drown me?"

"You know the fellow, I don't."

Her small shrug might have meant anything as she turned away, leading Parker's horse. Shafter dismounted and followed. In front of the low adobe station a stagecoach looked stubby and abandoned without teams in the harness. Light streaming from the open station door silhouetted roughly dressed teamsters loitering and talking.

Joan looked small and bedraggled as she walked to the men. *Like a half-drowned kitten,* came to Shafter, fully cynical because he knew now she was a real part of the threat that increased each mile he advanced toward her town of Grenada.

The teamsters saw her and stared; one tall, lanky man started forward. "What happened, Miss Joanie?"

Her rueful laugh reached Shafter. "My horse stumbled in the ford, Sam. Did McCloud come through?"

"He an' Curly Ames, on beat-out hosses, McCloud roarin' for fresh ones." Sam spat to one side and cocked his head with avid interest. "Vince come later. Somethin' wrong? They didn't say."

"Uncle Rufe is sick." Joan left the man holding Parker's horse and walked into the station.

The loiterers stared silently as Shafter tied his horse at the short rack and went inside. The large room was filled with steamy warmth, cheerful lamplight, men and women seated, standing. A spare woman with an apron over her gingham dress was solicitously conducting Joan through a doorway at the back of the room.

A wide fireplace, of adobe, also, held *snapping* cedar chunks; close to the heat a large smoky coffee pot steamed. Shafter caught a tin cup off the hearth edge and poured coffee.

Standing close to the heat, holding the jacket to dry, also, he sipped the coffee and wondered what was ahead. For he was going to Grenada, Shafter knew now. And when he thought again of Johnny Carr, his mood turned more flinty than the massive Con McCloud would ever be. He would clash with that bull-shouldered man, Shafter knew now—and he looked forward to it.

Con McCloud and Curly Ames rode their punished horses into

Grenada in the chill quiet before dawn. Houses that should be dark at this hour were showing light; when the mud-spattered horses entered the plaza at a sweating trot, the Palace Bar displayed more life and light than usual. McCloud's questing eyes noted everything. In a peculiar, personal way he had never put into words, even to himself, this was his town; here Con McCloud was supreme. To the west, Rufe Wolcott's immense XR Ranch reached mile upon endless mile, dominating this part of the territory. All of that, the two Wolcott mines, the smelter, much of Grenada itself, was under McCloud's unquestioned authority. Men obeyed or got out quickly. McCloud never bragged of it; it was his life. He was Con McCloud, backed by Rufe Wolcott; that was enough; he had made it so.

But when Curly Ames brought his foam-specked horse alongside and spoke in tired hoarseness for the first time since they had left the relay station—"Sid's place had a big night, looks like."—McCloud merely grunted. He was frowning over a vague restlessness he could sense in the night. The town was not asleep, as usual, at this hour.

Men were loitering on the wide boardwalk in front of the Palace. Sid Lutz, the owner, should have been home in bed, but Sid, elegant in frilled white shirt and tailored Kansas City suit, was one of the group. Sid peered toward them and moved expectantly to the walk edge.

Curly was wistful as he looked at the Palace lights. "A short snort'd help right now."

McCloud ignored Curly and Sid Lutz and reined over to the other side of the plaza, Curly following in silent resignation. A few years back, Rufe Wolcott had built a spacious new home a short distance west of the plaza, walls of thick adobe, roof flat, in the custom of the country. There were wings, patios, a walled garden behind, sheds, stables, outbuildings. And now the windows glowed with light; buggies and saddle horses waited at the hitch rack in front.

McCloud dismounted, curtly ordering: "Saddle me a fresh one."

Until now McCloud had never entered the big house without knocking. He shouldered in hurriedly and heard voices break off into uneasy silence. Men and women were waiting on Rufe's fancy plush and brocade chairs and sofas; they gazed in mute unease as McCloud closed the door.

His demand was quick and harsh to Henry Peck, cashier of Rufe's bank: "How is he?"

Peck, slightly built and nervous, with a trimmed mustache he was in the habit of flicking with the back of a forefinger, said uneasily: "Asleep, I think."

"Doctor with him?"

Mrs. Peck, small, brisk, usually smiling, who avoided McCloud when she could, spoke from the same sofa: "Doctor Jim is tending a miner's wife with her first baby."

McCloud's grunt was annoyed. His stare moved from face to face. Every man here had prospered in some way because McCloud had willed it. They were finished in Grenada when McCloud decided. Dave Bracken, who managed Rufe's general store, had snatched a cigar from his mouth and was sitting in stiff unease. Tibbons Wolcott, a graying clerk in the same store, a distant kin of Rufe's, hunched solemnly beside his larger wife. Only Buck Manning, who ran the smelter, lolled at ease in a comfortable rocker, legs crossed lazily. Amusement was on Buck's face as he reached for the cigar cocked in the corner of his mouth and asked: "Where's Joanie?"

"Back in Azul," McCloud said shortly.

Buck's short whip of a body, pointed face, and sandy, rumpled hair gave him the look of an alert terrier as his amusement grew. "And Vince?" Buck prodded.

"Azul!"

"He'll be along," Buck guessed. His amused eyes roved around the room. "Everyone waiting," Buck said. "Wondering what'll happen next. You, too, McCloud?"

"I'm here now!" McCloud told them all coldly. "The lot of you can go home!" He stalked out of the parlor, toward the back of the big house.

The housekeeper, Mrs. Prince, a widow, angular and tart-tongued, who McCloud had never liked because she was supreme next to Rufe Wolcott in this big house that was the heart of all that Rufe owned, was dozing now with her mouth open in a cane-seated rocker outside Rufe's bedroom door. She roused with a start, catching at the India shawl around her shoulders, as McCloud's heavy steps came to her.

"Don't bother him." Her whisper, her disapproving eyes resented him as she indicated the door, slightly ajar. "Doctor told me to keep everyone away."

"Get 'em out of the house." McCloud spoke softly, if his harsh rumble was ever soft. "All of them. Hear? And stay away from his room while I'm in."

Mrs. Prince bridled. "Since when do you give orders in this house, McCloud?" She was acid, scornful. "Doctor said. . . ."

"Get, you!" He was so malevolent, a bulking threat, that her eyes popped with fear. She scurried away.

McCloud took his first step into Rufe's bedroom. An uncertain step, as if cautiously tearing a veil, never seen, never mentioned, but always there between Rufe and himself. It crossed his mind now that he had lived apart from Rufe all these years, never sharing Rufe's personal life. Their talk had been of business, little else. The curious glance McCloud cast about the bedroom was amazed. Rufe was not miserly; he had spent lavishly on this big house. But Rufe's own bedroom was less than McCloud's room at the hotel. Rufe's hotel.

A cheap gun rack hung on the side wall. The plain chest of drawers, shabby wardrobe, two chairs with sagging splint seats, the worn, faded rag rug were not as good as the hotel afforded. The narrow wood bed looked cheap and not too comfortable. McCloud moved quietly to the bed, uneasily conscious that this plain room revealed something unsuspected about the man who lay quietly under a rumpled sheet. Just what, McCloud was not sure.

Even Rufe's tumbled, graying hair against the pillow looked different. Rufe seemed different; his aloof shrewdness, quiet, stubborn, canny drive were gone. It had been a thing to feel, to sense confidently, when with Rufe. Now the furrowed, leathery face was a placid mask against the pillow. McCloud swallowed.

"Rufe . . . ? Wake up, Rufe. We got to talk quick." Rufe had been staring up at the ceiling, not asleep. His eyes moved in silent demand.

"Joanie had an accident in Azul," McCloud said hurriedly. "Shook her up is all, but she's stayin' in Azul tonight."

Rufe held silence, as he often did while McCloud heavily sorted out thoughts and put them into words.

"We're in trouble," McCloud said in thickening strain, unusual in him. The doubts and premonitions held in through the long night broke now in a confession only Rufe would ever hear. "Big trouble . . . an' I ain't sure what to do." McCloud jerked a blue bandanna from his hip pocket and rubbed dried road mud off the sprout of dark stubble on his jaw. "Rufe . . . I saw Shafter. Remember him? I saw him, Rufe . . . like a dead man riding into Azul last night, alive again. Still young, Rufe. Whistlin', too, just like he used to." McCloud shook his head, fighting off the mood. "Wasn't him, of course . . . couldn't be. No dead man comes back after twenty years."

Rufe's eyes watched silently. Mocking him? Rufe would do that. McCloud's fist clenched on the bandanna. "His name's even Shafter. That explains it. Remember the kid? The Shafter kid? It's him, Rufe. And he come to Azul to meet that fellow Carr, that keeps books for Lyd Adams."

When McCloud talked like this, Rufe always listened, saying nothing, letting McCloud talk it all out. Like now.

"I ain't spoke of everything that's been happening lately. I been watchin'. Carr was askin' around about the old days. Ain't hardly anyone left, but Carr's been to 'em all. Now this Shafter comes to Azul to meet Carr . . . like a dead man ridin' back after all these years, set for. . . ."

McCloud broke off, standing motionlessly, watching the glistening intensity of Rufe's stare.

"Rufe!"

A chill wandered across McCloud's skin as a tear welled slowly from the corner of Rufe's left eye. It rolled down the leathery furrows of Rufe's cheek—Rufe's suddenly, frighteningly placid cheek. A cheek, McCloud realized, a face, that was not moving, not showing any expression at all.

"Say something, Rufe!"

McCloud caught under the sheet. Rufe's hand was limp in his grip. The hand dropped slackly when McCloud let go. And now the glistening agony of trying to communicate was frighteningly plain in Rufe's eyes. McCloud's voice blurted unnaturally, even to his ears, thick, desperate words.

"I'll get the doctor here quick, Rufe! He'll do something! You got to talk! I ain't sure what to do about this young Shafter! What's he here for? What's he mean to do? I have to take care of him, too?"

Only Rufe's eyes looked back. A groan wrenched from McCloud as he started out of the room in an ungainly, plunging run. Always there had been Rufe backing everything—and now McCloud felt abandoned and alone. Rufe had to talk.

Sometime in the night red sparks bloomed on the horizon ahead like a miniature, fiery flower. Shafter watched the sparks fade and vanish as he rode leisurely toward Grenada. They would be from the Wolcott smelter. Ahead of him somewhere Joanie Wolcott was driving the buggy she had borrowed at the stage station. She was dry, comfortable in clothes provided by the stationkeeper's wife. Their solicitude had been a lesson in how a Wolcott was regarded in this part of the territory.

He had dozed in the saddle, and dozed again, with the queer sensation that he was moving back into the past, like riffling the pages of a book long closed. The first blaze of sunrise was slanting across black mountain crests in the east when he reached the first pole corrals and small houses of Grenada. Long ago there had been a few squat adobe dwellings strung along the road, and the Grenada store, a pungent, shadow-filled little store smelling of oiled leather, coffee beans, salt meat, and chili peppers. Here was a town now, a plaza, criss-crossed streets of houses. Shafter reined into *Brad Hampton's Livery & Feed*—a large plank barn with an open runway.

The wiry young man who stepped out of the small office had an impudent grin that brought a smile to Shafter's tired face as he dismounted stiffly.

"Feed and water . . . might rub off some mud, too."

A glance at the gelding's hip brand. "From Donnelly's barn in Azul." A puckering, good-natured look estimated Shafter. "Rub you, too, mister?"

"Mud all the way from Azul," Shafter said wryly. He yawned and pulled the carbine from the boot. "How's Rufe Wolcott's health this morning?"

Quick, reserved, he got his answer. "You with the Wolcotts?"

"Never saw the man. Last night in Azul I heard he was sick."

"He's dead . . . just before daylight." Suspicion had switched to dawning speculation. "Like to buy a good livery barn cheap? Makes money. You won't believe the price I'll make for a quick sale."

"You Brad Hampton?"

"That's right. I own free and clear . . . everything."

"Why sell if you're making money?"

"My reasons wouldn't apply to a buyer." This Brad Hampton was earnest. Looked honest, too. "He'd do well. I'll take the pay out of his profits." And when Shafter stared quizzically, smiling faintly, Brad Hampton said ruefully: "No catch to it. I'm not a rabbit, but I know when to jump."

"Rufe Wolcott's death have anything to do with it?" It had, Shafter saw. "I'll make a guess," he said. "Con McCloud."

"I could live with McCloud. Vince Wolcott is in the Palace Bar now, bragging what he'll do when he's top man around here." The impudent smile had tension, bitterness. "I'm high on Vince's list for attention. Why waste time fighting him in a town he'll be running?"

"Why not?"

"Not worth it."

Shafter chuckled. "One way of looking at it. Jump fast if you can find a buyer. Good luck."

Now small things he would have ignored had meaning. Ahead of him two men halted in the middle of the dusty plaza and talked earnestly. They turned to watch a rider spurring through the west end of the plaza—looked like young Curly Ames, who had ridden to Azul last night for Joanie Wolcott. Other men in the plaza stared after the rider. Something taut, uncertain, almost apprehensive was hanging in the early sunlight.

Shafter was on the south walk of the plaza, pondering it, when he heard a trotting buggy team turn into the plaza behind him. The team slowed, stopped abreast of him.

"Will you step into that saloon, sir, and tell George Ross that his sister is waiting?"

He was gaping, Shafter realized, like a burro miner just in from the mountains. The smiling, vivid girl on the buggy seat had a red mouth, a provocative arch to her brows. Her cheeks had a natural bloom, untouched by wind or sun.

"The Palace Bar, ma'am?"

"The sign does say that, I believe."

"What does George Ross look like?"

It was a transparent excuse to linger and take in the crisp freshness of her linen skirt and jacket, the butter-gold hair under the stylish little flat-brimmed hat. She realized what he was doing and was amused.

"Look for a Boston Irishman with a build like a dock walloper and a red broken-up face. He'll have a glass in his hand, no doubt . . . and he'll be talking to an audience."

Shafter laughed delightedly; all this in Grenada, first thing. "You seem to know him well, ma'am."

"Who should know him better than his sister?"

Something more than amusement in that statement? A breath of bitterness, a shadow of the cynical? Something there. Shafter caught it and tucked the thought away, because this Boston Irishman brother must be linked to the Boston syndicate interested in buying the Wolcott properties.

"I'll tell him, ma'am."

Should have made some excuse and walked on. Vince Wolcott was in the Palace. Last night Joan Wolcott had warned in all earnestness: *Grenada won't be friendly to you.* Another pretty face, more trouble, Shafter guessed in resignation as he pushed through the half doors of the Palace.

In the yeasty-sour warmth the long bar reached back in impressive length. The long bar mirror in a scrolled mahogany frame, tiered bottles, ranks of polished glasses were not surpassed in Azul. Overhead lamps were still glowing pallidly, and the group of men at the back end of the long bar was listening to one man. The easy, fluent voice had a twangy brogue. She was right; she knows him. The man held a glass; a hard black hat tilted back on his head. He had a compact look in the suit of Eastern cut with narrow lapels. Couldn't miss this one. Sunlight had burned the face red; some past violence had bent the nose, mashed a cheek bone, broken the face that once must have been handsome in a raffish, merry way. Any urge to pity vanished before the expansive magnetism on that broken face.

The sister waiting outside had some of the same—a quick-smiling, readily laughing warmth, reaching out to charm and disarm. *Easy,* Shafter reminded himself. *Easy now.* Nine men, he counted, and Vince Wolcott was one of them. Sighting him, he stepped out in darkening temper.

"Get back to Azul! You're in the wrong town!"

"Grenada, isn't it?" Shafter said, walking back. And to the red, broken face behind Vince: "You're George Ross?"

A blond eyebrow lifted; the glass came up in a fist with misshapen knuckles. "Ross it is, my friend." The man was smiling as he drank; over the glass edge his eyes were level and estimating.

More there than a smile and easy talk. That, too, Shafter tucked away. "Your sister asked me to step in and say she's waiting."

"The attentive Priscilla," said George Ross. Annoyed? Shafter was not certain as laughing magnetism came again on the broken face. "A refresher, friend, for your trouble?"

Vince Wolcott's gray suit, soggy-dark last night in Azul, had dried wrinkled and shapeless. The pointed, arrogant face had not been shaved or washed. Last night's flushed, driving excitement was a higher flush of unreasoning anger now, whipped by whiskey.

"Out! Out of town, damn you!" Vince exploded loudly. "I'm

telling you!" Thick, slurring, but he was steady on his feet, knew what he was doing.

Shafter had suspected this. He had to decide now, minutes after entering Grenada—placate the Wolcotts and buy time, or meet their mood. How much time would he buy? What would it be worth?

The Boston man spoke to Vince. "A man to his likes and dislikes." He was watching the carbine in Shafter's hand. "This gentleman," Ross suggested to Shafter, "has the black grief over his uncle's death not three hours ago. He is *the* Wolcott now, no doubt. The town is his. A ride where you came from, friend, would be healthful."

"Probably," Shafter agreed. Two of the men seemed to be miners. One had a ranch look. The moon-faced bartender was standing with both hands slack on the bar, stare unwinking. A gun undoubtedly under the bar, waiting. "Last night in Azul," Shafter said, and his slow, tired smile came tightly, "a man named Jess Parker dropped me from behind with his gun barrel while I was talking to this one."

"Better a shillelagh," said George Ross judiciously, humorously. "And afterward a glass and handshake."

Vince said loudly: "Jess gave him a taste! Now he'll learn. . . ."

"I learn," Shafter said. "Once, I can't help. Twice, I can."

He used his palm. The full-armed slap *cracked* like a board snapping, driving Vince's chin around to the shoulder. The second mighty slap sent Vince head down against the bar. He bounced off to the floor and weakly fingered the dusty boards.

"Greedy, drunk, and bragging . . . not grieving," Shafter coldly informed the blank silence. "Anyone else?"

A glow spread on the Boston man's broken face. "A Kilkenny clout and a carbine in the other fist is a full hand. Do I hear different?"

"He's yours, if you can stand him," Shafter said, and walked out. To the girl waiting in the buggy, he called: "I told him!"

Radiantly Priscilla Ross called back: "Thank you, sir!"

She was watching him walk on, Shafter knew. He throttled an impulse to look back. His thoughts shifted to Joan Wolcott. How would the death of Rufe Wolcott affect her? With Vince *the* Wolcott now in full command, giving orders?

Lights had still been burning inside the big house when Joan had stepped out of her mud-splashed buggy in the graying dawn. McCloud greeted her in the big parlor where he must have been pacing, chewing the unlighted cigar he pulled from his mouth.

"Rufe's dead. Go help that sniveling housekeeper!"

Only that, leaving her desolate, suddenly and completely lonely. From now on, Joan realized as she walked back to find Mrs. Prince, it would be like this from McCloud, from Vince—brushed aside, ignored, openly resented. And now that leathery, remote old man would never hear that she did have gratitude for all he had done for her. She had no inclination to tears, a shabby substitute for all that might have been said and done. This sudden, desolate feeling would probably pass, but what would replace it? Everything she had known since a small girl had abruptly ended. Now she knew what a kindly buffer Rufe Wolcott had been against the world.

In the hours that followed, with Mrs. Prince still dissolved in tearful futility, Joan found herself issuing orders and arranging for the difficult day ahead. Rufe Wolcott's death was more than a family matter; he had towered, dominant over all this part of the territory. Friends and enemies would converge on Grenada and the house.

She heard McCloud leave and return. Men stamped into the parlor, talked, and departed. Some two hours after sunrise, Mc-

Cloud loomed in the kitchen doorway. "Feed me!" he ordered curtly.

Mrs. Prince turned away; the Mexican woman at the range froze. "Biscuits are in the oven," Joan said evenly. "Ham and eggs?"

McCloud grunted assent and turned back. Mrs. Prince spoke tremulously under her breath: "He acts like everything is his'n now."

"It could be," Joan said dully.

When she carried the hot, smoking platter into the dining room, McCloud had taken Rufe's high-backed chair at the head of the table. He bulked there, dominating table and room. In the kitchen, Joan heard him smacking and chomping, noisily slurping coffee. He called harshly for more biscuits. She was placing them on the table when Vince burst into the dining room in disheveled haste.

"I want a man run out of town!" Vince's fury was almost inarticulate.

"Well, run 'im out." McCloud reached for a biscuit without turning his head.

"He's armed!"

"Get a gun."

"Vince! Don't do anything foolish!" Joan urged in quick concern.

"Keep out of this!" Vince told her violently. He was wild as he blazed at McCloud: "I'll have this Shafter hauled off in a wagon and dumped for the coyotes!"

McCloud lurched around in the chair, biscuit forgotten in his hand. "That fellow in town?"

"He jumped me in Sid's place!" Vince was frantic with rage.

So the man had come, after all? Making trouble again! "What was said?" Joan asked hurriedly. Not until later in the day, when she heard how Shafter had contemptuously slapped Vince helpless, did she understand Vince's glare of livid aversion.

McCloud was still twisted around in the chair. "Where is he?" McCloud asked heavily.

"Took a room at the hotel and went to bed."

Slowly McCloud turned back to his platter. "Turn in an' sober up yourself. I got more to do than mess in your whiskey quarrels."

Vince glowered and stalked out. And minutes later, in the kitchen, Joan heard McCloud leave the dining room without finishing his breakfast. Now Shafter was in real danger. But he had come stubbornly to Grenada; he could face his own rashness, Joan decided resentfully.

Shafter came groggily awake; vigorous knocks were *rattling* his door. The booming voice of Lyd Adams followed. "You in there, Shafter?"

"*Uhhh* . . . coming."

Mote-spangled sunshine streamed through the window with a warm, yellow, late-afternoon look. The solid sleep had helped. When he pulled on clothes and opened the door, Lyd Adams walked in.

"Welcome," she said genially, "to Grenada." The green hat with bright red ribbon had an absent tilt on her carroty, gray-streaked hair. She grew brisk. "Might be we'll meet again. I'll walk to the livery barn an' say g' bye there."

"More trouble?" Shafter guessed, lifting brows.

"There will be. I just come in from Azul an' heard how you tangled with Vince."

Shafter chuckled; he felt good, felt alive again. "Vince tangled with me."

"Duck eggs," said the big woman grimly, "hatch ducks. But this egg you're roostin' on is hatchin' a full-growed, hungry buzzard. Rufe's dead. Vince is flyin' high. You got time to leave, happy an' ign'rant of what happens to men McCloud or Vince draws a bead on around Grenada."

Shafter grinned. "I run under cover of your skirts?"

"No shame for the borrow of 'em. You don't have the short end of a blind canary's chance if you stay around much longer."

"I've been called things, never a canary. I can't sing." Still smiling, he asked: "Where did Johnny Carr live?"

"In a little 'dobe house at my coal mine acrost the river. Ain't no use looking for Joanie Wolcott over there."

"The last person I want to see."

"Sensible, if it ain't reasonable. What else'd bring a young rooster on to Grenada?"

"It was easier last night to come on than ford the Palomas again."

"I've heard better excuses," the big woman said bluntly. "Anyways, you can head back to Azul safe an' happy now. McCloud lives here in the hotel, but he ain't around."

"No skirts protecting me when I go out," Shafter said flatly.

"Have it your way. Good luck, young feller. I'm still partial to you, but I had to unload my conscience and get you safe."

Sunset was blazing on high, scattered clouds when Shafter walked into the runway of Brad Hampton's livery barn. He was bathed, shaved, fragrant with barber water. He had eaten; his soft whistling past his teeth was contented. When young Brad Hampton emerged from a stall, he asked: "Sold your barn yet?"

"I heard how you handled Vince Wolcott and decided to stay," Hampton said. His gaze was admiring. "Been me, after that, I couldn't have slept all day. I'd have been jumpy."

"Who said I was sleeping?"

"When a man slaps a Wolcott down in Grenada, he's

noticed," Brad Hampton said dryly, leading the way back in the runway.

Far in the west, bold mountains were screening the plunging sun when Shafter reached the belt of green *bosque* bordering the river. Already blue shadows were clotting under the *bosque* willows and cottonwoods, and the sharp reports of a bullwhip and bawled oaths of a teamster lifted ahead.

A long jerk line hitch of ten straining horses was hauling a lurching, high-sided coal wagon hub deep through the river. Shafter put the gray gelding into the crossing and the teamster, jerk line in one hand, long whip in the other, yelled from his saddle: "Quicksand upstream there!"

Shafter waved thanks.

Beyond the river, the gouged road ruts climbed into a belt of low hills dotted with gaunt cholla cactus. When he looked back, the roofs of Grenada and bold stack of the smelter were visible. Southwest of Grenada the mountains raked uneven crests against the sky, still bright with stained afterglow. Northwest the open range reached into twilit hazy distance, vast and empty. Not exactly empty. Out there in the immensity of distance were boyhood memories, long forgotten, now back.

Lyd Adams's coal mine was not much; he had not expected much. The deep ruts swung off to the left past a small sign with an arrow pointing: *COAL*. A long mile from the sign, the mine was cradled in a fold of the hills—a black tunnel mouth in the steep slope, a short timber trestle ending in a loading bin under which the big wagons could drive. Large piles of black mine waste were somber in the thickening twilight. *OFFICE* was painted on the padlocked door of a small adobe building. No one was in sight.

Somewhere ahead a dog barked; a distant door slammed, and Shafter rode on toward the sounds. In the velvety shadows beyond a bend of the hillside, he found a close huddle of small adobe houses. The miners, he supposed, lived here. Behind the first house a well pulley was *creaking.* There was enough light, barely, to make out a woman balancing the dripping bucket on the well curb, and turning toward the approach of his horse.

Her eager voice called: "*¿Querido?*"

It meant "beloved", and he chuckled. "Sorry," he said. "He'll be along, probably. I'm looking for John Carr's house."

"Across from the office." She was disappointed. And, as he rode to her, a gasp, sudden, frightened, greeted him. "*¡Aie!*" She darted away, leaving the bucket toppling to the ground, *clattering* and spilling water.

"Wait!" Shafter called sharply. "It's all right!"

But it was not; she was a young, fleeing shadow, as terrified, as elusive as she had been last night when he had trapped her in Johnny Carr's dark hotel room, and she had reached for her knife. He hit the ground running—and stumbled over chunks of stove wood scattered on the ground.

III

Shafter might have caught the frightened girl if he had not tripped on the length of stove wood. A large mongrel dog rushed, snarling at him. He caught the chunk of wood off the ground and the dog veered away and turned, barking furiously. By then the fleeing girl had vanished in the thickening night shadows between the huddled adobe huts and sheds.

Other clamoring dogs were coming. Holding the wood, Shafter ran to the back of the small hut and hammered on the weathered, unpainted door planks. A slit of light reached out around him as the door opened a scant foot.

"A girl was at the well. Does she live here?"

The old man, peering out at him, was a native, a gnarled ancient with scanty white hair, deep-furrowed, leathery face, and watery eyes that blinked uncertainly. Fright broke suddenly from the old man in a protesting wail that made no sense at all against the background clamor of the dogs.

"In the name of God, *Don* Miguel . . . go to rest."

One hand was frantically making the Sign of the Cross as the other hand slammed the door and bolted it inside.

Shafter lifted a fist to hammer again—then shrugged, and turned back to his horse. He knew now that the girl was the young Marina Griegos who he had caught in Johnny Carr's room in Azul. This must be her home. She worked across the river for the Wolcotts. She could be found. But what had the old man blurted in terror? Understanding hit Shafter as he settled in the saddle again, and with it something close to awe. His father had been Big Mike Shafter—Michael—Miguel to the natives. And an old man's filming eyes peering at a shadowy figure had seen Big Mike alive once more. Twenty years had been wiped away. A dead man had stood there, still young, still vigorous, breathing hard and talking curtly.

At first it was a sad thought. Then it was a warming thought, filling him with pride. He had never suspected that he looked so much like his father. And, in a way, Big Mike had returned—in his son. Finally Shafter smiled slightly at the old man's fright. There should be a way to put it to use. He was thinking about it when he reached the deserted little adobe hut on the outer edge of the wide mine yard. When he stepped down and tried the door, it opened.

A flaring match inside revealed a framed photograph on a table against the wall, and there was no doubt now that Johnny Carr had lived here. The frame around the photograph was French-crafted silver, purchased in Marseilles, Johnny had casually said years ago. And the smiling young mother inside the frame of silver, the four children with her—three small boys and a doll-like little girl—were enough for any man's bursting pride.

The match burned close to Shafter's fingers as he stepped close and looked. A second match put flame in the small glass lamp on the table. Holding the lamp, Shafter looked around the low-ceilinged room, mud-plastered, lime-washed. A sagging sofa. Two cheap chairs. A rocker with a folded blanket on the sagging seat. A shelf holding four books—law books with cracked leather bindings dingy with age and use. There was Johnny's past—four old books from a law career of such prestige that life had indeed been champagne for Johnny. And all of it had come to this—grubbing in the ledgers of an isolated frontier coal mine, that and finally dreaming of wealth again. *Had Johnny's letter been so fantastic after all?* Shafter mused as he turned away from the books. Johnny was dead now, killed, no matter what the doctor in Azul had said. Mike Shafter had been watched and followed in Azul. Johnny's mind, skilled in legal maneuvers, had been keen to the end. Wasn't it possible old Johnny had known exactly what he was writing about?

The lamplight and wavering shadows moved ahead of Shafter into the other room, the bedroom. There was Johnny's scuffed leather trunk, lock forced, contents undoubtedly ransacked as Johnny's carpetbag had been last night in Azul. The room was quiet. Not a sound as Shafter paused inside the low, narrow doorway. Some compelling impulse moved his glance to the left—and he almost jumped back, almost caught for his handgun. For the lamplight was glinting on eyes watching him. Baleful eyes.

Then the burly, motionless figure of Con McCloud, somber in the same black suit, a revolver in one big fist, took shape against the mud-plastered wall, not lime-washed in here. Shafter lifted the lamp to see better and said with a soft bite: "Don't the Wolcotts pay you enough to keep you from stealing from a dead man . . . or have they run you off now?"

McCloud stirred against the wall, as if some vulnerable chink in his emotions had been jabbed. "Nobody throws me out!" There was harsh, suppressed violence in it.

He wouldn't be this way if he wasn't worried. Keep him talking. "You're only another ramrod," Shafter said in blistering contempt. "An over-muscled bully Rufe Wolcott had use for, and about through now, because he was the only Wolcott that had any use for you."

McCloud said thickly: "I built everything for Rufe. I made it. Ain't anyone else can run it now and hold it. Rufe knew so. It was his an' mine."

The man believes it. Narrowly Shafter calculated the fierce emotion he was uncovering. It sounded like a burning, cloudy obsession, not capable of putting together and holding all that Rufe Wolcott had left. "So you built everything?" Shafter jabbed again scornfully. "But who owns it now?" There was an air of unreality about this—the lamp glowing in his hand, the burly McCloud, gun in his fist, being coldly baited and reacting with harsh emotion.

"Rufe's gone now," McCloud said. His head dipped; his shoulders hunched; he had the look of a baited bull facing threat. "What's left is mine. Rufe meant it so. And I had an idea you'd show here after dark, Shafter. Shuck that belt an' gun."

"And get shot like a butcher's steer?"

"Up to me . . . everything's up to me now. You going to unbuckle that belt? Rufe knows what's needed!"

"Does he?" Shafter said—and now nerve ends were crawling. This man's mind is twisted; he's twice as dangerous—apt to do anything.

McCloud's gun muzzle was tilting up; he was a massive, malevolent figure, driven by hazy shadows flitting through his heavy mind. This close, his shot would not miss. Shafter did the only thing he could think of.

"The lamp!" he shouted suddenly, and hurled the lamp. The

heavy mind did what he hoped—McCloud's eyes jumped instinctively to the hurtling lamp. The gun muzzle flicked up, smashing a deafening shot that racketed and blasted between the confining walls. And what followed was awesome. The lamp shattered in mid-air. Glass fragments and spraying oil blossomed into a crimson, hurtling fireball. McCloud swore loudly as he dodged. His second shot was wild; his dismayed yell followed as the blazing oil showered on him.

It was an incredible sight. In the eerie, flickering glow that filled the room, McCloud had become a massive, frantic figure wreathed in smoky flames. The fire was licking up around his face as he dropped the gun and lunged forward, eyes closed, slapping frantically at chest and face. Shafter had dodged aside and caught out his gun. For a long moment he held there in fascination. Heat and oily smoke swept around him as he watched McCloud run against the bed and reel away, beating wildly at himself. A moment later, eyes closed, McCloud ran blindly into the solid adobe wall. Small flames were licking off the floor, off the bed, and off McCloud, who shouted thickly as he turned the wrong way, half stunned, and lunged wildly into the front wall. A strangled yell, helpless and raging, broke from him.

Shafter holstered his gun again and gulped heat and smoke and ran to the man and caught an arm. "This way!"

He should have known better. McCloud wheeled blindly. His clubbing fist smashed Shafter's chest; he caught a fold of the buckskin jacket and the stench of lamp oil and heat of the flames came hard against Shafter as they reeled off balance and crashed on the bed.

As they fell, Shafter twisted from under. His hip ground against his holster as they rolled off the bed and fell heavily to the floor. Shafter tried to reach his holster and McCloud's clawing hand was already there. Panting, coughing in the oily smoke, they struggled for the gun in nightmarish silence. Shafter's leg rolled painfully on the gun McCloud had dropped. It offered some hope, suddenly, where hope was dwindling. For McCloud's hand had reached Shafter's gun; his immense strength, despite Shafter's grip on the thick wrist, was pulling the gun from the holster. McCloud's thumb, Shafter realized, was cocking the revolver. Shafter tried to block the thumb and failed; the jolting discharge roared into the holster and the bullet tore down through Shafter's leg.

This, then, was the end; a gunshot had killed his father in this same Grenada country; now it was his turn. And a thought like that was enough. Hampering McCloud's wrist as best he could with one hand, he caught down at the floor with the other hand. Fingers closed on McCloud's discarded gun. He brought the heavy weapon up in a desperate slam to McCloud's head. All the berserk rage drained from the huge man; he wavered stupidly, as Shafter struck again, and rolled away from the collapsing figure, and struggled to his feet, sweating, gasping.

The room was almost dark as he lurched through smoke into the next room, a gun in each hand. The air was fresher in here.

Coughing, trying to get breath, he dragged a match into flame on the front of his jacket and held the light down to his leg with a shaking hand. Pain had not set in fully as yet, but already blood was soaking through the pants. The bullet seemed to have gouged through flesh above the knee, evidently missing bone and knee joint.

He looked back into the bedroom. The last of the smoky little flames were dwindling away. But there was a chance that bed blankets and mattress might smolder alight and ignite the floor. He limped back in, noticed his trampled hat, and caught it up.

McCloud lay inertly. By the man's slack arm, Shafter dragged him into the front room, through the door into the open night.

McCloud would live and make more trouble, Shafter's dark thought came as he did one last unnecessary thing. He limped inside again, put the framed photograph on the table inside his sweaty shirt. Blood was oozing from his leg as he limped out to his horse and pulled into the saddle.

The shots had not drawn anyone from the houses around the bend in the hillside. The night was peaceful as he left McCloud there on the ground and rode back toward Grenada. Once on the dark road he dismounted and, without light, tried to bandage the wounded leg. But more than a skimpy bandanna was needed.

A long time later, it seemed, he located Lyd Adams's house in Grenada by asking a strange man walking in the thick shadows on a side street. She lived in a frame dwelling of two stories on another unlighted street east of the Grenada plaza. The front yard held flower beds; vines massed on porch trellises. The window shades were drawn, but, when he limped to the porch and knocked, the door was quickly opened.

Antagonism came as he looked at Joan Wolcott standing in lamplight from the parlor that opened off the entrance hall, where stairs went up. She was startled and cool.

"Lyd said you were returning to Azul. Do you have to stay in Grenada, making trouble?"

"Trouble?" He thought of all that had happened in the past twenty-four hours that could be traced to these Wolcotts. "You haven't started to see trouble," he said in rough temper.

Lyd Adams's amiable call lifted back in the house. "Who is it?"

"Shafter."

"Here in town still?"

"Yes."

"I might've knowed it," came in resignation. "Tell 'im to come in."

In cold silence, Joan walked ahead into the parlor. When she turned and saw him clearly in the brighter light, her startled glance went from the red smears on his hands to the blood-soaked front of his pants.

"Wh-what happened?" Suspicion came instantly. "Vince . . . ?"

"McCloud," Shafter said shortly.

Lyd Adams hurried in. "I thought we had it settled. Grenada ain't a place. . . ." She stared. "Already?" the big woman said grimly.

"He met McCloud." Joan sounded uncertain now.

"I ain't surprised. He was bound to meet McCloud." Lyd Adams looked at Shafter narrowly. "He dead?"

"Not this time," Shafter said briefly.

"Soon as you get another chance at him, huh?"

"When he finds me."

She looked at his red hands, the great dark stain still spreading on his pants.

"If it's gone this far, Con'll find you," Lyd Adams said grimly. "He's that way, bulldog-like when he gets locked with a man don't give way to him." She switched to briskness. "Your horse out front?"

"Yes."

"Who knows you come here?"

"I asked a man where your house was."

"Who was he? Reckon you wouldn't know. Did you ride through the plaza?"

"No."

"That's somethin', at least. You figger this man got a good look at you? Seen that blood?"

"The street was dark. He didn't seem interested."

"He will be when he hears Con McCloud bellerin' and huntin'. Joanie, take him back in the kitchen and get his pants open whilst I get his horse outta sight in the shed." She turned back, asking keenly: "Where'd it happen?"

"In Carr's house at your mine. McCloud was inside. He seemed to be expecting me."

"I should've known you meant to ride over there, after your askin' where 'twas. We'll go into that soon as I put your horse up. Joanie, make sure the kitchen shades are pulled down."

In the kitchen, Joan silently indicated a chair by a scrubbed pine table. She looked even younger than last night in Azul. The plain black dress suggested mourning for Rufe Wolcott; narrow white cuffs, a small lace fichu kept the dress from being drab. Faint violet shadows had come under her eyes; grief and lack of sleep, he supposed as he tossed his hat on the table and sat down.

Joan's remark was openly hostile again. "I haven't forgotten how you helped me last night. I'll do what I can, help Lyd get you out of town, if we have to cover you in a wagon bed and haul you out." Joan bit her lip. Vince had said this about Shafter this morning—haul him away in a wagon for the coyotes.

Shafter's lean smile was not friendly. "If you can't drive the wagon more safely than a buggy. . . ."

The range was hot. Joan filled a tin basin from the heavy iron teakettle, took clean towels from a drawer, selected a sharp knife from another drawer.

"I'll have to cut your pants leg."

"Just so it's not my throat."

"That," Joan said evenly, "might stop more trouble. Sit still."

She brushed a strand of black hair off her forehead, bent over the leg, and carefully slit the cloth to the bottom. Shafter wet a towel in the tin basin on the table. "I'll do the rest."

"Will you sit quietly?"

She cut the blood-stiff bandanna away and firmly took the towel from his hand. Capable wench, her dislike boiling against him—as his was against her and all she was a part of—but the curve of her high-boned cheek was intent and her hands were gentle.

Before she finished wiping the leg, Lyd Adams returned hurriedly through the back door and looked at the leg. "Ain't that a sight?"

She took a whiskey bottle from a cupboard and sloshed whiskey into the raw wound. Shafter winced, reached for the bottle, and drank. His squint at the leg was speculative.

"A tight bandage should do."

"In the morning," said Lyd Adams with the gusty assurance of one who had often seen bullet wounds, "that leg'll be stiffer'n a shot goat. Prob'ly enough fever an' pain to lay you out. Joanie, this ain't your business."

"I think it is."

"Nope. You ain't McCloud, you ain't Vince. Reckon you can forget it happened?"

"I'll not mention it, if that's what you mean."

"Exactly what I mean. Supposin' you go home now an' rustle some sleep. You got a hard day tomorrow with the buryin' and all."

"The burying. . . ." Joan murmured it under her breath; she stood motionlessly in the black dress with white cuffs and fichu; she looked young and unhappy over sudden thoughts. A slight shake of her head banished whatever it was; her words to the older woman were cool and convinced. "You know you're making trouble for yourself. McCloud won't rest until he's finished this . . . whatever it is." Her look went to Shafter with renewed dislike, frowning a little, questioning.

"Ask McCloud," Shafter said. He was evenly sarcastic. "He's yours . . . the big bull in the Wolcott corral."

Lyd Adams chuckled. "I told Shafter that about Con. And Shafter, I reckon, totes some idea now about what a tangle with

McCloud means."

"I," said Joan distinctly, "am thinking about you. No one but you, Lyd." She paused. "There's Vince, too."

"I'll get used to it," the big woman said good-naturedly. "Don't worry about me. Anything McCloud starts won't be a surprise. And Vince ain't man enough to start a ruckus unless he gets someone else to do it. Shafter'll make out."

"I'm under obligation to him. I want to be certain he gets away safely."

"A chance to help a pretty young girl," said Lyd Adams archly, "makes a man obliged to her. He can brag inside an' strut."

"If he lives long enough," Joan said coolly as she walked out of the kitchen.

Lyd Adams followed her. Their voices murmured at the front door, then the door closed, and Lyd Adams returned with a bed sheet and began to tear off long strips of clean bandage.

"Joanie," she said, "will be here tomorrow to look after you." And at his quick, dour look, her chuckle came. "It ain't a plot. McCloud and Vince don't like Joanie. Rufe's Queen Mine has faulted out. Tryin' to pick up the ore again has cost Rufe heavy. That's not the kind of gamblin' Vince wants. He's sure to sell to that Boston syndicate. Sell the house, too. It's time for Joanie to get out and make a new start." She dropped to her knees in front of him and began to bandage the whiskey-reeking leg. "Now, then . . . what happened over at my coal mine?"

Briefly Shafter told her the surface facts. "Johnny Carr was my friend. I wanted to see where he'd worked and lived. McCloud was there."

"Likely he followed you. . . . Hold still while I wrap tight. McCloud keeps after a man who crosses him. He don't forgive an' he never forgets."

Shafter's grin lacked warmth. "It can work both ways.

Someday a man will take McCloud's trail and not stop. And when that happens. . . ." Shafter thought about it, his smile thinning to a tight line. "McCloud," he guessed slowly, "won't know what to do."

Hours before the midday funeral of Rufe Wolcott, a thin haze of stirred dust drifted through the plaza. The sounds of wheels, of passing horses, and feet scuffing the walk boards came through the second-story front window of the hotel room where George Ross, the Boston Irishman, was writing on sheets of foolscap with slashing strokes of a stub pen. His broken face with its mashed cheek bone and crooked nose lacked the smiling magnetism that it could hold—and usually did hold—in public. Collar of his pleated white shirt open, sleeves rolled back on hairy, muscular arms, Ross wrote with fierce intensity.

Occasionally he poured a drink from a bottle at the back of the table and tossed it down without water before catching up the pen again. Finally he lighted a cigar and strolled to the window. He was looking out at the thronged plaza, smiling faintly over his thoughts, when Priscilla Ross entered the room.

"I haven't any black to wear, George. Will this do for a funeral?"

In the dark blue suit and blue hat, she had more than ever the vivid look of butter-gold hair, pink New England cheeks, and red, smiling mouth. Ross glanced at her and shrugged. "You'll do. Who cares anyway?"

"I care. Are you ready?"

"You're going alone."

"To a funeral? Have you seen how many people are in town?"

"Do what I tell you!" He walked to the whiskey bottle.

"You're drunk!" Priscilla said hotly. "After all, when I come West to see how you make all this money. . . ."

"Shut up!" Angry and rough, it invited an instant, stormy rift between brother and sister. He drank the full glass, and coughed this time and brought the back of his hand across his mouth. "You see what I let you see, not what really goes on."

"Like a magician?" Flushed and furious, she added: "And you are drunk, so missing the funeral is probably best."

"Drunk on gold."

"Well, well . . . a bottle of gold." Priscilla's shrug was eloquently disgusted. "Sleep it off, George."

Since yesterday strain had been building in Ross, pulling nerves and uncertainties tighter. Now he became tensely quiet and deliberate. Priscilla's eyes narrowed as she recognized a dangerous mood.

"Directly after the funeral," Ross said distinctly and very quietly, "the lawyer is opening the will . . . and then Vince Wolcott is coming here to sell. I talked him into it. The papers are about ready to sign. Get close to that girl you've made friends with . . . that Joan Wolcott . . . and make some excuse to wait at the house until she gets back from the lawyer's office and tells what happened."

"I like her too well to spy on her, George. Vince Wolcott will tell you when he comes . . . if you try to think clearly."

"I want it from someone else, also. Don't argue."

"Why?" She was deliberately stubborn. "Why two people?"

He became quieter and biting. "Because the Queen Mine is shut down. They lost the vein. Because the last blasting two miners did in a new drift exposed bonanza silver and gold. I've seen it and it's fabulous."

"But I don't see. . . ."

"You'd better see," Ross said with venomous calm. "Where d' you think all the money you spend back East comes from?"

"From you, George. You've told me. . . ."

"And I'm telling you now. Listen, this is damned important to you, too. I've got to tell you to make you understand. Those two miners knocked off work without going back into the drift. They never went back. That bonanza ore is exposed up there in the mine, but all work in the Queen was stopped the next morning. Men in town here would kill for the chance to work it for a week."

"But I don't see . . . after all, it can be guarded."

"I'm not through. Use your head when I am. Manning . . . Buck Manning . . . who has charge of the mines and the smelter went in alone that evening to block out work for the next day. He found the bonanza strike. Only Manning and myself know. In a couple of hours now, I'll have the Queen sold separately to me, as a faulted mine, worth very little. I can swing it."

"It's dishonest," Priscilla said without hesitation. "Isn't it? Vince Wolcott doesn't know. This Manning . . . both of you. . . ."

"Manning saw his chance and traded what he knew for a share. The only way he'd ever get it. D' you think he'd get it from Vince Wolcott? Or the price wouldn't go out of sight to me? Now do what I tell you, or no more money from me."

"You are drunk . . . whiskey, and gold, too."

Ross watched her go. He knew her weaknesses; she would obey. He poured one more drink, a half glass, and stepped over and put the bottle on the marble top of the washstand, to sit untouched. Even thinking of that bonanza ore, high on the mountain a few miles away, waiting to be discovered at any hour, drew nerves to the snapping point and invited whiskey. And, in two hours or so, when young Wolcott walked in to sign the papers that littered the table, he needed a clear, cool head.

Few tears were visible in the immense gathering at Rufe Wolcott's funeral. Joan was not surprised; she had not expected to see grief, and was dry-eyed herself. Vince, as she expected, was the center of attention. And Con McCloud. They were taking Rufe Wolcott's place—and Rufe Wolcott had indeed been king of the Grenada country. From this day on, jolting changes would affect the lives and fortunes of many present. Uncertainty was in the air, and apprehension and calculation.

Joan rode to the cemetery in Lyd Adams's washed and polished buggy—and, as they joined the long, gathering line of other buggies, wagons, buckboards, and saddle horses behind the black-plumed hearse, the lonely, empty feeling came back. All she had known since a small girl had ended—and what was ahead now?

Lyd Adams was a magnificent, formidable sight in rustling purple grosgrain silk and a hat of black straw piled with wired red roses. "All this fuss," Lyd remarked dryly, "must be makin' Rufe snort." Even a funeral could not subdue the big woman. When Con McCloud rode a sleek-curried horse up from behind, Lyd bent out her side of the buggy and spoke in a hoarse, booming whisper of false sympathy. "That han'some face looks like it got throwed under a calf stampede, McCloud. How'd it happen?"

McCloud's black hat could not hide the bruises on the side of his head; heavy nose and forehead were battered. Pale little blister patches were visible on his jaw. His stare held dislike as he rode on.

"That"—Lyd Adams chuckled—"blowed his bile. I'd've rubbed Shafter into him, but he'd have knowed Shafter come to the house last night and likely was still there."

"Shafter . . . ," Joan said under her breath, looking after McCloud, "I thought . . . I mean, last night it looked like McCloud had caught Shafter and . . . and punished him."

"What you're tryin' to say," said Lyd Adams with a grim smile, "is that Shafter like to ruined McCloud. Ain't a man ever left McCloud lookin' that way."

"Something like that," Joan confessed, frowning.

"This Mike Shafter is a hunk of man, might as well get used

to it," Lyd said cheerfully. "Me, I'm partial to him, even if he is stubborn an' bull-headed." She changed the subject. "You was told, I guess, that Judge Dixon means to read the will soon's we get back? I got to listen. Seems I'm mentioned."

"I'll have to listen to the reading," Joan said listlessly, her own uncertainties moving in again. A thought made her add: "I always believed that Uncle Rufe secretly liked you."

"If he'd ever said so, I'd have ducked from whatever he was aimin' to skunk me with," Lyd said frankly.

Joan never forgot the reading of the will a little later. Judge Horace Dixon had been a circuit judge, and could be one again if he tired of his lucrative practice in mining law and Spanish grant claims. His unpretentious office was on the north side of the plaza, and, when Lyd Adams turned her buggy to the hitch rack, the dapper, sallow figure of Jess Parker was standing on the walk nearby. Parker ignored them—but he was a symbol, Joan thought resentfully, of the disturbing, foreboding changes already taking place. Vince was already taking over; what Vince wanted was being done; McCloud's wishes no longer counted. Parker was waiting there, of course, for Vince to come out of Judge Dixon's office—and it was not a good omen for Vince's future.

Lyd Adams swept through the judge's waiting room into the office behind, and her booming confidence to Judge Dixon reached every waiting ear.

"Looks like bein' late saved us from gettin' tromped in the rush."

This office with its faded Brussels carpet, large copper spittoon, shelves of law books, sagging horsehair sofa, and cluttered roll-top desk had been familiar and friendly to Joan. Now the office was filled with tight, unfriendly, suspicious tension.

Already seated were Tibbons Wolcott, the graying clerk in

Rufe's general store, and his sizable wife, Henry Peck, cashier of Rufe's bank, and Vince, and others. Mrs. Prince, also—and Con McCloud, standing at the back window, looking out, a burly, silent figure solidly apart from the others.

Vince scowled at Lyd Adams and spoke arrogantly to the judge. "Does she belong in here?"

"I believe so." Judge Dixon was courteous. Standing by his roll-top desk, thick gray hair rumpled as usual, he spoke mildly to them all. "Decisions must be made, so I called this meeting in unseemly haste. The will itself will be probated and a matter of record. But these brief extracts will resolve uncertainties." Glancing at a sheet of paper he lifted from the desk, the judge read: "Title and immediate possession of the Grenada house, with all contents, to Miss Joan Wolcott. To Tibbons Wolcott, five thousand dollars, payable within two years, by the co-executors."

Tibbons held solemn silence. His larger wife burst out: "Only five thousand . . . after nigh ten years here?"

"Five hundred a year, Lucy, ain't bad for a death watch," Lyd Adams said genially. "More'n you could've got elsewhere."

"You aren't in the family, Lyd Adams! Judge, who are these co-executors?"

"Myself, ma'am, and Lyd Adams, without bond."

Joan hardly heard them; she couldn't, of course, afford to keep the big house, but he had remembered her.

The judge was continuing: "To Dave Bracken, five thousand. The same to Missus Prince. And five thousand dollars each to Henry Peck and Manuel Sisneros Griegos. All payable within two years."

Con McCloud turned quickly from the window. He was frowning. "Is that last one the Manuel Griegos from Cincos Hermanos?"

"From Five Brothers?" the judge translated. He seemed at a loss. "I haven't heard of the settlement."

Joan explained. "Cincos Hermanos isn't on a map. It isn't a settlement, only a place in the mountains, beyond Skull Cañon, where Mimbres Apaches burned six wagons and left heads on stakes across the cañon as a warning. The Griegos families are scattered in small cañons west of there. Five brothers settled back in there, and old Manuel was one of the sons."

"You seem familiar with the clan," the judge said dryly. "Perhaps you can help us notify this man that he was mentioned in the will."

Lyd Adams had listened with amusement. "Old Manuel lives over t' my coal mine, Judge. His boy works in the mine. Marina, the granddaughter, works in Rufe's house."

"Why'd Rufe leave him all that money?" McCloud insisted.

"I can't say," the judge said briefly. "Now, then, I'll omit smaller bequests. To Vince Wolcott, five hundred dollars, payable within a week, plus thirty dollars on the first of each month for ten years."

"A dollar a day?" Vince's blurted question had a strangled sound. And when the judge nodded, Vince blurted again: "Why?"

Judge Dixon, Joan had heard, had ordered men hanged when he was on the bench, and had not lifted his voice. He was calm now. "An attorney doesn't require reasons for a clause in a will. This was done day before yesterday, when Rufe Wolcott had reason to believe his illness was serious."

McCloud's relish punched at Vince. "Now you'll muck rock in the mines or chouse steers, and jump when you're told."

"Enough of that, McCloud." The judge was terse and sharp. "You're here to listen."

"I'm here to get what Rufe meant me to have."

"I'm coming to that."

Vince was standing up. It seemed an effort. Vince looked blindly around and started out of the office, each step faster,

faster, until he was almost running when he reached the front door. It slammed after him.

The judge had turned, looking after Vince; he frowned, and was still frowning as he looked down at the notes in his hand. His words were deliberate and carefully precise. "To Con McCloud, twice his present wages, plus a five hundred dollar bonus on the last day of each year in which he has worked for the estate of Rufus Wolcott. If the estate should be sold, five years' pay and bonuses shall be given to McCloud for past services. All other properties and assets, and full control immediately, under the advice and with the consent of the executors, are left without other reservations to Miss Joan Wolcott."

The abrupt silence that followed had a blank, stunned quality.

Joan could feel it, and the eyes on her, they were thinking: *why her?* And Joan herself was thinking the same thing with the same stunned blankness.

McCloud's heavy challenge reached at the judge. "What else did Rufe say?"

"Nothing more." The judge was watching McCloud closely and thoughtfully.

"Five hundred? For me? That's all?"

"The five hundred is a bonus each year," Judge Dixon said slowly and distinctly. "Plus double pay. Do you understand that, McCloud?"

He might have been explaining to a child. The thought almost touched Joan's mouth with a smile—Con McCloud a child. Silence filled the office again; it drew out second by silent second, and suddenly tension was in the air. McCloud was not himself; he was acting strangely. The puzzled shake of McCloud's head seemed an effort to clear muddled thoughts.

Without looking, Judge Dixon tossed the page of notes to his desk. The paper tilted on the desk edge and slid off to the worn carpet and the judge did not notice. His searching gaze was on McCloud. Small blisters on McCloud's muscular jaw were turning livid as blood surged darkly behind them. McCloud shook his head again; his mutter, rumbling and almost inaudible, sounded as if he were arguing with himself.

"Wasn't Rufe. He never said that . . . just a paper. . . ."

Again Judge Dixon explained with grave care. "It was a legal will, McCloud. The court. . . ."

The man's big hand impatiently swept talk aside. Looking at the floor, frowning, McCloud's mutter argued with himself again. "He tried to tell me and couldn't talk. Tears were in his eyes while he tried. I saw 'em . . . tears. First time Rufe ever did that. He was trying to tell me. . . ."

It could have been pathetic, that heavy mind groping for what it had believed. It was chilling. The burly figure in front of the window had loomed over their lives too long. Save, perhaps, over Judge Dixon and Lyd Adams.

The judge tried again, a tighter note of clarity in his patient words. "When I drew the will, McCloud. . . ."

"You!" McCloud said in a louder voice, looking up. He nodded, as if his thoughts had fastened now on one unquestioned fact. His deep chest lifted in a breath as his scowl considered the judge. "You did it!" McCloud said, still louder. "You said it . . . not Rufe!" The scowl sought Joan. "And you!" McCloud said harshly, moving away from the window.

"We'll discuss it later," the judge tried to say, and McCloud ignored him. Flushed fury had surged through the man.

"I helped him get everything!" McCloud said loudly. "From nothing! Rufe knew it! It was mine like it was his! He said so plenty times! And then a rag-tail girl he took in an' kept underfoot stole it while Rufe couldn't talk!"

"McCloud. . . ."

The judge was not able to say more. In one of his roaring,

awesome rages, McCloud was shouting as he advanced.

"You two did it! Stole it from Rufe an' me!" His big fist chopped a furious gesture at Joan. "You, girl! All you ever did was take from Rufe! But you don't steal from McCloud!"

For a moment Joan expected the fury to strike her, to turn on the judge. She had seen McCloud like this, berserk, and knew what he could do. But he shouldered past her, past the judge. He was talking thickly to himself as the front door banged behind him.

Lyd Adams drew a breath that sounded shaken; the first unsteadiness, Joan realized, that she had ever heard in the big, gusty, confident woman. It was a measure, in a way, of what had just happened.

Soberly, grimly Lyd Adams broke the silence that held all of them again, even the judge, who stood in frowning, serious thought. "This ain't new in McCloud. Think back. He's been comin' to this. Worse the last year or so. While he had orders to follow, he didn't seem much different. Only they were his orders, more 'n' more, the way they seemed to be workin' in his head."

The judge's nod agreed, and he added more. "Rufe Wolcott knew it, which was why his will gave McCloud no authority at all. Provided for his help and loyalty if they continued, yet recognized that McCloud might have to be dropped."

"He can't work for Joanie now. And that ain't all. He's movin' in a fog. He's got an idea set in his head an' he'll hold to it. He's dangerous." Lyd Adams was positive. "Can't something be done about him, Judge?"

"Nothing at the present time," the judge said slowly. "I remember a case when I was on the bench . . . an attempt by family and friends was made, but the man had a certain reasonable way of talking. He laughed, he joked in court, and explained remarks and answered questions in an apparently normal manner. So normal that he gained sympathy from most people who heard him, as McCloud will probably do when he calms down and gives his version. . . .”

“McCloud sounded reasonable to me,” the large and challenging wife of Tibbons Wolcott said spitefully. “Everything to a girl who never did anything for it. McCloud'll convince people. . . .”

“Undoubtedly,” the judge said briefly. “And the case I mentioned, madam . . . within a year seven people were dead because a dangerous man wasn't stopped while there was time. Are there other questions? No? I believe, then, that is all for the present.”

Shafter was shaving, and thinking about Johnny Carr's letter, Johnny's death, and the tangle of mystery Johnny had left, when the idea came, full-blown, as fantastic as the letter Johnny had mailed to Colorado. Yet the perfect answer for what had to be done to get at the truth about Johnny's letter and all that had happened since. Shafter grinned at his lathered face in the mirror. Why not?

Two days ago Lyd Adams, downstairs in the kitchen now, cooking breakfast, had returned from the funeral of Rufe Wolcott with the amazing news about the Woicott will. For two days Mike Shafter had spent most of the time in this upstairs bedroom while fever burned in his leg and pain jumped each time he moved. Thank the bull-built McCloud for that and for Johnny's death, but now Shafter grinned again, and finished shaving.

The dark wool pants he was wearing, the gray flannel shirt he pulled on, had been bought yesterday by Lyd Adams. He was clean, he was rested, he was smiling when he limped downstairs to the kitchen.

Lyd Adams turned from the range and thick bacon strips sizzling in an iron skillet. "I had an idea you'd be prowlin' this mornin'. Coffee there by your plate."

Pain walloped the leg as he sat down, but not like yesterday. Across the coffee mug Shafter was casually humorous. "How is she doing in Rufe Wolcott's boots?"

"Half the territory is already holding breath over it," the big woman said dryly.

"Any trouble from McCloud?"

"He got middlin' drunk in the Palace, first time in years. Talked to anyone who'd listen and plenty were willin'. A schemin' girl and lawyer had tricked a sick man, anything that happened now would be deserved."

"How many believed him?"

Lyd Adams opened the oven door and glanced at pans of baking bread. She caught up a long fork and turned bacon strips, and her voice was dry again and blunt.

"They've listened to McCloud for years and jumped. Easy to believe him now, especially with some agreein' to suit their own ideas and plans."

Shafter nursed the hot coffee mug between his palms. "Someone," he suggested, "will have to take McCloud's place. A girl can't do all the things McCloud did."

"Joanie would try if she thought she could. That's what Rufe liked about her. Spunk. Lots of it. He told Judge Dixon she was the best he could do. But she's only a girl, and a young one, and likely to make a mess of what was left to her."

"In what way?" Shafter asked thoughtfully.

Lyd Adams's snort lacked any illusions. "Every way." She was emphatic. "Men that Rufe stamped on will be at Joanie. Some who didn't have the nerve to take on Rufe and McCloud will try her. And she'll make mistakes. She's bound to think like a girl instead of thinkin' like a man, which she'll have to do. She'll be soft when she should be hard, and lose her temper when she should be cool."

Shafter was smiling. "McCloud lost his temper."

"He was McCloud, with Rufe behind him. Joanie will take men serious she should shrug off. She'll ignore men who ought to be settled hard and quick. She'll think all her friends are still friends. She's a woman and she'll act like a woman," Lyd Adams said with sober conviction as she reached for another egg. "She needs a man who can be like McCloud when needed, and will stand up to her when he knows he's right. And think like Rufe Wolcott when needed, and do what Rufe would have done."

"A large order," Shafter said.

"Not a man in sight who fits."

Shafter drank more coffee and put the cup down gently. "Try me."

The egg Lyd Adams was breaking almost missed the skillet. Her startled look was frowning. She turned back to the range in silence and spooned hot grease over the eggs.

"Last night there was a shootin'," she said abruptly. "First man killed in Grenada in over a year. Riff-raff is driftin' into town already. They mean to try Joanie quick."

"Expected it, didn't you?"

"I did," said Lyd Adams grimly. "There's been a day marshal and a night marshal who never amounted to much. The sheriff's in Azul. McCloud was the deputy in these parts."

"He's still deputy?"

"Not for long. The man who takes his place will get it. Judge Dixon will see to that."

"Even me?"

The big woman put breakfast on the table—eggs, bacon, slabs of steaming bread, stewed prunes, a hot apple pie. She sat down and frowned across the table.

"I wouldn't wish McCloud's job on any man I was partial to," she said bluntly. "He'll be the man has to be killed so they can get at Joanie. And Joanie won't be easy on him. I can tell you this, too. Joanie's in trouble already. Long on property and short on cash. A young stranger with health an' good sense would keep out of it."

Shafter speared a prune with his fork and grinned over it.

After a moment, Lyd Adams said briefly and grimly: "I'll talk to Judge Dixon. He'll decide."

IV

The mountains southwest of Grenada looked nearer than they were. The high, green blotches were forest; the smoky-purple gashes were cañons; two livid scars on a shoulder of the nearest mountain were mine dumps smearing down the rocky slopes. George Ross, the Boston Irishman, was looking with rapt fascination at the distant mines when he rode into the broad, sun-baked smelter yard west of Grenada. A man, Ross was thinking—any man—usually had only one chance at swift, spectacular riches. With envy, he'd watched it happen to others. And now it had happened to George Ross—bonanza silver with high gold values discovered in a drift of the Queen Mine that had been driving through worthless rock. For six tormenting days only two men had known of the strike.

Wind eddies swirled acrid smelter fumes down from the sooty top of the smelter stack. Ross coughed and grimaced, then his scowl came again at the memory of how close he'd been to buying the Queen from young Vince Wolcott as a faulted, almost worthless mine. It had taken the will of a dead man, intruding like a blocking hand, to upset a faultless plan. For two days now resentment had boiled in Ross, and corrosive uncertainty and mounting tension had blotted out all else. There was still hope, had to be hope, for a chance like this would never happen again.

Ross was barely aware of the thick adobe walls of the main smelter building, the hammering stamp mill beyond, the buckboard team and three saddle horses waiting at the office hitch rack. Buck Manning, who managed the smelter, the mill, and the two mines on the mountain came quickly out of the office as he dismounted, and in Manning an expectant tension was visible.

"Men in the office," Manning warned under his breath as he came close.

They walked out into the open yard—Ross, solid and conservative and Eastern in his narrow-brimmed gray hat, gray suit and neat cravat, and polished black shoes. Buck Manning, indifferently wearing soiled ducks and cotton shirt, was short and sinewy, with a terrier-like alertness in his question.

"Any luck with Joanie Wolcott?"

"I found her in Wolcott's old office above the bank." Anger tightened Ross's broken face with its mashed cheek bone and bent nose. "She sat there . . . just sat there looking at me from an empty head. Not a question out of her. Not even an expression. No interest at all. Finally she said she was selling cattle and horses if I wanted them, but nothing else."

Buck Manning was rueful before Ross finished. "I should have warned you. Listen, I've seen that girl before she was seventeen, sitting cross-legged on a blanket by one of the loading chutes up at the mines, beating muleskinners at quick five-card draw while they were waiting to load. Joanie was listening to you. Thinking, too, as fast as you were. If there was an empty head in the office, it wasn't Joanie's."

"What sort of girl is she?" Ross demanded with quick attention.

Manning did not hesitate. "A maverick. Ran wild, you might say, with no one paying attention to what she did."

"How wild?"

"Make no mistake there," Manning said coolly. "She's welcome in church. By the ladies."

Ross shrugged disinterest. He was looking again at the mine dumps on the mountain. With renewed tension, he said: "All I could think of last night was that high-grade ore exposed back in the Queen." He struck a fist into his palm. "Someone may find it! That drift has to be blasted shut until I can do something with this Wolcott girl."

Manning was sarcastic. "Who'll carry in the sledges and drills, and beat out the blast holes? And lug in powder and fuse? Me, the boss? You, the gentleman from Boston, with a million in his pocket?"

"Mostly stock they'll issue," Ross reminded.

"Stock or cash, those miners aren't blind or fools. We'd be like a brass band marching into the Queen. No one's going into that drift while the mine is closed. The men see enough tunnels, stopes, and drifts while they're working."

"Someone might go in." The tension was still in Ross, ridging muscles on his broken face. "One look at that ore, if a man knows ore . . . have you assayed any more of the samples we brought out?"

"Last night." Manning licked his lips. "Still better than two thousand dollars a ton."

"A thousand tons of it. . . ."

"It could be a pocket, fifty tons or less," Manning said sharply. "A mine doesn't stay in bonanza forever."

Ross said irritably: "I've seen 'em stay long enough. Even the low-grade in the Queen may have enough value to smelt. Don't think in a small way."

"I know mines."

"So do I. How d' you think I got this face?"

Manning shrugged, and Ross said savagely: "I got it from mucking in cow camps, mine camps, and dirty little towns, looking for investments that might interest some of the sharpest pocket-slitters between Bangor and the Chesapeake. Ice in their blood, locks on their money . . . and not interested in scruples if they were shown a hundred percent and better. If I connived, misrepresented, and hacked at a man until he let go cheap, I got a small cut and a pat on the head. But never enough to swing a large deal of my own."

"And your face?" Manning reminded coolly.

"An accident. I tried to blow a little one-horse mine tunnel shut one night and a premature shot blasted rock in my face. I had to hide out with half my head blown in and almost died."

Buck Manning swallowed. "Your mine?"

"The man who'd found wire gold in it was found dead," Ross said coldly. "But it was only a pocket. Never paid out after I bought it cheap. All I got was this face. I mean to do better here. Smelt five hundred tons of that Queen ore for me . . . and in five years I'll own all Wolcott left, and twice as much. He hasn't scratched the chances here. He was a small man with little ideas."

Buck Manning said slowly: "Half I smelt is mine. That agreement we signed is court-proof." Manning's glance at the broken face was almost furtive. "If you don't think so, Ross, you'll be surprised."

Ross offered a cigar, bit the end off another, and said more calmly: "There's enough. First get the Queen. And five weeks to do it. No more. I had a Boston letter yesterday, telling me to drop this in five weeks and go to Denver. They have something else in mind."

"Five weeks?" Buck Manning suddenly looked worried. Then calculating.

Ross's twisted smile was not pleasant. "Don't get ideas," he suggested. "If I can't turn it, if I have to leave, I'll take the girl into the Queen myself and show her the ore. I'm your only chance . . . and five weeks to keep that high-grade undiscovered and get title to the Queen."

Buck Manning lost his temper. "Serves me right. What do you think you can do in five weeks, the way things are now? Vince Wolcott . . . yes! Joanie Wolcott is something else! She's got everything . . . and she'll keep it!"

Ross struck a match on the bottom of his shoe and got the cigar going. He was completely calm now. "She got it through a will," he reminded, looking at the end of the cigar. "Who would inherit from her?"

"Vince Wolcott is an equal cousin. I suppose. . . ." Manning broke off, startled. "Wrong man, Ross," he said flatly. "I'll help steal a mine, and convince myself it's the only chance I'll ever have. Rufe Wolcott was alive when I went to you, and little enough I'd have gotten from him and McCloud for the news that the Queen was in bonanza. But a mine's one thing. A dead girl is another."

"I only asked a question," Ross reminded coldly. "Do you think Vince Wolcott doesn't know the answer? Or some of his friends who'd profit if he inherited?"

"That's their business." Buck Manning was caustic. "I had my hands on bonanza ore and it's slipping away. Five weeks!" Buck turned, squinting toward the mountains. "Never be a chance like it again," he said sullenly. "Everything broke just right this once. Now it's gone sour."

"This isn't penny poker with loafing muleskinners," Ross said curtly. "I've hacked good men down in less than five weeks. Last night I hired this Con McCloud to manage everything for the syndicate after they buy and we get the Queen."

Manning was startled. "You're crazy, because McCloud's crazy now. I heard what happened in Judge Dixon's office. McCloud's worse than powder in your pocket with the fuse lit."

"In the girl's pocket," Ross corrected. "McCloud thinks she and the lawyer stole everything. All he can think of is getting it away from them."

"Crazy!"

"Of course. We want him that way." Ross was gazing toward the mine dumps again in the same tight fascination. "McCloud claims he can take almost a thousand prime steers from the girl tonight."

"Drunk, too," Buck Manning said disgustedly. "Take 'em in his pockets, I suppose?"

"I didn't ask him," Ross said calmly. "But he's going to try."

For the first time, Buck Manning was apprehensive. "All I had in mind was a mine that might be picked up cheap. Now it's rustling, now it's Vince Wolcott inheriting from Joanie."

"All she has to do is take what she's offered and quit," Ross said coolly. "Hack her savagely enough and she'll be sick of it fast. She needs money already."

"Money?" Buck Manning was skeptical. "She's got all the money in the world."

"Property and liabilities," Ross corrected. "Rufe Wolcott's reputation made him safe. She's different. Who has confidence in a young girl? She's got to sell cattle and horses quick to get money she needs at once."

"She told you everything, I suppose," Manning said sarcastically.

Ross was amused. "In a way . . . she's taken a liking to my sister, has her staying in the Wolcott house now for company. Two girls close like that chatter secrets."

"Your sister, too?" Distaste flashed on Buck Manning's face. "If I get half the Queen, I'll still feel dirty."

"But you'll take it," Ross said dryly.

At Lyd Adams's mine across the river, coal thundered down from a loading bin, banging and slamming against the high sideboards of the empty wagon beneath, and spewing black dust toward Mike Shafter as he rode past. He wheeled the gray gelding into cleaner air and lifted a hand to the grinning, dust-blackened face at the chute, and rode on around the bend in the hillside to the cluster of small adobe houses where the miners lived.

There was noise and life now in the bright midday sunlight; dogs began to bark, small children stopped playing to stare at the stranger who turned his horse in behind the first house. The bucket that young Marina Griegos had dropped in fright when she had recognized him was on the wide, adobe well curb. The chunk of stove wood he had tripped over was on the ground where he had dropped it. And the back door that the old man had hastily bolted in his own fright at sight of Mike Shafter was padlocked on the outside now.

Pain raveled like a hot wire through the bandaged leg as Shafter limped to the door and knocked, and knocked again without an answer. He ignored the dogs, not so bold in daylight, and limped to the next house. The children, he noticed, had disappeared. Make something of that, more than a stranger was the reason, he guessed.

The middle-aged woman who answered his knock looked through a scant foot of open door with a blank expression that did not change when he smiled.

"I'm looking for the old man who lives next door," Shafter said. "Where is he?"

She said—*"¿Quién sabe?"*—in a voice as blank as her face.

"You don't know where he's gone?"

"¿Quién sabe?"

"Well then, where's Marina Griegos?"

Another monotonous *"¿Quién sabe?"* had a slight shrug this time for emphasis.

A voice behind Shafter said dryly: "You're wasting your time, young man. There's no information here for you if you try every house."

He had halted his horse quietly by Shafter's horse, a ruddy man with graying hair and calm dignity. Broadcloth suit, light straw hat, and walking shoes marked him a townsman. As Shafter thanked the woman and limped back to his horse, the stranger rested folded palms on the saddle horn and regarded him closely and speculatively.

"I was beginning to suspect there'd be no talking," Shafter agreed, catching up the reins of his horse. He looked up at the man. "You seem to know why, sir."

"Yes, I do, Mister Shafter." And when Shafter's eyebrows lifted inquiringly, the man smiled faintly. "Your limp," he said. "From Con McCloud."

Shafter stepped up, and winced as the leg came down hard against the saddle leather and pain jumped through it. "Has to be Judge Dixon," he guessed.

"It is. I saw you ride by the mine office and followed you. Mind telling me, Shafter, what you're after here?"

They were reining back toward the coal mine, holding down to a walk. "I wanted to talk about Johnny Carr," Shafter said. True, as far as it went.

"You knew Carr, I understand."

"We were friends." Shafter waited, and reminded: "Why no information back there?"

"Oh, that?" Dixon's thoughts had wandered. "Yesterday McCloud came here looking for old Manuel Griegos, who lives in that first house. Used his fists on Pete Griegos, the son, trying to make him tell where old Manuel had gone. Now the son is gone, also, and none of them will talk about it. Not even to Lyd Adams or me, certainly not to a stranger."

Carefully Shafter asked: "What did McCloud want with the old man?"

Dixon was thoughtful. "I wish I knew. McCloud is a dangerous man now. Whatever drove him into a rage at Pete Griegos could be dangerous to old Manuel. Probate will show that Rufe Wolcott left five thousand dollars to Manuel. McCloud was disturbed when he heard it." Dixon shook his head. "The will of a wealthy man," he said slowly, "can sometimes drag into the open the mistakes and hates and long-buried skeletons of a lifetime."

The long jerk-line spans of horses were hauling the loaded coal wagon away, and another wagon was moving under the loading bin when Dixon dismounted in front of the low hut where Johnny Carr had lived.

"Come in," he said.

The stench of oily smoke still lingered inside as Dixon walked directly to the shelf that held the four old law books. "Carr often stopped at my office for a visit. He seemed familiar with the law and courts . . . more so than these four books would account for. Perhaps you can explain."

"If Johnny didn't explain, why should I?"

"I have a reason for asking."

Shafter looked around the small, shabbily furnished room again, thinking once more of all that Johnny had been. "He probably wouldn't mind now," Shafter decided. "He was an attorney, one of the best in the East, he hinted."

Dixon was watching him closely. "You believed the man?"

"I always believed Johnny."

"Was his name Carr at that time?"

"No."

"He abandoned the law then, gave up prestige and no doubt a handsome income, and changed his name. Was it scandal? Disgrace?"

"Johnny had taken his wife and four small children to Europe. He sent them back several weeks before his own return, and their ship went down at sea. Johnny blamed himself. He should have kept them with him, should have returned at least on the same ship. He might have saved them or gone down with them. He waited until there was no hope, and changed his name and began to drift."

Dixon said quietly, glancing around the shabby little room: "He went down with them in his own way. I think I understand him better now." A direct, probing glance considered Shafter again. "The facts I know about you," Dixon said bluntly, "are these . . . you carried Joanie Wolcott to her hotel in Azul, and pulled her out of the Palomas crossing when her horse lost footing. You came on to Grenada after being warned away. In the Palace Bar you used the flat of your hand on Vince instead of a gun. You've had serious trouble with McCloud already, yet, dangerous as it may be, you want McCloud's job."

"At least," Shafter said wryly, "you've checked on me."

"You also own a small stageline and a small mine in Colorado. You came to Azul to meet John Carr and found him dead. An interesting pattern, Shafter."

"What sort of pattern?"

Dixon moved one of the chairs to the table, sat down, and plucked an envelope from inside his coat. He thrust the enclosure back in his pocket, produced a pencil, and continued to speak as he wrote on the back of the envelope. "A pattern of trouble," Dixon said dryly. "Also some suggestion of a level head and responsibility. And, not the least, the approval of Lyd Adams." He handed the envelope to Shafter. "If I'm mistaken, we'll soon see the last of you, or we'll bury you and try again."

The bearer, Michael Shafter, will replace McCloud, and be discharged only by me. He will see that the trail herd on Bajada Mesa is delivered to Boswell and Terry at Fort Kinfadden.

Horace Dixon

Shafter's glance was quizzical. "Just who gives me orders?"

"Joanie Wolcott, mostly," Dixon said, getting to his feet. A fleeting look of humor touched his eyes. "I suspect she will not be easy on you. But, as executor, my orders will stand. You will understand that, young man, even though Joanie may choose to forget when it suits her."

"She can't fire me?"

"No."

"But I'll have two bosses?"

"I have three," Dixon said. "Probate court, my conscience, and the wishes of Rufus Wolcott. And the strictest," Dixon added reflectively, "is conscience. Now, then, this herd must reach Kinfadden without delay. Joanie may have left for the ranch. If she has, talk with her there." Dixon hesitated. "Can you make the ride with that leg?"

Shafter said—"Yes."—briefly, and had an idea the older man had been about to say more but had decided against it.

Night had closed in when the narrow ranch road Shafter was following began to twist and climb through low hills blotched with scattered scrub and small cedars. The stars were a misted spatter in a disturbed sky. To the southwest, lightning streaked and glowed through dark cloud banks. Rain again—Shafter's thoughts jumped to old Johnny Carr who, even in death, must be finding a lean streak of macabre humor in this. *We can't lose, Michael, unless we're killed!* And Johnny had lost. The Wolcott girl had many riches in sight—and Mike Shafter had hired to help her keep them.

She had left for the ranch before he had returned to Grenada. That settled, he had leisurely eaten at a café on the plaza. Then, taking his time, he had bought extra cartridges, a canteen, belt knife and sheath, slicker, and blanket, replacing gear he had left at the feed corral in Azul. For miles he had been riding on the night-shrouded sweep of XR range that Joan Wolcott now owned. And when he speculated on her reception of Judge

Dixon's order, his smile came faintly; without doubt he would be somewhat less than welcome. The black clouds in the southwest were pushing closer. Distant thunder whispered across the hills. The first clouds moved overhead, wiping out the stars.

He rode out of the hills as a damp wind was sighing through the cedars. Spits of rain began to peck his face. He unstrapped the new slicker and pulled it on some minutes before a belting downpour started.

The blackness was intense. From the saddle, the muddy slope of road was only a guess in the invisible curtains of rain. He let the gelding follow it. After a time the rain slacked off, then came hard again, and, finally, eased once more to a light drizzle.

A few threads of light ahead, to the left a little, were the first warning in the wet blackness that the road might have reached the XR headquarters. A horse nickered ahead. The gelding answered and veered toward the slits of light. And, suddenly, the darker blot of a house loomed close in front, and the threads of light were seeping around drawn window shades. The gelding halted beside the horse that had nickered, then snorted uneasily and moved away.

Shafter stepped down on muddy ground, took one step, and lurched off balance. His startled oath came as he wheeled around and reached down to the arm he had stepped on—a slack, outflung arm that did not move as he touched it.

The horse took a sidling, nervous step away. Speaking soothingly, Shafter found the reins looped over the horn. His other hand groped to the stirrup and found a foot twisted, locked in the iron.

In blackness and tapping rain, with the skittish horse poised to bolt, Shafter pulled the new belt knife from its sheath on his hip. The edge was keen and sliced through the stirrup leather; the iron, the foot locked in it, and the hoisted leg, dropped to the ground with a soggy *thump.*

Shafter tossed the reins to drag; a slap moved the horse away. Slicker open, shielding against rain and wind, he flared three matches in a sputtering burst. One quick look down and he flipped the matches away and turned to the house.

Voices were murmuring inside. A woman's laugh cut off as his muddy feet *thudded* on the planks of a roofed porch. The door opened as his fist lifted to knock, and bright lamplight struck his eyes to a squint. Joan Wolcott, framed in the light, looked at the dripping slicker and up at his wet face. Laughter on her countenance turned startled and frowning as she tried to see past him. "Is Lyd Adams . . . ?"

He said—"I'm alone."—and he was thinking: *Two days . . . and pants. Brown wool pants tucked in soft leather riding boots, a man's brownish-red blouse. Not another woman in Grenada would have dared dress like this and ride out astride like a man, a lithe, slender young man.* But this girl who owned half the town now, half the country around, could do as she pleased—and obviously meant to.

Her comment was reserved. "You've taken the wrong road to Azul and back to Colorado, Mister Shafter."

Two lamps were flooding light through the room behind her. The Boston girl, Priscilla Ross, was seated on a sofa, as vivid tonight as Shafter remembered her in the early sunlight in the Grenada plaza. The same smiling radiance as she looked toward the door, the butter-gold hair, the long-limbed, graceful poise of a girl from the East, not yet tanned, toughened by this harsher country. A wide-shouldered man standing near her in jeans and plaid shirt was not George Ross, her brother.

"I took the right road," Shafter said briefly. "Bring a lamp to the porch here." He turned back to the horses, adding, "There's a dead man waiting for attention."

He was lifting the muddy, inert thing that had been a man

when steps pounded off the porch. A lamp in the doorway pushed light through the misty rain. The wide-shouldered man stopped by Shafter, looked at his burden, and blurted: "That's Waco Jordan! Here, I'll help!"

"I've got him."

Shafter slogged heavily to the porch, where each girl was waiting with a flickering lamp. The Boston girl's eyes widened when she saw what he lowered to the rough planks. She swallowed and looked away.

"He was dragged by a foot and trampled and kicked," Shafter informed her coolly. "Doesn't leave a man looking like much." He pulled back what was left of the torn, abraded coat. "And shot through the chest."

Joan Wolcott was pale but her voice was steady. "Waco was smiling when we left him on Bajada Mesa."

"One of the men with the trail herd?" And when she nodded, Shafter guessed: "Then you have trouble there." He glanced at the wide-shouldered stranger. "Who is this man?"

Her look flashed resentment. "This is Art Blaisdell, the foreman. He's taking McCloud's place."

Shafter knocked water off his dripping hat and looked at Blaisdell with closer interest. Pushing thirty, the man stood lightly, confidently, wearing his gun easily. Light-brown hair made his weathered face look darker. His nose was straight, mouth unsmiling as he said with edged curtness: "You brought him in. Now what happened? What's your business here?"

"His horse dragged him in. I found him waiting in the mud out there while you were enjoying yourself inside," Shafter said briefly. He reached under the dripping slicker and handed the envelope to Joan Wolcott. "From Dixon," he told her.

Priscilla Ross spoke unsteadily: "I . . . I'll go in. This is the first time. . . ."

"Probably not the last time if you stay in Grenada," Shafter assured her.

The look she gave him as she started in with the lamp held wide-eyed revulsion. Boston, plainly, did not deposit battered bodies on the doorstep.

Joan Wolcott was reading the penciled words on the back of the envelope.

"Art. . . ." She brought her lamp closer and read a second time, as if unbelieving. Anger was lifting a red wave into her face. "Take this lamp in, Art, and . . . and close the door. I'll talk with Shafter."

"Something wrong, Joanie? Want me to . . . ?"

"Not now!" She waited until Blaisdell, scowling and reluctant and puzzled, carried the lamp inside. When the door closed, her tight voice said: "You . . . in McCloud's place?"

"It says so."

"But I told Judge Dixon this morning that Art Blaisdell was my choice!"

"Dixon had his reasons, I suppose."

"Reasons? What reasons could there be?" She was a slim, straight shadow, furious and suspicious, in the darkness that had closed around them. "What do you want? What are you trying to do? When you rode into Azul the other night, McCloud said you meant trouble."

"McCloud said that?"

"Exactly that."

"Then you're saying that McCloud knew me."

"Of course he knew you." Hers was a scornful voice whipping out of the darkness. "You passed us in the Azul plaza, and McCloud recognized you and was afraid of you."

Shafter said dryly: "Interesting, but the man couldn't have known me, so he couldn't have been afraid of me."

"Don't tell me I'm blind or lying. I saw it happen."

So it had happened; his memory flashed to the wrinkled old

man across the river. *In the name of God,* Don *Miguel . . . go to rest!* And again the unreal feeling came that Big Mike Shafter—that tall, laughing father the small boy had worshiped—was riding this Grenada country again. There was some truth in it; a man lived on in his sons.

"What trouble did McCloud expect?" Shafter asked with close interest.

"He didn't say!"

"So you followed me," Shafter said with irony, "to the Azul plaza in the buggy . . . curious, no doubt."

"Of a shabby stranger who meant nothing to me?" her scorn flashed back. "No. Con McCloud whipped what little pride I had, reminding me that I lived on charity from my uncle and gave nothing back. He said I was needed to delay you a few minutes. And I was foolish enough to try."

"Why did he want me delayed?"

"I don't know!"

"But you did it . . . by wrecking your buggy."

"I won't deny it."

"You delayed me," Shafter said, and the rest of it rowelled his memory: *And you killed old Johnny as surely as if you'd entered his room yourself!*

The rain tapped ghost fingers on the porch roof—for ghosts were stalking around them—one ghost still tied to the broken, trampled, mud-smeared body at their feet.

"You're not on charity now," Shafter said evenly. "You're a wealthy woman, with more power than most women should have in their hands. Your man here has been shot. Start thinking about him."

"You won't quit?" her shaken anger challenged.

Shafter said coolly: "I will not, until I'm ready. Live with it, get used to it . . . because you've got me."

She whirled quickly and opened the door—and in the burst

of yellow lamplight she was slender and pale and hating him. Blaisdell stepped quickly into the doorway, as if he'd been waiting.

Her calmness was forced. "Art, the judge has hired this man for McCloud's job. Directed him to see that the herd reaches Fort Kinfadden. I'm sorry. There's nothing I can do at this time. Not while the executors have control."

Blaisdell's face hardened. "I can do something," he said, and chagrined anger was boiling up in the man as he stepped out on the porch. "I can run him off, Joanie."

She looked at Shafter—a woman with the sure knowledge a strong man was backing her—and the glinting temptation was stormy in her eyes. Shafter watched her, bracing for the reckless word that would set Blaisdell off. Slowly, reluctantly she got the wish under control. "Take his orders, Art," she said quietly.

"Everything?"

"As if he were McCloud."

Blaisdell's delayed moment of yielding broke in a short, angry, glowering laugh. "If you say so, Joanie. Let's watch him be McCloud."

"Don't waste your time," Shafter said dryly. "I'll be myself. This dead man won't be cheerful company for the ladies. We'll move him. Now . . . how far away is the herd? How big? How many men there?"

"On Bajada Mesa . . . about eight miles north. Five men, including the cook, there now. Today we tallied seven short of eight hundred head," Blaisdell said with surly exactness. "The rest of the crew is on the west range, about twenty miles, throwing another herd together. Eight men there, and a cook." Blaisdell's rasping resentment finished: "And I rode here with the ladies to see them settled for the night, and was ready to start back."

"Five men," Shafter said, letting scorn edge it. "Eight

hundred head ready to move . . . the rest of the crew out of reach . . . and the ramrod off coddling two girls who thought nothing of riding out from Grenada alone."

Blaisdell was rigid, his mouth a tight, strained line, his antagonism on a taut thread as Shafter lashed him coolly, deliberately, shoving him back where he'd been—ramrod—before he'd been led to the heights and offered wider horizons. Wide enough, Shafter guessed, to include marriage, perhaps, with this girl who had offered so much. They had known each other a long time, obviously, and she had turned to Blaisdell in need and trust. A handsome man like this one could get ideas—and perhaps his ideas were right. But not tonight.

"I don't know who shot this Waco Jordan," Shafter said coldly. "We'll get out to the herd and see."

Joan said: "I'll go, too."

"Can't be bothered with you," Shafter said flatly.

Easy to say, easy to move the dead man back to a wagon bed and cover him with a tarp, easier to rope a fresh horse out of a corral and switch saddles.

Half an hour later the rain had stopped. Holes were opening in the clouds. The short-coupled roan under Shafter was running effortlessly—and she was riding with them. Breath wasted ordering her not to come. Priscilla Ross had protested. Blaisdell had spoken against it—and there she was, slim and straight in slicker and hat, astride like a man—her horse, her ranch, her cattle ahead. She had said with cool stubbornness—"It's my trouble."—and had silenced Blaisdell with a sharp reminder: "Art, you're not being paid to tell me what I can do!" Probably the first time, Shafter had guessed, that Blaisdell had heard crisp, unyielding authority in her voice. But not the last time—even with marriage—Shafter thought sardonically now as he looked over at her in the dim starlight. Two days—and she was changing, trying to fit the boots that Rufus Wolcott had left her to fill. Judge Dixon, executor, Shafter was beginning to guess, might have had shrewd reason for hiring a stranger who had clashed unyieldingly with her. Art Blaisdell was a competent man, but his temper was reckless and explosive.

They were following a dim trail of wheel ruts and horse tracks that skirted rugged hills. Blaisdell's explanation was grudging. "Water and some cliffs on the south side of Bajada Mesa make it a good holding ground."

The clouds had opened still more when the sweep of level mesa reached out before them and the hills on their left chopped off in a curving line of low cliffs.

Joan said: "I think I can see the wagon."

"Then you've pushed luck too far," Shafter said flatly. "Drop back."

Her quick, angry glance turned to him. "I meant to," she said, and reined back.

Wet earth and grass muffled their advance. "How far from the wagon is the bed ground?" Shafter asked, and Blaisdell's—"Close in."—was brief.

"Have a look. I'll ride to the wagon."

The pale blob of chuck wagon canvas lifted like a fat mushroom near the dark cliffs as he advanced through patchy starlight and shadows, listening for the bawl of a restless steer, the soothing keen of a man riding night herd. The quiet took on a brooding, waiting intensity. No horses in sight, hobbled or on picket. Only the silent wagon, a rained-out cook fire. And then as he reached the wagon, dark cocoons on the ground were bedrolls. Shafter swung his horse sharply to the left and flung off.

The cocoon he bent over had blankets and man rolled like a swathed mummy in the dirty-gray ground sheet of heavy canvas. He yanked the folds of canvas back, jerked sweat-wet blankets off a figure so bound with turns of saddle rope—and a shirt rolled tight and tied across the mouth—that the whole might have been the first exotic layer of burial wrappings. The sheath blade off his hip cut through the rolled shirt.

"What happened?" Shafter demanded of the gaunt, sweat-glistening face as the knife slashed at the circles of rope binding the arms to the body.

Faint mouthings gobbled first; shuddering gulps sucked in the cool night air. Then the cursing came in tearing whispers that gained strength. "Woke up with my head busting! Like a damn' dead man in a coffin!"

"You were lucky," Shafter said. "Waco Jordan was shot."

He ran, limping, to the next cocoon. And when a grimy towel was cut from a bearded mouth, the first wrenching sucking in of breath spewed back oaths so violent that Shafter's mouth cracked in a twisted smile.

Five men, Blaisdell had said. He found four—and Joan Wolcott rode in as the rush of Blaisdell's horse arrived from the bed ground.

"Cleaned out!" Blaisdell said furiously. "Joe Dumbarton's out there with the back of his head caved in!"

The cook, the gaunt, lurid man Shafter had found first, was coaxing shavings into flame in the dead char of the fire as rapid questions shaped what had happened. Three men caught asleep in their bedrolls. The fourth grabbed by two men as he dismounted at the wagon in darkness and rain. The dead man had been struck out of the saddle as he rode night herd. And Waco Jordan had died for less reason than a man should. Waco had lost his last half plug of tobacco while riding in from the herd, and had started back to the bunkhouse for more tobacco, his brand, which none of the other men carried.

Shafter's guess was as good as any for the present. "They met Waco and shot him, and his horse dragged him in."

Guns and horses had been taken. Blaisdell spurred off to the small pocket cañon where the remuda had been held without guard behind a brush fence across the cañon mouth. Coffee boiled over the snapping fire. Shafter carried two tin cups of coffee to the side of the chuck wagon where Joanie Wolcott was standing alone.

She said stiffly—"Thank you."—and over her cup burst out in protesting bitterness: "Two men dead tonight merely because they worked for me!" She sipped at the coffee. "Rustlers were afraid of McCloud and Uncle Rufe!"

Shafter regarded her thoughtfully. "Stop feeling sorry for yourself," he advised. "Rustlers have killed men before. You aren't the first owner with worries. Take that Boston girl back to Grenada and forget this."

She glared. "You know I won't."

"Then keep out of the way."

Anger stained her cheeks as he turned away, and he guessed that her moment of weakness had passed. He was at the fire, planning what could be done, when the dead man was brought in across a saddle. Blaisdell returned a few minutes later.

"Remuda cleaned out, too!" Blaisdell said in thick anger as he swung off by the fire. His glower speared Shafter. "Your worry now, mister!"

The men had gathered and were watching without friendliness.

"Three horses we can use," Shafter told them. "So two of you can go with me."

"I'm going!" Blaisdell made it a challenge. When Shafter nodded agreement, Blaisdell added a grudging suggestion. "Curly Ames there spends part of his time cleaning out the lobo steer killers. He can track like an Apache. Knows the country better than any of the crew. And he's cat-eyed at night."

"Curly, then," Shafter said. "Miss Wolcott's carbine is on her saddle. The dead man's gun was left under his slicker. As soon as we water the horses, we'll leave."

They rode west off the bed ground on a trail churned into the damp earth by the long columns of heavy steers. Three men, armed rustlers ahead of them. And rustling, Shafter was deciding, was too pat an answer. Too obvious. The bank draft of the beef contractors at Fort Kinfadden was urgently needed in Grenada. This would delay the draft or block it completely. When reasoning reached that point, Joan Wolcott was the obvious target, a $1,000,000 target and only one inexperienced girl in the way.

Blaisdell brought his horse over and asked in sarcasm: "Going to ride in and clean 'em out?"

"With luck," Shafter said, "we can scatter the herd tonight, and get the rest of the crew from the other end of the ranch for a fast roundup. Got a better idea?"

"No," Blaisdell conceded after a moment with more respect in his voice.

A little later Curly Ames dropped back beside them.

"Near as I can guess," Curly said, "they've got to make a swing south into the ranch now, or head for Salt Flat Draw, that'll take 'em off these mesas into the breaks and badlands. And we can short-cut to Salt Draw. It'll wring out the horses but'll put us up near even with them."

"Blaisdell . . . ?"

"I'd short-cut," Blaisdell said without hesitation.

Half an hour later they were leading the horses up a precipitous, brush-choked slope where boots slid in the wet earth and rocks rolled out underfoot and clashed against other rocks as they plunged down. When they topped the high ridge, the somber mass of another ridge soared up ahead of them. More clouds were sliding across the exposed stars. Shafter estimated them and panted: "Curly, can you get us through this and down on the other side if it's black and raining?"

Between deep breaths, Curly chuckled. "I can get us to the top . . . an' we can fall down."

It was the first break in the silent hostility. Sweating effort and danger ahead were bringing them together. Rain held off. Breaks in the clouds let thin starlight through as they topped the next ridge, descended some distance, and climbed once more through scattered pines. This was a belt of high, stony ridges without pattern, gouged, gullied, and eroded. Curly Ames, leading the way, seldom hesitated. When they finally halted on the edge of a steep slope, plunging into shadowy depths, still another bolder, higher ridge loomed beyond.

"This cañon," Curly said, "will put us near the head of Salt Flat Draw. Got to get down in it and follow it up, but it's dry and easy ridin', and we've saved. . . ."

Shafter cut in: "Listen."

Ghost sounds were riding the wind eddies swirling over the cañon rim. They became the distant, tired bawling of weary cattle echoing and batting through the cañon.

Blaisdell was startled. "Sounds like they're coming toward us!"

"Where does this cañon go?" Shafter asked.

Sudden, cracking strain filled Curly Ames's reply. "Nowhere!"

"Pockets at the end?"

Blaisdell said harshly: "This is Blind Cañon! A quarter-mile rock chute at the end, sloping down . . . and then nothing!" Anger sweated in the man's words. "Three hundred feet straight down to the edge of the breaks! The fools . . . thinking they're in Salt Flat Draw and driving a herd to that!"

Shafter was already throwing off, ignoring the jolting pain in his leg. "Can we get the horses down here?"

Curly, hitting the ground at the same moment, said: "Have to lead 'em! Keep in my tracks!" Curly and his horse dropped away into the first steep pitch down to the clotting shadows in the cañon bed.

Shafter followed, loosening small cascades of earth and pebbles, and more of it *rattled* past as Blaisdell came after him. And the ghost sounds of the advancing herd funneled through the cañon toward them in an eerie, rising tide.

Blaisdell's horse slipped. Shod hoofs clashed sparks from rocks—and, when the danger passed, Blaisdell was swearing under his breath.

There was no trail, only steep, rain-softened earth and rotten rock, and angling reaches past sheer drops. Curly Ames seemed to move with tortoise caution. Actually all three of them were descending recklessly, driven by the thought of unreasoning cattle and high-strung horses pouring through the dark cañon. Increasingly, to Shafter, it seemed like a ghost herd. Nothing was visible, but the bawling and clashing of horns and hoofs grew into a tide of sound that brought the night alive and quivering.

Blaisdell's harsh voice lifted behind Shafter: "I'm going to warn 'em with shots!"

"Hold it!" Shafter interjected.

Blaisdell ignored him or failed to hear. The smashing report of his handgun spewed a muzzle flash that must have been visible far up the cañon. And then another—another—another—the echoes hurtling back, piled sound on sound, racketing, crashing from side to side of the cañon, racing away in diminishing waves. And below them, only a little up the cañon, other men, other guns, that had been invisible, opened fire at them, and another roaring crescendo of sound filled the cañon.

A ricocheting bullet screamed close to Shafter's head. He could only swear helplessly. The remuda, he guessed, was being driven ahead of the herd; men behind it were starting to fight through what must seem an ambush. And now there was no way to reach them with reason, to shout warning of what was ahead.

Curly Ames's horse broke into a stumbling trot, following Curly's plunging run across the last, less steep reach of brush-dotted talus slope. Shafter followed him and hauled into the saddle.

Far up the cañon other guns were firing, and, when Shafter heard the echoing reports, he knew their chances were running out. Those distant guns were stampeding the herd. Horses and cattle were coming through in one mass of fear-driven flesh.

Curly Ames, in the saddle, also, was hesitating as Shafter reined up beside him, gun in hand. "Try to scatter the remuda!" Shafter called. The deep, pounding rumble of charging horses came at them as he spurred down the final slope.

V

The bolting remuda was a sweeping clot of shadows at which Shafter and Curly Ames burst from the cañon side, shouting, firing handguns. The shadows screamed, whinnied, dodged away from this new threat; the front of the racing mass broke apart like an opening fan, disintegrating, scattering, wheeling, veering up the cañon sides.

A hurtling shadow slammed into Shafter's horse, spinning it half around before careening away. Shafter wrenched the bit, spurred mercilessly, and drove his buffeted, reeling horse on across the cañon floor to safety. His gun was empty. Curly Ames had vanished. He pulled up on the opposite slope, reloading swiftly. Blaisdell's charge across the cañon had scattered more horses.

The last of the remuda raced past, riders following. And close behind came a new wave of sound—a chilling, churning roar of big steers stampeding blindly in full panic.

"Shafter!" It was Blaisdell, swinging his horse in close. "Those men went by us!" Blaisdell's voice had the high, keening note of complete futility. "Can't turn that herd! Can't stop 'em!"

"Those men!" Shafter said again.

Guns down the cañon were winking viciously back at them—in grisly farewell—receding with each shot as the two strange riders raced on ahead of the stampeding herd—on to the hideous moment when hope would break into screaming, helpless awareness. . . .

Silently Shafter and Blaisdell turned their horses farther up the cañon side. The great wave of clashing sound hurtled by below them while they watched helplessly. Shafter's voice battled the tumult. "Might stop the drag riders!"

"And get shot for trying?" Blaisdell shouted back.

But when the churning thunder swept past and Shafter rode recklessly down among the stragglers, Blaisdell was beside him, gun firing also as they tried to turn back even a few. Plunging shadows began to swing aside, slow, wheel back. Curly Ames suddenly was helping them, and shortly, in relative quiet, they came together, looking warily upcañon.

Blaisdell's question was hoarse and puzzled. "What about those drag riders?"

"Didn't get by us!" Curly said. "I was watchin' for them!" Curly began to swear with a wild, helpless sound. "I hate even to ride down the cañon!"

Shafter said with tight, grim hope: "Those two men with the remuda still had time to get up the cañon side. Keep together. Watch for them." But when the dark cañon sides began to rise sheer and press in, Shafter halted again. "We can stop anything here that didn't get by us."

They waited; in silence they turned back a few straggling horses and steers.

Finally Shafter said: "We're putting it off. Let's get it over with."

They rode slowly now, until the footing began to tilt down and Curly Ames dismounted.

"From here on I walk," Curly said flatly.

A few stars winked through slits in the drifting clouds as they all walked, leading the horses. Wet sand and gravel underfoot had been churned and pounded. Their steps seemed to *crunch* loudly, for ahead lurked hackle-raising, gruesome quiet that caught throats, dried mouths as the blackness in front of them suddenly became the full arc of star-specked sky reaching to the far horizon.

They halted gingerly on the edge of space, and an updraft wind swept a warm, alien stench into their faces, and brought up from far below a rustling, moaning stir of movement that held them mute.

Shafter turned away first, his harsh voice exploding: "How do we get down there? I've got extra cartridges!"

Blaisdell said thickly: "Have to go back to the head of Salt Flat Draw and down." He began to swear. "The fools! Blind, bumbling fools, taking this cañon by mistake!"

"Wasn't a mistake. They knew where they were!"

"How could they know?" Blaisdell said violently.

"The others didn't come on," Shafter reminded. "You heard 'em stampede the cattle. They had darkness and steers running ahead of them. All they'd have had to do in the Salt Draw was follow down into open country, but they turned back."

"Taking this cañon deliberately don't make sense," Blaisdell said stubbornly. "They killed two of our men. They rustled the herd and remuda. Now you're saying they threw it all away. Not a dime of profit for anyone."

"The herd for Fort Kinfadden is gone."

"Who does that help? Joanie Wolcott's got more money than

she knows what to do with. Doesn't hurt her."

This man, Shafter realized, had been busy running the ranch and had scant awareness of anything else that might be happening. "How long before another herd is ready for the trail?" he asked Blaisdell.

"Three, four days," Blaisdell guessed, "if the crew at the other end of the ranch ties into it."

"You'd better take charge there. That herd is needed fast at Fort Kinfadden."

The pale blob of Blaisdell's face turned toward him. "You've got Con McCloud's job, mister, but I still take orders from Joanie Wolcott." The man was harsh and hostile again.

"Then remind her of Judge Dixon's orders," Shafter said, unruffled. And before the man could blaze back, he continued: "We scattered some of the remuda. You and Curly Ames can drive horses back to the chuck wagon. And you said that Curly can track."

"Best man at tracking I know."

"Curly," Shafter said, "I want the men who turned back, want at least one of them tracked down. If you run out of sign, try to back-trail on Waco Jordan from the house. Try to find where he met the men who shot him, then back-trail on them, and find out where they came from."

"Yes, sir," Curly said uncomfortably. "That is . . . if Miss Wolcott an' Blaisdell say so."

"They will, because the men who did this may try again," Shafter said absently, another thought prodding him. "We know what happened, but if we say rustlers who didn't know the country got into the wrong cañon by mistake, they'll feel safer and might get careless."

"It's probably the truth," Blaisdell said shortly.

"Then you'll be telling the truth," Shafter said dryly.

★ ★ ★ ★ ★

In the first gray hour of dawn, Shafter had lost all concern about what others might be doing. He was alone in a sickening nightmare of savage reality. The end of Blind Cañon was an insignificant-looking notch far above. Around him the gouged, eroded badlands broke against the talus roughs at the base of the long line of cliffs. In front of him horror was piled on horror. The barrel of his handgun was hot. The shots he fired bounced sound off the cliffs, booming away into empty distance. He was a sweating, lonely figure, cursing helplessly as he worked. With rope, saddle horn, and snorting horse he was endlessly dragging death aside to get at broken, still-living carcasses that needed the mercy shot.

They found him that way, limping and haggard, his long rope, borrowed at the chuck wagon last night, his boots and his hands smeared red. Gun sizzling. Extra cartridges in his saddlebags almost gone. He had sighted the four riders in the distance, appearing and disappearing in the badlands. When they reached him, he glared from bleary eyes. Talk was not needed; they had eyes, too.

"Men under there!" Shafter said harshly, and turned back to his work.

Joan Wolcott had come. He had suspected she would, and with her was the gaunt cook and the two men who had been left afoot at the chuck wagon.

The crimson-gold blaze of sunrise quickly burned the last clouds away—and the buzzards came planing down through the high sky currents. And more buzzards—and still more—until an immense, obscene umbrella of soaring wings was circling overhead when they dragged out two men, dead and broken from the long screaming fall or the rain of hurtling carcasses that had followed.

The first was a man about forty, with a black mustache. The

second was younger, unshaven for days, jeans and coat well worn. Their pockets yielded knick-knacks and a little money, no letters or writing at all. Shafter looked at the bodies, laid side-by-side in an open space. His eyes were bloodshot, his voice had a flat, harsh weariness, lacking any pity now.

"Anyone know them?" he asked.

Joan Wolcott stood with them, biting her lower lip. More than ever in the brown pants and brownish-red man's blouse, she had a slender, boyish look, with tired pallor now on her face. Earlier he had noticed her turning away from the heaped carcasses, dashing her blouse sleeve across her eyes. That had been her moment of weakness, bludgeoned out of her. Now her strained voice was steady. "I don't think I've seen either of them before."

Noah Law, the gaunt cook, gazed up at the notch far above where Blind Cañon ended in space. "Blaisdell said they'd have to be strangers to get lost an' end up like this."

"Someone in Grenada or Azul will know them," Shifter guessed. "We'll pack them in."

Shortly after that they left, the two dead men lashed across a horse, two of the crew riding double. None of them looked back as the cloud of wings closed in. For the most part they were silent as they rode slowly back up the long, twisting Salt Flat Draw to the higher mesas.

In Shafter the sick fury of the past hours was burned deeply. He would never, he suspected, be quite the same again. Not in this Grenada country, at least, for this blood bath of destruction, he was convinced, had been deliberate. When he reined back to Joan Wolcott's horse, she looked away, ignoring him.

"Did you order Blaisdell to take charge of the men at the west end of the ranch?" Shafter asked impersonally. "And tell him to get that second herd ready for the trail fast?"

"I did."

"And tell Curly Ames to track the rustlers who turned back?"

"Yes."

"I can't give you orders," Shafter said, still impersonally. "But this happened, and more of it can happen. You should stay in Grenada."

Her glance came around, looking steadily at him. "No," she said evenly, "you can't give me orders, and you never will." Abruptly she struck the saddle horn and stormy inner emotion blazed out. "What do they think they can do to me? What do they think I am . . . a helpless woman who'll not fight back?"

Anger brought her vibrant and alive, flushing and feminine. He found a needed moment of humor in the sight. "I don't know what anyone thinks," Shafter told her. "But to fight, you have to know who you're fighting."

"Everyone now!" She was bitter. "Uncle Rufe and Con McCloud made it that way. McCloud especially. I've seen it in people's eyes, even when they were smiling at me. I was a Wolcott, also. Now I'm fair game, even for you. Con McCloud said in Azul that you meant trouble, and ever since there has been trouble wherever you appeared. As soon as you wormed your way into McCloud's job, this happened!"

"So now the rustlers are working with me, and I killed your Waco Jordan last night?" Shafter said with irony.

"They were strangers, too, obviously!"

Shafter gazed at her with shortening temper.

"Well, prove it," he said. "Meanwhile, I'm working for you."

He rode on ahead again, whipped by the constant pain in his feverish leg, rowelled by the conviction that what was ahead for this Joan Wolcott—and for Mike Shafter, too, now—was going to be ruthless. The pattern was plain. All that Rufe Wolcott had handed to one young girl was going to be torn from her, if possible. For she was not, and never would be, a Rufe Wolcott, a Con McCloud.

Sometime before daybreak, Con McCloud spoke harshly to the stranger named Selby. "You talk too much."

"So now I can't open my mouth?"

"A man works for me does what I tell him."

Selby yanked his horse back where Vince Wolcott and Jess Parker were riding. The three of them heard Con McCloud's voice up ahead—an eerie sound in the black night—for McCloud was riding alone now. And the massive man seemed to be carrying on a low-voiced argument with some other man who was not there.

Selby was a cold-eyed man, quick with his gun, resentful now. "Gabbing to himself!" Selby said venomously. "Listen to him. Time somebody called him to taw."

"Who's stopping you?" Jess Parker said coolly.

Vince's reaching hand tugged an urgent, silent signal on Jess Parker's coat sleeve. Vince reined back his horse, and moments later Jess dropped back with him.

"Tell Selby to keep quiet," Vince blurted under his breath.

"Waste of time," Jess said indifferently. "Selby's mean when he's stirred up."

"Listen, Jess . . . you two don't know. We were in Blind Cañon. I thought so when we turned in, and told McCloud. He told me to keep quiet, and he sent those two strangers you picked up in Azul on ahead with the remuda."

Jess asked cautiously: "Did McCloud have an idea men would be waiting for us?"

"Of course not," Vince said thinly. "But McCloud knew what was waiting. That cañon ends in a straight down drop, Jess! And McCloud headed in there and got the herd running before he turned back. That was all he wanted anyway. He never meant to get those cattle out in the breaks and away, like he told us."

Brush scraped past their stirrups. Ahead in the black night the slap and scuff of the other two horses pushing through more brush drifted back, and Jess Parker's voice sounded thick. "He sent those two men out front, and let them ride to a drop?"

"Yes."

Jess swore softly. "How crazy in the head is McCloud? You know him better than I do."

"I'm afraid of him now, Jess," Vince said tightly. "Do you think he'll turn on us?"

"I don't know. Mostly he seems like usual. But we know he's not."

"Talking to himself," Jess muttered. His short, angry laugh followed. "I can handle him. He came to me when he wanted men for tonight."

"He sent those two men on ahead," Vince reminded in the same thin voice.

"But not you, not me. Know why? I told him you had wanted him in charge of everything, if you'd inherited. He said Rufe Wolcott had wanted it that way, too, and it was going to be that way. The girl is the one to worry. If she's out of the way. . . ."

Vince broke in nervously: "Anything happens to Joanie, I'll be blamed."

"Not if it happens while you're in Azul, or out of the territory."

Vince said sullenly: "I'm here, me, who was going to own it all!"

"You'll get it if you don't weaken." When Vince said nothing, Jess added coldly: "If I don't think for you now, you'll end up swamping out saloons for hand-outs. You know it. I know it. Are you going to let me handle McCloud, and whatever has to be done?" When Vince rode in moody silence, Jess Parker was satisfied.

First dawn was the slightest graying of thin clouds as they rode down a long slope dotted with the vague shapes of green juniper bushes, many head-high to a rider. McCloud's horse dropped down the low bank of a small wash, to a shallow channel in the middle that carried water from the night's rain.

The four of them dismounted, and, while the horses drank greedily, Selby's resentment broke venomously at McCloud.

"Just because you ran into trouble last night, you're bustin' our tails all over god-knows-where, gabbling to yourself. I've had. . . ."

"Told you to keep quiet!" McCloud's rasping voice cut in.

The two men were gray-dark shadows standing close on the damp sand by the gurgling water. Selby's venom clashed against the sound: "Quiet, hell! Ain't a man livin' who pushes me. . . ."

The bulky shadow that was McCloud moved silently, suddenly, and seemed to envelop Selby. The man's wild oath choked into a dwindling gasp—into silence.

For frozen seconds the two shadows seemed locked in a monstrous, affectionate embrace—then McCloud's bulk slowly separated. The shadow that was Selby stood motionlessly, head bowed as if in mute supplication, then without sound in what looked like writhing, macabre twitching, Selby fell forward, his chest and face splashing violently into the water.

McCloud's bulk seemed to crouch slightly, hovering over the jerking figure, which made no move to escape or turn over. McCloud's words had eerie unreality. "Told him, didn't I, Rufe?"

The water chuckled, gurgled around Selby's submerged face. Vince sucked a half-strangled breath and edged away. Jess Parker's hand stopped him; Jess reached to the gun inside his own coat as McCloud's bulk came to full height, peering toward them.

"He knows now who's boss . . . you two know?"

"You're boss," Jess said cautiously. "Vince wants it that way, don't you, Vince?"

"Sure," Vince said thickly, "sure . . . sure. . . ." Jess Parker's fingers digging savagely into his shoulder stopped it.

McCloud was in range clothes, bulky canvas jacket, cartridge belt, holstered gun—a massive, shadowy figure slowly rubbing his forehead now under the black hat brim. "That Shafter too, Rufe. . . ." McCloud clenched the hand, stared at it, shook his head as if dispelling fog. "We'll split up here," McCloud's harshening voice, normal again, said as he moved to his horse.

Vince whispered desperately: "Selby's face . . . under. . . ."

"Quiet," Jess breathed. "Want to join him?"

Vince turned blindly to his horse and said no more as they rode from the chuckling water; only when McCloud was out of sight did Vince wrench out: "Crazy! What'll he do next, Jess?"

"How do I know?"

"I don't want any more of him."

"I'll do the thinking," Jess said coldly.

A single telegraph wire, often damaged and silent, linked Azul with the southeastern Colorado settlements, and east through Kansas. Telegraph messages to Grenada were forwarded by stage mail, and this early afternoon when George Ross emerged from the cubbyhole of a post office west of the hotel, his mouth corners were white with sudden strain. At the edge of the walk, Ross stopped and read the telegram again.

Withdraw commitments and leave by fifth next month if not completely successful.

It was a routine message. He had received telegrams like this in other towns, during other negotiations. But never when the full promise of real wealth for George Ross himself—wealth and all that would go with it, including power—had hung in sweating uncertainty that needed time to work out. He had counted on twenty-one days more, at least. Now it was nine days. Nine days. . . .

Ross crumpled the telegram as Charley Doane, the town marshal, spoke at his elbow.

"I told Buck Manning he better watch his bank trips now. Looks like Buck thinks so, too."

Doane was a well-fleshed man with a loose, friendly mouth and convivial purplish veins in his prominent nose. He was looking at a buckboard rolling into the plaza with an armed guard riding a horse on each side, and Buck Manning on the seat beside the driver with a shotgun across his lap.

"Trouble expected?" Ross said. A man could be sweating inside while he smiled like this and talked easy nonsense. While frustration stormed through him as he thought of the silver-gold ore—bonanza ore—still undiscovered in the Queen Mine.

"He better look for trouble." Worry lurked in Doane's eyes. "McCloud and Rufe Wolcott kept the hardcases out of town," Doane said glumly. "Now they're coming in."

"You're the law," Ross said, and gave the man a cigar.

Doane sniffed the Manila Perfecto and carefully placed it in a shabby leather case holding cheap stogies whose dark, rank tobacco almost made Ross grimace. Glancing unhappily at the badge on his coat, Doane said: "I don't fool 'em, don't fool myself, ain't anything behind me now."

"Miss Wolcott is behind you."

"That," said Doane, "is what's wrong." He shook his head and started across the plaza toward the red brick bank building.

Nine days. Ross lighted a cigar and tried to think. The wooden box in the buckboard held, he knew, silver-gold ingots, silver bars, and smaller gold bars, being transferred from the smelter to the bank. From Buck Manning he knew the details. Only a small part would be from the single Wolcott mine now working. The rest would be custom metal, milled, concentrated, smelted from custom ore hauled in from other mines as far away as five or six freighting days. Smelter assays and returns were delivered to the bank, and drafts issued to the ore shippers. Two independent assayers in Grenada were often commissioned by shippers to check against the smelter assays. All that was familiar to Ross as he watched the buckboard halt in front of the bank.

Buck Manning, wearing a blue broadcloth suit today, stepped down to the walk, and stood there, holding the shotgun while the driver and one of the riders grasped iron handles at each end of the box and got it off the buckboard with visible effort. Lurching, straining, they carried the box into the bank.

Ross stopped an impulse to follow the marshal across the plaza. Buck Manning had sighted him, and a week ago, inside the bank, he had watched the same thing that was happening now. Watched it carelessly then, Ross remembered, with none of the intent calculation tightening inside now. They would be carrying the box into the vault. Henry Peck, the slightly built, nervous cashier, would be at the door of the vault, flicking his blond mustache with the back of a forefinger, as was his habit. Buck Manning, grinning and genial, would enter the vault with Peck, and unlock the box. Together they would check the contents. Peck would sign a receipt. Manning would leave an envelope stuffed with smelter reports—and one more bank trip would be finished.

Ross was narrowly turning the whole procedure over in his mind as he walked on to the hotel, and upstairs to his room overlooking the plaza. Standing at one of the front windows, he saw Buck Manning emerge from the bank without the shotgun. Usually Buck crossed to the Palace Bar; this time he walked through the late afternoon sunlight to the hotel. When Ross admitted him to the room, Buck's grin was tight.

"Don't ask me what would have happened if we'd been held

up," Buck said. "I sent two men on ahead to stand on the roofs with rifles, watching." Buck went to the whiskey bottle on the table against the wall. "The marshal was sweating." He poured a drink, downed it, reached for the water pitcher, then smacked his lips and looked at the label on the bottle instead. "Nice . . . if you can afford it," he said, and his look at the strained waiting on Ross's broken face was amused. "Relax," Buck advised. "I rode up to the mines this morning. No sign of anyone going into the Queen."

"Three days . . . more luck already than we've a right to expect," Ross reminded tightly. "Someone will get in there and see that ore."

"Doing anything about the Queen now is the quickest way to make those miners curious," Buck said coolly. "Let it sit there. You've got over twenty days to make Joanie Wolcott sell . . . and I'll eat all the bonanza ore anyone else finds in the Queen before then."

Buck opened the cigar box at the back of the table, sniffed a cigar, and transferred a handful to the inside pocket of his coat.

"Those cost sixty cents each," Ross said coldly.

"I'd have guessed more," Buck said carelessly. "Do you know that Joanie Wolcott and your sister went to the ranch yesterday?"

"Yes," Ross said shortly.

Buck helped himself to another cigar and bit off the end while he studied Ross. "Joanie," he said, "oughtn't to have gone. And I wouldn't want my sister loose on that ranch while Con McCloud was encouraged to rustle cattle. The man might do anything, especially to Joanie, and anyone with her." Buck stared at the unlighted cigar. "Are you sure McCloud wasn't encouraged to do something about Joanie Wolcott while she's out there on the ranch?"

"Not by me," Ross said curtly. "But it might have been a good idea."

"No," Buck said softly. "I told you once. I'll take half the Queen Mine if we can get it, but not with Joanie Wolcott on my conscience." Buck stepped over and dropped in a chair. "Don't forget that."

"Your elastic conscience," Ross said with irony, "is safe today." The bed *creaked* as he sat on the edge. His broken face with its bent nose and caved cheek bone lacked all the smiling magnetism it carried in public. It was an ugly, twisted face now, with only a hint of the debonair handsomeness that once must have existed. Yet, oddly, not even now was the face repulsive, Buck Manning's fleeting thought came, for the mashed features were striking in their own ugly, nearly brutal way. They had strength; they had confidence as Ross soberly inquired: "How much coal do you keep in reserve at the smelter and mill?"

"Not much. The wagons haul coal every day from Lyd Adams's mine across the river. Before the spring floods, we stock enough to last until the water drops."

"If you ran out of coal, you'd have to close the smelter and mill?"

"True," Buck agreed. He was intent now, weighing the questions.

"You're coking coal in that row of stone beehive ovens," Ross said. "How long will the coke supply hold out without coal to recharge the furnaces?"

"About the same."

"How much smelter metal is the bank holding now?"

Buck grinned. "I'd say too much. With Rufe Wolcott sick like he was, and the roads tied up with the rains, I think there's near ninety thousand dollars' worth of metal in the bank. Peck, the cashier, is getting nervous, the way strangers are gathering in town." Buck chuckled. "If it was my metal, I'd be nervous, too."

"Mostly it's metal smelted for outside mines?" And when Buck nodded, Ross said: "Drafts have been issued to the mines?"

"Yes."

"And now the smelter owns the metal?"

"Smelter . . . bank," Buck said, "right hand . . . left hand, all the same. Joanie Wolcott owns them now. When the smelter account gets low, it borrows from the bank against the metal. Matter of juggling figures. And most of the mines leave their draft money in the bank. It's safer here in Grenada. They can. . . ."

Buck broke off as someone knocked. He came to his feet as George Ross opened the door and Priscilla Ross entered the room.

She had come without a hat. Her butter-gold hair was windblown. She looked tired, yet she brought a vivid tautness into the room that held Buck Manning's eyes in cynical admiration. He remembered and caught off his hat.

"I was just leaving," Buck said.

"Oh, don't bother, Mister Manning," Priscilla said with obvious distaste. "I know about you." She read his look of irony; resentment kindled in her eyes and tone. "And I see you know about me." Her glance ran over them. "Partners," Priscilla said with stinging resentment. "Were you partners in what happened last night on the ranch?"

Buck's hardening question was swift. "Anything happened to Joanie Wolcott?"

"Were you expecting something to happen? You were, weren't you? Both of you waiting here, hoping. . . ."

Ross caught her arm. "What about the girl?"

"I won't be mauled, George, even by you!" His square hand with broken knuckles released the arm. Priscilla rubbed the spot. "Last night rustlers killed two of Joan's men, and stampeded cattle over a cliff by mistake."

"Over a cliff?" burst from Ross in startled uncertainty. "How many cattle?"

"Hundreds," said Priscilla tightly. "Two of the rustlers went over the drop, also. That man Shafter is bringing the four bodies in to the undertaker who has the saddle shop around the corner."

Ross stared at her, frowning. "Shafter? What does that fellow have to do with it?"

"Judge Dixon hired him to replace McCloud, even though Joan wanted Art Blaisdell, her ranch foreman." Priscilla's suspicion rested on them. "Is this killing and rustling part of the scheming to get Joan's mine?"

"Rustlers," Ross said sharply, "and cattle over a cliff aren't a worked-out mine."

"I suppose not." Priscilla drew an uncertain breath. "But I still don't like what you two are doing, or what I'm doing . . . spying on someone who trusts me."

Buck Manning's quick look studied her face with new interest.

Ross, unmoved, said impatiently: "In business, you do what needs to be done."

"Then I don't care for business."

"But you like to spend money," Ross said, controlling anger. "When I make money, you get money. When I don't, you'll do without." His voice turned brusque. "Would you rather pack and start back East?"

Color crept into Priscilla's face. "And support myself from now on? That's what you mean, isn't it, George?"

"You could marry."

Buck Manning watched resentment, defiance build under her deepening flush, and watched it slowly crumple into acceptance. In a low voice, Priscilla said: "You've been generous, and I've taken it for granted, haven't I? And . . . and you need me now, don't you, George?"

Disgustedly Buck turned to the window and stared cynically

out at the plaza. Behind him Ross was saying: "I need all the help I can get." A tone Buck Manning was getting used to—exultant, feverish, fiercely convinced—came into Ross's words. "I'm going to be rich. Nothing will stop me now. And you'll have more money than you can spend, Priss."

Her breath of a question held pleading. "Do you have to do it this way?"

"This is the one chance I'll ever have," Ross said roughly. "You'll have to get friendly with this man Shafter as quick as possible. Find out why he's here in Grenada . . . why that lawyer hired him . . . and what he thinks he's going to do in McCloud's job. I want to know all about him."

Priscilla's—"I'd rather not."—was barely audible.

"Do it!" Ross said sharply.

She either gestured or nodded, and went out without speaking again. When the door closed, Buck Manning turned from the window.

"Now," Buck said bitterly, "you know how a crazy man planned to take a thousand head of cattle. Not rustling . . . killing!"

"What difference?"

"The difference," Buck said, "is that one is rustling, the other is destroying. And a man who's destroyed hundreds of live animals deliberately won't stop now." Buck's voice was lifting accusingly. "He's turned killer in that crazy, fogged-up head! And you've hung him around your neck! And around my neck, too!"

"Read this telegram," Ross said curtly. While Buck took the message and scanned it, Ross crossed to the table and the whiskey bottle.

Buck said sharply: "Nine days? You've got to pull out in nine days?"

"Yes."

"Joanie'll never sell that quickly. We'll chuck it. All of it."

Ross swiveled around, bottle in hand, lips drawn off his teeth. "Run from a fortune?" His scorn whipped viciously. "Chuck the one chance to control all this Grenada country . . . and a good part of the territory, with luck . . . because one stubborn girl is in the way?"

"What else?"

"Your guts are gone, Manning, if you ever had any. One girl. Drag her playhouse down around her. Tear it to pieces. Rub her face in it until she screams and runs. What does she think she inherited . . . dolls and Sunday school and loving friends?"

Buck looked away from the broken face and blazing eyes, and licked his lips. "I don't want any of that," he said sullenly.

"You've got it," Ross said more viciously. "You demanded a signed agreement about the mine, and a copy for me. Did you stop to think my copy will finish you with any decent job, that you'll never be trusted again?"

"It'll do the same to you."

"Will it? My job is to get truth about any property I'm interested in. The agreement about the Queen Mine doesn't say I'll profit. It merely gives you your greedy half of any ore mined in the Queen if title passes to me or anyone I represent."

Shocked by the brutal truth, Buck swallowed hard. Now he knew, suddenly, how Priscilla Ross had felt.

"Well?"

The contemptuous certainty in it made Buck hate even himself as he asked sullenly: "What can I do?"

"Hire all the hardcases that have drifted in. Get more from Azul. They'll be blamed for anything that happens."

Buck licked his lips again. "What will happen?"

"We'll need this man Shafter, and Doane, the marshal, out of the way first."

Buck walked blindly over to get the drink he needed. An

avalanche he had started himself was burying him, sweeping him along. Ross was worse than McCloud would ever be, for the madness now in Ross had a cold intelligence. Help the man and probably be rich—refuse and be broken. Buck downed his drink, hating himself for what he was going to do.

Mike Shafter had been awake almost thirty-six hours as the light spring wagon he was driving rolled through the final miles to Grenada. Twice he had overhauled heavily loaded ore wagons, and the startled bullwhip men had denied knowing the dead rustlers under canvas in the wagon bed. He was dozing fitfully on the jolting wagon seat when a slamming gunshot close by made him yank the team rearing and catch blindly for his handgun.

"Hold it!" Young Curly Ames sat his horse by the roadside; a second horse on lead bore a dead man jackknifed stiffly across the saddle. "Fool trick," Curly said ruefully, riding to the wagon.

"So was driving asleep. That one of the rustlers?" Shafter asked, stepping down.

Curly, grimy, unshaved, stifling a weary yawn, joined him beside the lead horse. "Found him face down in run-off water in a wash. Three more riders had left him an' his horse there." An uneasy note entered Curly's voice. "Tracks in the sand were plain. He was close to another man when his neck was broke."

"Neck?" Shafter said sharply.

"Not a mark on him . . . bullet, knife, or rope. He fell over in the water an' stayed there, neck twisted to a snap."

Shafter bent, scanning the dead man's face. "Who knows the ranch well enough to steal those cattle so slick? Madman enough to run cattle and two men over the cliff? Strong enough to wring a man's neck like a chicken?"

Curly muttered: "It came to mind."

Shafter bit the word out. "McCloud. I hope so, at least."

Curly's puzzled squint drew more from Shafter. "McCloud is only one man, even if he's rousted up help. But if more than McCloud is behind all this, anything can happen now."

Curly nodded uncertainly. "The other three split up. Best set of tracks took me into another wash, following more run-off water, to the road. Sign had been trampled out in the road."

"We'll guess one man is in town now, maybe all three. Load this one in with the others," Shafter decided. "Tie his horse on back. Ride on in, and hitch in front of the hotel. Keep your eyes and ears open after I get there."

In the first red wash of sunset, the Grenada plaza had a peaceful look when Shafter halted the wagon in front of the Palace. But a cat could seem placid as it waited to pounce. The anger of the dawn hours whipped high again as Shafter limped through the swing doors of the Palace and ran a hardening stare over men at the tables and the long, polished bar.

The slap of his single word—"Attention!"—swiveled eyes to him. Quiet fell. Standing inside the door, Shafter said curtly: "Last night rustlers on the Wolcott Ranch killed two men . . . then got lost, evidently, and ran stolen cattle over a cliff. Some of the rustlers went over, also. Their bodies are outside. Fifty dollars a head for naming one! A hundred a head for naming any rustler who got away!"

Startled shock held them staring, until one voice blurted: "Who're you?"

"Name is Shafter . . . in McCloud's job now!" Shafter said coldly, and walked out, a marked man.

He was barely in the wagon, canvas flipped off the gruesome load, when the first men who bolted out of the Palace were gaping over the sideboards, mounting wheels, swinging over the tailgate. The sudden commotion in front of the Palace was drawing others from around the plaza.

Standing behind the wagon seat in red sunset glow, Shafter watched faces closely and answered questions. Who was friend? Who was enemy? No one was admitting knowledge of the rustlers. But as he'd expected, the bold legend of Rufe Wolcott was raveling before his eyes; if this could happen so quickly, the Wolcott girl would not last long.

Curly Ames was drifting through the crowd with detached innocence. Jess Parker was watching from the walk in open hostility. Ross, the Boston Irishman, was loitering on the fringe of the gathering, not interested it seemed in viewing the dead men.

Two minutes later Jess Parker yawned, as if awake last night and today. Shafter saw it because a vagrant thought had wondered if that sallow tinhorn, so friendly to Vince Wolcott, really had tried to drown Joanie Wolcott in the Palomas torrent. . . . Now Parker's yawn whipped suspicion that Shafter thrust aside as a lazy-mocking voice offside the wagon called: "McCloud was a lot of man! How good are you, mister?"

A quick eddy of movement left the speaker standing alone, a long-boned stranger, leather-dark, hat canted jauntily, a challenging grin backing the slender cheroot he had cocked in his mouth after speaking.

Shafter looked at the man for a moment. "I do what I have to," he said briefly.

A brown hand removed the cheroot and the man drawled: "You look full of blow to me. Got anything to back it up?"

Curly Ames was rising on his toes to see better. And behind Shafter the booming, blunt warning of Lyd Adams rang out: "Don't let that cozy smile bamboozle you, Shafter! If you don't know him, he's Bud Holland, pushing for another killing!"

A quick glance back saw the large, red-faced woman standing with Judge Dixon and Joan Wolcott. The three of them must have crossed the plaza from the judge's office. Joan had changed to a plain brown dress in which she still looked slender and young. She could not have rested much today. Her tired pallor was more obvious. She was watching without expression as Shafter turned back to the man. Even in Colorado, Bud Holland's name was known. Fury clawed Shafter's tired nerves as he realized what was happening. This was an execution, not a quarrel; this had been planned to remove Mike Shafter. "Come up in the wagon and satisfy yourself," Shafter said.

Holland removed the cheroot from his mouth. His drawl sounded amused. "No need to take that trouble. Pull your gun and show how good you are in McCloud's job."

The fury drove Shafter on. "You're not the only man, Holland, waiting to try me. Step up in the wagon where everyone can see."

VI

Leisurely and unruffled, Bud Holland walked to the rear wheel of the wagon. His long-boned figure stepped lightly on the wheel hub, and over into the wagon bed. Graying maturity touched the thick black hairs on his temples. Dark broadcloth suit fitted well. A plain, cedar-handled gun rode unobtrusively in an old, scuffed holster inside his open coat.

The man looked what he was, Shafter thought in cold rage—a more than competent gunman, calmly confident of breaking a stranger's nerve, or killing him if necessary. Even the lazy, jibing challenge had been neatly timed. All the Grenada country was represented in the faces looming around the wagon in tight, expectant silence.

"Closer!" Shafter urged harshly. "Close in, damn you, if you've got the nerve!"

Old Johnny Carr's legally brilliant mind couldn't have anticipated this—Mike Shafter standing in the front of a weathered ranch wagon, corpse-stiff figures at his feet, eyes gritty from lack of sleep, bandaged right leg throbbing and feverish—and any smashing second now the end.

Bud Holland's glance around in the red sunset seemed to grasp, suddenly, the position into which he had been maneuvered. He shrugged slightly. "Coming," Holland said calmly, and moved forward, stepping carefully between the stiffened bodies.

Gray-green eyes, squinting slightly, were watchful as Holland halted an arm's length away. His faint smile, seen close, had the relaxed tolerance of a man who seldom was excited by anything.

"Now!" Shafter said savagely. "Show them now! Neither of us will miss this close!" And, guessing, he added: "You'll earn your pay for this!"

The gray-green eyes estimated him unblinkingly. "Planned it, didn't you, pulling me in close?" Holland said mildly.

"You planned a public circus!" Shafter said in the shaking rage. "Now give it to them! Make it seven bodies in the wagon here . . . and I'm the one who'll be laughing at the way you earned your money!"

Something like admiration warmed the steady eyes. "Ready for it, aren't you?"

"Did you think I wouldn't be?"

"Listen to this, first," Holland said. Hands held carefully away from his sides, blue smoke drifting from the cheroot in his left hand, the man turned his back and lifted his voice in a drawl to the staring faces. "I was curious, I guess." His chuckle was audible. "Now I'm not curious." He reached down to the sideboard and vaulted out of the wagon. On the ground he looked around again. His cool question was challenging. "Any man got a remark to make about this? Like to try my nerve?" The silence was incredulous. Holland let it draw out, and then said dryly: "All of you saw it. Think it over. The next man who cuts this cake, better be ready to eat it."

"Holland . . . who paid you for this?" Shafter whipped at the man's back.

"If I took money for it," Holland said casually over his shoulder, "I wouldn't admit it."

The fury steadied in Shafter as he watched the long, neat figure move without haste to the walk, and across it into the Palace. Close, only Bud Holland could say how close! The hot, crimson sunset had a fresh and vivid reality. For in this moment by all logic Mike Shafter should be dead. Only the unpredictable whim of Bud Holland had given life back to them both, for a time at least.

A curious thing was happening. Shafter could sense it in himself. When a man's mind had accepted death in the next few seconds, and he lived instead, then, suddenly, he was free. What might happen in the future did not greatly matter.

It was an odd, relaxing sensation. Shafter almost smiled as his gaze sought Curly Ames in the crowd.

"Curly. Drive this wagon to the undertaker's, and then to the livery."

Faint perspiration was visible on Curly's strained young face. Curly's—"Yes, sir."—held a new note of respect.

Shafter left the wagon on the other side. Staring faces moved out of his way as he walked to Judge Dixon, Lyd Adams, and Joanie Wolcott.

"I'd like to talk to all three of you . . . alone," he said briefly.

Lyd Adams's shrewd glance searched his face as they moved out of earshot. "If you ain't quittin'," the big woman said, "you're to stay at Joanie's house, in Rufe Wolcott's room."

"Appreciate her kindness, but the hotel will do."

"It wasn't Joanie's idea."

"To be exact," Joan Wolcott said coldly, "I said I'd rather have a skunk in the house. Lyd is going to stay with me, but there seems to be an idea I need a male nurse, also."

"Be simpler to lock you in your room." Her flush brought his chuckle, easing the last of the rage. But when they paused on the walk in front of the judge's law office, he was terse again. "Taking McCloud's job seemed like a good idea yesterday, even with two bosses. Now it won't do. If I stay in the job, I want full authority."

Joan flashed: "Authority over me?"

"You, too, ma'am."

"Ridiculous! Judge," Joan said hotly, "I told you that McCloud said in Azul this man meant trouble. We've had trouble ever since he appeared. Now he has some new scheme."

"He has a reason, I assume," the judge said calmly.

Shafter gave the gray-haired, ruddy man a thoughtful look. "Several reasons. Those cattle were run over the cliff deliberately last night. I think McCloud had a hand in it, but I can't prove that as yet. Now this Bud Holland was hired to get me out of the way."

"By McCloud?" the judge suggested.

"No, McCloud's kind would try it himself, I think."

Lyd Adams was listening in frowning silence.

Joan said: "I can't believe even Con McCloud would . . . would do that to a herd of cattle. . . ."

"It's done, whatever the reason," the judge said briefly. "Things are getting out of hand. You must face it, Joan." A glint was in the judge's estimating glance at Shafter. "You'll quit, young man, if you can't have Rufe Wolcott's full authority?"

"All but legal signatures and financial details."

"You have some plan?"

"No, but I can't make plans if I take orders and run errands for two sets of bosses." Shafter was cool, detached. The odd, new feeling of being alive when he should be dead, of being free of worry about it, was gaining strength. "If someone wants me out of the way, then more trouble is coming."

"Art Blaisdell can be here by tomorrow and do anything this man Shafter can do," Joan insisted. "We can trust Art."

"And you'll take charge of him," Shafter said calmly. "He's a good man where he is . . . on the ranch. He's needed there."

The glint had brightened in the judge's eyes. "Lyd, what do you think?" he inquired.

The big woman was blunt. "A man bent on hangin' himself ought to have enough rope."

A slight smile warmed the judge's gravity for a moment. "Hang yourself then, young man. Lyd Adams and I, as co-executors of Rufe Wolcott's estate, give you full authority from this moment." The judge cleared his throat. "For all practical purposes . . . and we'll let it be known before dark . . . you are Rufe Wolcott now."

Shafter nodded. He felt no different. And he must be mistaken about the slight twinkle of satisfaction that seemed to back the glint in the judge's eyes. "I'll sleep on it at Miss Wolcott's house tonight." His bloodshot, gravelly eyes considered Joanie Wolcott's flushed defiance. "The first order," Shafter said, "is that Miss Wolcott stay in her house after dark tonight, where she'll be safe."

"Don't say it, Joanie," Lyd Adams said quickly and dryly. "You've butted up against a stubborn young man who just missed bein' killed for you. Takin' his orders, meek and grateful, is the least you can do."

"Meek and grateful?" Joan said in a stifled voice. "I'd rather have Con McCloud back! At least we know what to expect from him!"

Con McCloud was talking to himself, muttering, when he heard goats blatting not far ahead through the belt of mountain forest. Minutes later he reined up on muffling needle duff under the tall yellow pines, and squinted into the glare of the setting sun, across a brush-studded sweep of rocky mountain slope. McCloud's head was aching again as his frowning gaze weighed the scattered goats, a single mongrel dog, and a dark-skinned native boy out there in the open.

The dog barked, the half-wild goats froze warily as McCloud rode into sight. The boy jumped up from the rock where he had been sitting, and stared with sudden fright at the burly, silent rider approaching. A command in Spanish, thin and shaky, silenced the dog as McCloud pulled up.

"Speak English, boy?"

"*Sí, Señor* McCloud."

"Know who I am, huh?"

"Sí, sí." The boy had snatched off his raveled straw hat. Thin, wiry, in another year he would be ten, almost a man. "You are," he said in stumbling English, lips trembling, "the *Señor* McCloud, who is only a little less than God and *Don* Rufe Wolcott, who is with God now."

"Hold still, boy." McCloud bent from the saddle and caught the thin, brown neck at the back. The dog rushed in, barking furiously. McCloud drew his belt gun and shot the dog. The goats scattered. The small neck went rigid in McCloud's big hand.

"Don't lie to me!" McCloud said heavily as the boy's mute gaze watched the last convulsions of the dog. "I know this Cincos Hermanos country, and these Griegos families back in here."

"S-sí, señor. . . ."

"Where's old Manuel Griegos hiding out?" McCloud's grip tightened. "Who's he staying with?"

"*Señor* . . . my neck. . . ." McCloud squeezed; the boy moaned, stammered: "Fabien Griegos . . . weeth Fabien, his cousin. . . ."

McCloud released the neck. "I know Fabien's place. You better be right!"

The boy edged to the dead dog, and went to his knees as McCloud rode down the rocky slope to the narrow little valley at the bottom, where water glinted in a small, sandy channel beside a horse trail that was also a deer trail. When McCloud reined to the left, up the valley, the boy rose cautiously, fearfully to his feet, and began to run in the opposite direction, toward the high, screening pines. This was the business of men, and—even sniffling like this over a dog—nine years old was almost a man.

Shafter rolled up to a sitting position on the bed edge, fighting sleep fog. "Yes?" he called. This was Rufe Wolcott's room; in this cheap, narrow bed, Rule Wolcott had died, and a legend had ended in the Grenada country. He hadn't dreamed the rapping on the door.

Priscilla Ross, the Boston girl, answered through the door: "Mister Peck didn't come home last night."

"Peck?" Shafter said vaguely.

"Henry Peck, cashier of the bank."

A small tocsin of warning snapped Shafter sharp awake. "Drunk?" he suggested.

"His wife was just here to tell Joan. Peck doesn't drink."

"Women?"

"Missus Peck trusts her husband," Priscilla Ross said severely through the door. "In every way. Last night he went back to the bank to work on the books. He wasn't home when she went to sleep. He's not at the bank now. No one has seen him this morning."

Shafter came to his feet, reaching for his pants. "What does Miss Wolcott think? And Lyd Adams think?"

"They left early and said to let you sleep, but I thought you should know this. Joan said last night you were giving all orders now."

Sunshine was streaming through the window; he had slept late, too late. "Peck," Shafter guessed, "has to unlock the bank door and open the safe."

"And it's almost time for the bank to open." Her voice was warm, friendly. "Hot coffee and breakfast are waiting."

Last night she had held towels, fresh strips of torn sheeting, while Lyd Adams had cleaned and re-bandaged his bullet-torn leg. The Wolcott girl had not come near him.

"Three minutes," Shafter said.

Hauling on clothes swiftly, he looked about the room again, at the shabby wardrobe, two chairs with sagging splint seats, worn rag rug. Money had been spent generously on the rest of the big house—but only this plain, cheaply furnished room for Rufe Wolcott himself.

He was still puzzling over it when he found the dining room, and breakfast and Priscilla Ross waiting at the long table. She was crisp, fresh in the linen skirt and jacket she had worn the first morning he had seen her.

"A different man this morning," Priscilla commented with amusement as he took the high-backed chair at the head of the table, where his plate was waiting. She was vivid, provocative again. "Rufe Wolcott's chair," Priscilla murmured. "What orders do you have for me, Mister Shafter?"

He chuckled as he reached for the platter of ham slices and eggs. "Always have breakfast ready."

Priscilla laughed. "A promise. And now that you're king of the Grenada country, in Rufe Wolcott's place, what are you going to do?"

"Probably get shot."

"You seem to expect it." Sobering, Priscilla reached for her cup. "Why, Mister Shafter, should anyone want you dead?"

"Mike Shafter," he suggested, "Mike. . . ."

"Priscilla, then." Her renewed smile was an effort. "Why,

Mike? Who would want you dead?"

"Be interesting to know."

"How will you know?"

Humor tightened as he cut into a ham slice. "I can make mistakes until I'm dead. Anyone else gets one mistake."

The cup was unsteady in her hand and she put it down. "Then what, Mike?"

He looked up as the door into the kitchen opened. A young native girl came in with a silver coffee pot on a silver tray, and Shafter pushed back his chair and stood up. Her eyes widened, dark and enormous again with fright. The tray crashed to the floor; she whirled back into the kitchen.

"Been looking for her!" Shafter threw at Priscilla Ross, and bolted after the girl through the steaming pool of coffee spreading over the wide floor planks.

He caught up with her in the range-warm kitchen, fragrant with cooking odors. The lush young Griegos girl halted with a gasp as his hand clamped on her arm. She turned, trembling.

"Now we'll talk about John Carr's hotel room in Azul," Shafter said sharply. "And who killed him. And why."

Behind him young Curly Ames said softly and unsteadily: "She's my girl, Mister Shafter. Let her alone."

Curly had been eating breakfast at a small table in the corner. His earnest young face was tight; his hand under the table edge held his gun, Shafter guessed. Curly's girl—who would have suspected? Shafter released her arm and looked more critically. Young—but she had matured early. Pretty, with her olive skin, fine black hair, large dark eyes. Not so innocently helpless. When he looked back at Curly, Shafter was remembering the thin-bladed knife she had whisked from the low neck of her dress in Johnny's dark hotel room.

"I caught her in Carr's room, Curly. No light in the room. She said . . . 'He's dying, I think.' . . . when I stepped in out of the storm. Then she pulled a knife, and got away in the dark . . . and Carr was on the bed . . . dead."

"I know," Curly said. He was still poised stiffly on his chair, hand under the table, young face desperately determined. "She thought you were Mister Carr when you walked in. Marina had been waiting for him." Curly licked his lips. "She wanted to tell him that Mister Wolcott was probably dyin'. I'd seen her when I got to the hotel, an' told her." Curly swallowed; he was unhappy. "When we heard Carr was dead, I told her to keep out of sight. We knew you'd blame her. Marina went across the river to stay with her father an' grandfather, and you found her there."

Priscilla Ross was standing frozen, listening, in the doorway. The bank, Shafter remembered, trouble at the bank. His trouble now. But this first.

"Curly," Shafter said, "put up that gun and answer some questions."

"Ain't a thing to hide." Sheepishly Curly stood up, holstering the gun he had been holding under the table.

"You've done well at keeping quiet," Shafter said coldly. "Now, why was this girl waiting in Carr's dark room with news about Wolcott's health?"

"Wasn't much reason, I guess." Curly was embarrassed. "Me an' Marina was sparkin' on the quiet. She's a mite young. Carr took meals off an' on at their house over by the coal mine. Marina liked him. She says he asked questions about the old days around here, questions all the time."

"What questions?"

"All kinds. Even about folks in the house here. About Mister Rufe an' Con McCloud. So, when I seen Marina in the hotel, an' told her Mister Rufe looked a goner, she thought to tell Carr. Few days before, he'd asked how sick Mister Rufe was. Seemed interested. It was rainin' and blowin', and, when his door opened, she waited inside, sure he'd be along any minute."

Rufe Wolcott. Con McCloud. Now some of the scrambled mystery Johnny Carr had left was sorting out. *We're rich, Michael.* But the riches in this Grenada country had been scooped in by Rufe Wolcott, helped by McCloud. "Old Manuel Griegos, his son Pete, and your Marina vanished," Shafter reminded.

"Uhn-huh." Curly was frowning. "They took off to kinfolks in the Cincos Hermanos hills, west of here. Came back quick last night. McCloud was out there at sundown yesterday, lookin' for Marina's grandfather. One of the kid relatives sent McCloud wrong, and got word to them."

"McCloud was hunting old Manuel Griegos? The one Rufe Wolcott left money to?"

"Five thousand dollars," Curly said. "Makes Manuel a rich man when he gets it. And Manuel thinks McCloud means to kill him on account of it."

"Why?" Shafter prodded. "Why kill an old man who's been around all these years?"

"Might be old Manuel knows," Curly said, shrugging. "Marina says they can't get much sense out of the old man. But he's scared blue of McCloud."

"Where's the old man now?"

"I don't rightly know," said Curly blandly.

"I want to talk to him."

"If I see him," Curly said with the same bland lack of expression, "I'll tell him."

Priscilla Ross broke her intent silence. "The bank, Mike. . . ."

"I know," Shafter remembered. "Curly . . . seen Henry Peck this morning? He didn't come home last night."

"No, sir." Curly smiled wanly. "I got me a room at the hotel an' died. This morning I got your saddle out of the wagon an' cinched it on that lead horse I brought in yesterday. He's out front."

Priscilla Ross walked to the front door, also. She was thoughtful. "Joan was right, wasn't she, Mike? You didn't just happen to be in Azul and Grenada. You had a reason, some reason connected with the Wolcotts . . . ?"

"You heard what I heard." His excitement was surging. Close, now, to the mystery old Johnny had left—and exactly in the right place, near the secrets of Rufe Wolcott's past life. "It seems," Shafter said calmly, "that John Carr was interested in the old days, and I seem to have made a mistake about Curly's girl."

Priscilla was intelligent. "Why, Mike," she persisted as they walked out into the morning sunshine, "was this man Carr so interested in the past . . . and in the Wolcotts?"

"He was dead when I found him," Shafter reminded her.

"Well, then"—all laughter was gone from her face—"haven't you some idea of what's happening? Men and cattle dead, gunmen willing to kill, waiting. . . ."

"I can guess," Shafter said calmly. "An estate worth more than a million up for grabs. One girl, not very experienced, trying to take the place of a solitary old wolf like Rufe Wolcott."

"Mike. . . ." Priscilla's hand dropped on his arm. On impulse his other hand covered her fingers, which turned and clung. They halted, looking at each other. Priscilla's eyes closed; a pulse started to beat visibly in her neck.

"Pretty girls," Shafter said lightly, "come from Boston. If we were in the house. . . ."

Priscilla swallowed. "Thank you, Mike." Her opening eyes looked at him gravely before her slight smile came. "I think I needed that from someone like you, Mike Shafter." She squeezed her hand and drew her fingers away. "The truth, Mike, please . . . is Joan in danger? Really in danger?"

"I don't know," Shafter said honestly. "If she should die. . . ."

"Vince," Priscilla said, "would have it all?" When he nodded, she said under her breath: "He's asleep in his room now."

"Why didn't you tell me?" He bit back angry annoyance. "Are you certain he's asleep?"

"I suppose so. I didn't know it mattered, Mike. Joan told him he could live here in the house as usual, as long as he wished."

Scowling as he remembered Jess Parker's tired yawn yesterday, Shafter asked: "Did Vince say where he was yesterday or the day before? Anything unusual in the way he looked or talked?"

"No-o-o," Priscilla said uncertainly. "Oh, subdued and resentful of Joan, I suppose. He didn't try to hide it. Vince said he was tired, and went to his room."

"Watch him," Shafter said briefly. He was wondering if Vince had heard the commotion in the dining room, the talk in the kitchen—and whether it mattered if Vince had.

The growing fear in Priscilla's eyes escaped him as he walked out to the hitch rack and the bay horse Curly had left for him. Joan Wolcott, he was thinking as he rode toward the bank, was lucky to have a young friend like Priscilla Ross close to her in these critical days. He would have been amused by Priscilla's bitter thought as she watched him leave: *Joan should be grateful. Why couldn't someone like Mike Shafter care what happens to me?*

Her back to the door of the red brick bank building, tense, pale, braced against the almost frightening thing she was witnessing in the men and a few women pressing close, Joan saw the sharp, final run of Shafter's horse reach the bank. He flung off with a hard face. His slapping order—"One side, please!"—cut through the voices.

Way was made for him in hostile silence. He looked tall, lean, stern in the gray flannel shirt and dark wool pants. She remembered his cold rage yesterday as he had faced Bud Holland. Angry men in the crowd remembered, also; there was sudden, welcome relief in the way their anger muted.

"What's wrong?" he asked coolly, turning at her side to face the men pressing close.

"I thought I had friends." Heated scorn curled Joan's lip. "All they want is their money now. They want the bank opened quickly."

His cool tone did not change. "Can't blame 'em. Their money is in the bank." His voice carried. "Peck is late this morning. The bank will open late."

"He was in the bank last night! What happened to him?" challenged a belligerent voice. That was Sam Gilman, beefy, red-faced, always looking like he was sweating, always arguing. He owned some wagons, teams, hauled coal, ore.

A woman's shrill, worried accusation followed: "Henry Peck never disappeared before!" Mattie Sorenson, widow, frugal, whose acid tongue was seldom courted by any of the town ladies. Or men, either.

Under her breath, Joan said: "Judge Dixon is bringing a door key and the combination of the safe. Carl Phelps, the bookkeeper, is searching for Peck."

Someone called: "Here comes Dixon!"

Judge Dixon's mouth was a severe line as he unlocked the door in silence. Shafter's order to him was low and curt: "Step inside." Then his tall figure barred the determined surge forward of the nearest men. "No one inside until the bank opens!" He backed in, closed the door in their faces, and pushed an inside bolt over. The green shades were pulled down on the door and windows, giving a shadowed illusion of privacy. Unsmiling, jaw muscles tight, Shafter said: "I was told I'd give all orders."

Antagonism against this dark-tanned stranger who more and more seemed to dominate her life drove Joan to sarcasm. "Is anyone stopping your orders?"

He gave her a dark look. "I didn't send for the door key and safe combination."

"I did. I sent word to Judge Dixon." Hatred of the man was not the word: scorn, dislike, rebellion against his domineering ways backed her glare. "You wouldn't have done so, I suppose, Mister Shafter?"

"Worse thing you could have done, ma'am." His politeness was cutting. "As long as the safe couldn't be opened, they'd talk and wait and hope. Now you have to produce money, ma'am, cash money, to satisfy them."

The judge, hat in hand, gray hair rumpled, was listening, watching them closely. Some of the tightness had relaxed about his mouth. "That hadn't occurred to me," the judge admitted "However, it's done." The judge walked through the end gate in the banking counter and, consulting a slip of paper, slowly manipulated the safe combination, and opened the heavy door.

In silence all three of them looked into the shadow-filled vault—at the clutter of papers, silver dollars, smaller coins, and scattered gold eagles on the floor.

"I had hoped for something better," the judge said quietly. "I suppose Phelps will have to make a check and tell us what is missing."

Behind Joan, Shafter was terse. "What isn't missing is more important."

Joan said tightly: "I can give you some idea. Henry Peck showed me everything." She was heartsick as she entered the small, shadowy vault. Always the bank had been a point of solid stability. Rufe Wolcott had been quietly proud of it. Now it was her bank—and the angry suspicions she had faced outside had been justified.

"Buck Manning brought bullion from the smelter yesterday. It's gone. All the gold money seems to be gone . . . and . . . and the paper money." Her voice shook, and she despised herself for showing weakness in front of that grim-faced Mike Shafter, looking silently at her. "Part of the silver dollars are gone."

Shafter's curt question seemed to boom in the shadowy confines of the small vault. "Is the note file there?"

"I don't see it. Henry showed me the file. It . . . it was here. . . ."

Shafter said evenly to the judge: "The note file makes it plain enough. Peck didn't do this. I doubt if he'd have made so much litter. He knew the notes were worthless to anyone but the bank. Whoever did this meant to cripple the bank."

"And succeeded," the judge said.

"If Peck was an honest man last night," Shafter said, frowning in thought, "he's probably dead now. Guilt in this can't hurt him."

Joan flared at the man as she started out of the vault: "You'd blame an innocent person for trouble which seems to happen every time you appear?"

Looking down at her, unmoved, he drawled: "Like the buggy wreck in Azul?" Her face flamed; his brief grin was ironic—then his cool words beat at her with relentless facts. "You've lost cattle. Lost men. Your bank is closed. Don't think there won't be more. There will. Riff-raff and men who won't bluff are still coming in. Rufe Wolcott ran this town and the country around with a short rein. When he wasn't respected, he was feared. Who's afraid of you, ma'am? How much respect and confidence did you see outside in those faces crowding around you?"

"Go on!" Her mouth was dry; now she did hate him because he was right. Frighteningly right.

His eyes were infuriatingly cool and detached, as if she really didn't matter much in his scheme of things. "If Peck's alive, calling him a thief will help him."

"How could it help?" This kind of anger clogged her throat, curled fingers into fists.

"Men everywhere will be looking for the fellow, which is what we want," Shafter said calmly. He turned, obviously brushing her from his thoughts. "Judge, is there a back door?"

Had there been the faintest hint of brief humor deep in the judge's gray eyes? A satisfied glint? Impossible, Joan decided, because there was nothing to be humorous or satisfied about.

The judge had brought a spare key to the locked back door. Shafter looked out at the open sweep of lots, some with sheds, all backed by an alley. He gazed at horse sign and light wheel marks outside the door.

"Peck, and the rest of it, went out this way. Must have answered a knock, or had a door unlocked while he was working in the bank last night." Shafter was thoughtful as he closed the door. "Can you borrow money in Azul, Judge, and get this bank open quickly?"

"Difficult, without the note file."

"Well, then, can you borrow against the Wolcott estate?"

"I can't say." Lines of worry and responsibility were drawing into the judge's ruddy face.

"If we can't pay out cash today, we have to give hope." Absently he adjusted the cartridge belt and holster that he seemed to wear as an afterthought. "Even ten cents on the dollar as soon as possible should keep them hoping."

"Everyone will be paid sooner or later," Joan said coldly.

His cool glance made the words seem foolish. "Later won't do, ma'am. You have payrolls to meet. Have to get the bank open, pay out some money to show good faith, promise more quickly, and try to carry on business as usual."

"Almost forty percent of the bank," said the judge, "is owned by others. Mostly large ranch owners and mine owners. Rufe got their banking business that way."

"That should help." Shafter drew a breath and smiled wryly. "We'll try."

He said "we" as if all this were a part of his life now. He had moved in, taken over. Resenting the man more than ever, Joan stood in the lobby beside the judge as Shafter opened the front door again. Expectant silence fell outside.

"Henry Peck is gone," his calm voice said. "The bank will close for a day or so while the loss is checked, and more cash money is brought in."

"Peck cleaned out the bank?"

"Money is missing," Shafter drawled, "and Peck is missing."

"We don't get money today?" The shout was Sam Gilman again.

"You don't," Shafter's unruffled drawl agreed. "And shouting won't help you. Blame Peck, not the bank. He'll be hunted. You know your money is safe."

Someone else demanded: "How do we know?"

Shafter looked toward the speaker. "Because the men who own the bank need it open. Miss Wolcott needs it. And you'll wait because you have to wait." Through the doorway, over the massed heads outside, Joan could see Curly Ames on his horse, watching. Shafter's voice lifted. "Curly! Bring my horse to the back!" He closed the door, pushed the bolt again, and grinned wryly once more. "Should give us a little time."

An angry hubbub of voices beat through the bolted door. Joan asked icily: "Time for what, Mister Shafter?"

"First, to get the bookkeeper in here, checking. You, ma'am, can assist. Judge, can you help me get new men to push that herd to Fort Kinfadden? I want Blaisdell and his crew in town, all but the cook."

He was checking the loads in his revolver with brown, muscular hands, which moved deftly, Joan grudgingly noted. "I'm only one man," Shafter said matter-of-factly. "Can't run all the errands, do everything that has to be done." He walked back to the rear door again to meet Curly Ames.

Under her breath, Joan said: "I don't trust him. Why did he take McCloud's job? What is he up to?"

Mike Shafter's crisp tones were audible outside the back door. The glint came back into the judge's eyes as they rested upon her. "Does it matter? You need him now, but I doubt if he needs you." The judge's smile was wry, also, as his hand dropped on her shoulder. "Take an old man's advice . . . sugar, not vinegar, catches flies. Catch this fly, Joanie, or you may regret it."

"You sound," Joanie said, "as if you know something that I don't."

"Why else would I have hired him . . . a stranger?" the judge said enigmatically.

Whistling softly past his teeth, Shafter reined into the open runway of Brad Hampton's livery barn, near the Grenada plaza. A saddled horse stood in the runway ahead of him, and Brad Hampton's voice spoke cheerfully from the loft above, on the left. "Be down in a shake."

"Any luck selling your barn?"

Young Hampton's grin was impudently friendly. "Not selling, with you the big boss of these parts now."

"How do others take it?" Shafter asked dryly.

"There's doubt," said Brad Hampton, "you can cut it." He pitched hay, rustling, down a chute.

Big flies droned in the warm shadows. The smell of feed and leather and horses hung pleasantly in the cavernous barn, inviting lazy idling. Shafter was palming the horn to dismount and roll a cigarette when warning cut sharply from the loft above. "Ahead of you. . . ."

His fast glance sighted a carbine barrel and hatless head with black, curly hair, easing furtively out from behind a bay horse in a stall ahead. The tense face, gaunt and bony and young, was desperate in purpose. Shafter's instant reaction carried him in a plunging dive down the left side of his horse. Brad Hampton was furiously forking a cloud of loose hay over the loft edge.

The slamming carbine report missed, and splintered wood somewhere behind Shafter. He struck the runway earth, hard and stumbling, catching out his handgun. His horse was swerving; ahead of him the other horse was bolting, reins dragging.

Hay showered over the stranger as he desperately jacked in another shell. Brad Hampton's pitchfork streaked down from above like a thrown javelin, burying sharp tines in the runway litter inches from the stranger, who flinched as his carbine barrel sought Shafter again.

For a fateful instant, Shafter forced steadiness, to aim. The heavy revolver in his hand bucked twice, the smashing muzzle blasts overwhelming all other sounds. The pitchfork handle was still whipping violently as blood welled red and bright at the stranger's hairline, over the right temple. Grotesque and jerky, he seemed to bow in macabre politeness. The carbine slipped from suddenly slack fingers. Eyes bulged in shock. The whites of the eyes rolled up blankly as the grotesque bow fell backward. Doubled and inert, he struck heavily, bounced slightly, and rolled to his side.

Brad Hampton had slid over the loft edge, down to arm's length, and dropped. He was panting, stammering. "P-paid 'im no mind till that sneak move!"

"Who is he?" Shafter dropped to a knee by the man.

"Rode in last night, busted an' hungry, on an old crow-bait gelding, rode-down more bony than he is," said Brad Hampton. "He hit luck in a stud game, he said this morning, an' traded up for that gray he'd just saddled when you rode in. Paid the boot with gold eagles and didn't bother to haggle. Said he might be leavin' town, and might not. Come to think of it, he had a funny manner, like he was half scared and didn't feel so good. Dead, ain't he?"

"Bleeding from the head like he is." Shafter felt for a pulse.

"He meant to kill you," Brad Hampton said. "Hadn't met you here, he'd've been out lookin' for you."

Shafter said nothing, concentrating on the limp wrist he held. "How far to a doctor?" he asked abruptly.

"Doc Kelton's house ain't far, if he's in. He covers a heap of territory, busy all the time."

"Worth a gamble," Shafter decided, dropping the wrist. "Hand him up to me, and get on his horse and guide me." They rode out of the barn, ignoring running men who had heard the shots, young Hampton leading, Shafter awkwardly balancing his burden. At a trot they cut through the plaza, watched by every startled eye. The doctor's house was adobe, behind a white picket fence. *James Kelton, M.D.* Brad Hampton hurried in ahead, shouting: "Doc! Doctor Jim!"

In a whitewashed room holding the stale, sweet reek of chloroform and sharper bite of carbolic, they stood beside a sheet-covered table while the doctor glanced quickly at a wound low under the right shoulder, then bent intently over the bleeding head. He was a young man with startling red hair, large freckles splotching his square-jawed face, and hands that looked big and awkward but were quick and gentle. He felt for a pulse with probing finger ends, thumbed up an eyelid and looked closely, and finally used a stethoscope for silent seconds.

"Not good," he said under his breath.

"Is he alive?" Shafter asked.

"Oh, yes." The doctor was calm, wasting few motions as he stepped to a glass-fronted cupboard against the wall and took out a hypodermic. "Not too much blood lost, either. But with bone fractured in the head, he may go off any minute, or hang on. Depends on the damage underneath."

"Do what you can." Smoldering anger still pulled Shafter's face tight. "While he's alive, no one is to get in the room with him."

"That," said the red-haired young doctor evenly, selecting a small bottle from a rack of shelves holding bottles and jars, "sounds like an order in my own house, from a stranger."

"It is," Shafter said sharply. He watched Kelton's eyebrow lift slightly, unimpressed, and his wry chuckle came. "I'm Mike Shafter, working for the Wolcott estate. This man took a shot at me. Never saw him before, so someone must have put him up to it. He might talk."

Kelton's close, keen look was followed by an easy grin. "So you're the man?" His shrug followed. "I don't take sides. Can't afford to. My wife helps me with cases like this . . . but I can't be here all the time, and she's not a guard."

"Up to me then to see that no one gets at him?"

"Exactly. Now, if you two will get out. . . ."

In the next room, a small waiting room with chairs around the walls, Shafter smiled faintly at Hampton. "Salty, but he might pull this fellow through. How much extra did you get for the horse trade?"

"Forty dollars."

"I cleaned his pockets on the way here. Seven double eagles and change in them. He was broke last night, so he raised about two hundred dollars fast."

"I'll ask around," Brad Hampton said. New purpose gleamed in his gaze. "My hostler can watch the barn. I can sit in the room here and see who's interested in him."

"Not your trouble."

The impudent grin flashed again. "I'm interested in how long you'll last," Brad Hampton said.

Shafter was wondering the same thing as he rode back to the plaza, smoldering and more uncertain than he'd been. This try had been cold-blooded, deliberate. He was only one man. Luck could run out quickly. The thought depressed him. Mike Shafter, dead, would never know how Joanie Wolcott came out in all this. Never know whether Johnny Carr's improbable dreams had any basis. He should, Shafter knew now in increasing gloom, have kept to himself here in Grenada, instead of brashly standing forth as an inviting target in matters that were really none of his business. It was not yet too late to get out of this. He was toying with the thought when he saw Curly Ames riding into the other side of the plaza at a fast trot that swerved toward him.

They met in the middle of the plaza, watched by dozens of eyes. Curly was glum, also. "No luck. Can't even be sure which way them wheel marks behind the bank left town."

"*If* they left town," Shafter said on impulse.

Curly stared. "You think Peck's alive, hiding in close? In his own house, maybe?" Curly wet his lips. "He kept a team and buggy in his barn. Dark as it was last night, he could've done something like that."

"You might take a look at his rig." Useless, but it would keep Curly busy. There was something suddenly more important, while there was time. Before all Mike Shafter's luck ran out. "Curly, don't hold back this time," Shafter said coldly and bluntly. "Where do I find old Manuel Griegos?"

Curly's dark young face set stubbornly, flushing. Then he yielded reluctantly. "I guess it's all right. Back of the Wolcott house. There's a bunk room ain't being used now. Old Manuel's holed up in there. Only Marina an' me know."

"I'll see him alone," Shafter said.

Rufe Wolcott had built on the grand scale. Behind the sprawling main house and flower-filled patios, a spacious rear yard was enclosed by a high, thick adobe wall, with an arched gateway at the side. Back here were sheds for horses, buggies, saddles, other needs of the large establishment and men in from the ranch. The bunkhouse was of adobe, also, small, apparently deserted. The locked door rattled to a knock.

"Manuel. This is Michael Shafter. Ames sent me."

Nothing happened. He'd been tricked, or the old man had slipped off to another hideaway. Then, slowly, a bolt scraped inside. Hinges *creaked.*

Shafter stared at the bent ancient with sparse, white hair, deep-wrinkled, dark face, watery eyes peering, blinking. "I'll talk with you now," Shafter said.

Fright or age quavered in the thin voice as a veined, lean hand made the Sign of the Cross. "God's will," Manuel Griegos said.

Shafter walked into the dim interior, which held three pairs of bunks, a pine table, chairs, small iron stove, and sand box in a corner. Wheeling a chair beside the table, he sat down and asked evenly: "What is God's will?"

This old man had known Big Mike Shafter, remembered the long-past years when a small boy had worshiped his tall, laughing father. Memories crowded in, moving, nostalgic. The past crept into the shadowy bunkhouse with them.

The blinking, watery eyes were sad and fascinated as they regarded Shafter. "A man, *señor,* is not killed, until his sons are killed."

Superstition! Old men like this were riddled with primitive beliefs. "But," Shafter said mildly, "God's will?"

"You have come, his blood and flesh and face. . . ."

It made nerves crawl slightly because it brought the long years, boy to man, into the quiet shadows with them. "I was young when Big Mike was killed," Shafter said, watching.

"Sí." The ghost of a smile crinkled the old, deeply wrinkled face. "So high." A hand measured from the floor.

Carefully Shafter asked the question that had lurked deeply in his thoughts, darkly suspicious, the last day or so: "Did Rufe Wolcott kill my father?"

"No, *señor.*"

That was settled. But not the tangle of mystery. Shafter spoke his groping thoughts aloud: "Wolcott left you five thousand in his will. All these years, old man, you've been around . . . and suddenly McCloud wants you. So the will must have made McCloud guess something that Wolcott knew all along. And God's will brought me back." Shafter leaned forward, voice sharpening. "Rufe Wolcott didn't kill my father. But he knew who did. And he knew you knew, old man. Didn't he? And now McCloud knows you know. He's afraid of you, afraid of me. He was afraid of me from the first sight in Azul, because I looked like Big Mike Shafter . . . back after all these years, back to find the man who killed Big Mike." Shafter's voice shook slightly. "Out with it, old man. The truth. This Con McCloud killed my father, didn't he? And you've known it all these years?"

Old Manuel Griegos sighed in soft submission. His watery eyes filmed, casting back. Listening, Shafter was a small boy again that last night when life had crashed down about him and his mother.

"I was on the road, *señor,* on my mule, when I heard the gun ahead . . . two shots. Then a horse coming fast. It was not a place to be, *señor.* I was off the road, hiding, when the young *Señor* McCloud, who was feared by men even then, went past in the moonlight . . . and I knew a man had died. When I found him, he was on the ground by his horse."

"And what happened," Shafter asked, the words hardening, "when you told what you'd seen?"

The dim room was quiet. Old Manuel Griegos gestured helplessly. "Who would have believed? *Señor* McCloud would have killed me, too. So I said only that I had found a man dead."

The chair scraped as Shafter stood up. "Has to be more to it than that. Why did Rufe Wolcott leave you five thousand dollars twenty years later?"

"Because he knew, I think, when he had owned the land of your father for two years. . . ."

Shafter cut in: "Rufe Wolcott bought our place?"

"Oh, *sí* . . . poor land, of little value, once part of the Ricardo Montoya Spanish Grant. Of me *Don* Rufe asked many questions about that night. Was *Don* Miguel Shafter dead when I found him? Had I seen anyone else that night? *Señor,* he knew, he saw it in my eyes, I think, and he said . . . 'We will forget that night, Manuel, eh? And because you are a good man, Manuel, you will work for me when you wish, and always your family will have food.' "

"But McCloud never asked questions?"

"He would have killed me if there were questions in his mind."

"Then Rufe Wolcott covered for McCloud for twenty years . . . and never told McCloud," Shafter muttered, trying to think through that puzzle. "And twenty years later, Wolcott left you five thousand in his will . . . so you'd keep quiet as long as you lived. Still protecting McCloud."

"Sí, señor."

"No," Shafter said flatly. "What an old man said after twenty years wouldn't matter much. Rufe Wolcott dead, McCloud running the country, able to handle you and any charges you made. There has to be some other reason."

The old man said simply: "McCloud wishes to kill me now."

"Not because he's afraid you'll put his neck in a noose for something that happened twenty years ago."

"No, *señor.*" The watery eyes were blinking in the dim light. Wrinkled, white-haired, stooped, he had been a younger man once; he had known Big Mike; he had found Big Mike in the night, beside his horse. His voice had a firmer, younger, relentless sound, or so it seemed. "A man," Manuel Griegos repeated, "is not dead until his son is dead. The son is back, asking blood for blood, as all sons must. And so the fear is in *Señor* Mc-

Cloud, and he wishes to close the mouth of Manuel Griegos while there is time. Is it not so?"

"Explains a lot, anyway," Shafter muttered. "Stay here safe, old man." He drew a breath. "McCloud is my business now."

VII

For Buck Manning the grisly nightmare was still savagely stark despite the brilliant mid-morning sunlight heating the dark slag heaps and sooted beehive coke ovens of the Wolcott smelter. No longer did Buck doubt that he stood beside a madman, and a second madman was riding into sight, heading toward them. Over the black-sooted brick dome of number one coke oven dangled the gruesome specter of the hangman's noose. The sickness knotting Buck's middle was a soul sickness, from knowing he was trapped in a destroying avalanche he had started himself.

George Ross, the madman beside him, spoke with brusque tautness. "How many more loads before that oven can be burning?"

"One more load, maybe," Buck muttered, haggardly watching the wagon piled with short lengths of wood halting on a higher bench of ground behind number one oven.

"How long before the next wagon?"

"They come in from the mountains when they're ready." Buck's words reached his ears like a gagging croak.

Who would guess that Ross was a madman? Only Buck Manning knew—and he couldn't tell. Buck's furtive glance saw a conservative Easterner wearing a gray hat with narrow brim, a fastidious cravat, and meticulously polished black shoes filmed lightly with yard dust. The man's broken face with bent nose and mashed cheek bone, usually warmly smiling, was hard with brute-ugly strength now, calmly confident. Last night in shrouding blackness, on the higher roadway behind number one oven,

Ross had been coldly controlled as they had lifted Henry Peck's body. In front of them now, the beehive coke ovens stood in a long row, each oven some ten feet in diameter, lifting a straight two feet or so, and rounding off gradually in a domed roof, which held a charging hole at the top. Coal loaded in at the top was burned in a fiery smolder some seventy-two hours while the clean coke formed. Then the water-quenched coke was removed through an arched port at the bottom, which was closed with brick when the oven was charged and burning.

Last night the blackness had been intense inside number one oven. The chunks of wood partly filling the oven had been heavy, difficult to lift and pile over the inert body, and a last flaring match had shown a gleam of pale cheek down under the jackstraw lengths of wood—as if Henry Peck were looking up accusingly. Buck Manning had been gasping, sweating, shaking, when he had climbed out through the sooty charging hole into the cool, star-hung night.

Ross said, frowning: "It would be better if that oven could be lighted off now."

"Not enough wood inside," Buck said thickly.

When Henry Peck had opened the bank door last night, his smile had been quick and friendly.

"This load of wood should be cover enough," Ross decided. "And when the oven is lit off. . . ." His slight smile was satisfied.

George Ross sounded, looked like the sanest man in all the Grenada country, Buck Manning's sick thought came, and the man was coldly, greedily out of his head over a bonanza mine he meant to have. Buck looked toward the mountains in the southwest, where two livid scars on the shoulder of the nearest mountain were the dumps of the two Wolcott mines. That highest dump marked the Queen Mine, with its vein of bonanza ore promising fantastic wealth if title could be obtained while the mine was still thought faulted and all but worthless.

It had seemed possible; it had seemed easy to get, with the help of this Boston man who represented Eastern syndicate money. Easy wealth. More chunks of wood were *thudding* hollowly into number one oven as they turned away. The sickness twisted Buck Manning's middle again; he had crossed the line; there was no turning back. Be rich now—or hang.

"You're sure that bullion from the bank won't be found?" Ross asked curtly.

"It's in the metal safe in my office, where it started from," Buck said. "No one can open the metal safe but me."

"We'll bury it tonight if there's a chance, and use only cash money from the bank," Ross decided. His chuckle was amused. "Using the girl's own money against her. Touch of the poetic in that m' lad."

Poetic. . . . Henry Peck's face had contorted in agonizing unbelief as Ross had tightened the twisted bandanna around his neck, and Buck had held him.

Buck looked over his shoulder at the approaching rider. "What about McCloud?"

"I want to talk to him in your office." Ross's voice was harder. "We'll need McCloud. Not much time left."

A continuing nightmare, even with bright, hot sunshine flooding the smelter yard, mill stamps beating in unendingly fast rhythm, the big coal and ore wagons unloading as usual. In the smelter office, the draft roar of reverberatory furnaces beyond the thick adobe inner walls was a muted *hum*—and McCloud and Ross might have been two completely sane men, talking quietly of inconsequential things.

Leaning back in the desk chair, Ross informed McCloud: "A stranger took a shot at this man Shafter an hour or so ago, and missed. Shafter creased his head with a bullet, and the man's probably dead by now."

McCloud was slouching in a chair by the desk, where he had sat almost daily through the years, listening, giving orders. Thick stubble covered his heavy jaw. He looked massive, sullen, but then he always had. The soiled brush jacket, sagging gun belt, and black hat yanked down gave him a rougher, wilder look than the tight, black suit he was in the habit of wearing around town.

"Dead," McCloud said slowly in a flat, harsh voice. He stared at the opposite wall and seemed to be listening.

If the man isn't dead, he'll be able to talk! crossed Buck Manning's mind in a flick of fright as he stood watching, listening.

McCloud's gaze went to Ross. "This Shafter's giving orders now, like he's boss?"

Ross said carefully: "Shafter's taken Rufe Wolcott's place. He's giving all orders." A new tightness had drawn Ross's broken face into an ugly mask. He was watching McCloud and choosing his words.

McCloud rubbed his forehead with a big, grimy hand. A deepening scowl creased his forehead. "Rufe told me I didn't do what was right," he said heavily. "Called me a coward for not makin' up my mind. Rufe said I knew what he wanted."

Ross wet his lips. "What does Rufe want?"

"Wants me to stop being weak," McCloud said in a harsher voice. "Wants me to fix the wrong they done Rufe and me by stealing everything." McCloud was talking louder, in growing excitement, while Buck Manning watched in chilling fascination.

Crazier than a locoed bull! Buck, sitting there, knew it now beyond any doubt.

"You'll have to do it," Ross said. "But how?"

"Take it away from them," McCloud said harshly. His big fist slammed the desk edge. "Smash everything! Kill! Rufe says I'm afraid! He says I ain't the man he thought I was, to let 'em do this!" McCloud lurched to his feet, glowering. "Rufe'll see I won't let 'em keep it!"

Ross drew a visible breath, watching the man. "You're right, McCloud. But you'll need help . . . men, and money to pay them. It's all ready for you, all the money you'll need, and men who'll do what you tell them to, as long as they're paid enough."

McCloud rubbed his forehead again, staring, and then nodded, scowling. "First I've got to look for a man over at the coal mine. Then this Shafter. . . ." McCloud's smile was not exactly a smile; it was a tight grimace. "He'll know how it is, too . . . come back to kill me and take everything, like Rufe thought he would."

Buck Manning swallowed in a constricting throat, thinking of the five dead men Shafter had brought in from the ranch, the cattle and men this bull-shouldered madman had sent off into empty space. That had been the start, a fogged-up brain turning to killing, with George Ross encouraging it. Now Ross was guiding greater destruction with a cool-planning mind even more twisted than McCloud's. And there was no way to stop it. The ingots of gold and silver in the metal safe across the office, Peck's body in coke oven number one, were sweeping Buck Manning along, also. Buck wanted to be sick, and he stood in a kind of growing horror, listening to the rest of it.

Curly Ames had waited outside the wide yard gate at the back of the Wolcott house, lounging restlessly in the saddle, nervously smoking. When Shafter rode through the gate, Curly said sharply: "Old Manuel all right?"

"Worried about Con McCloud," Shafter said soberly.

"I looked at Henry Peck's rig, back in his barn," Curly said. "Hasn't been out for days, his wife says." Curly's young face was drawn with mounting worry. "A muleskinner in the plaza says he saw McCloud riding toward town a couple of hours ago." Curly threw his smoke to the ground violently. "He's followed Manuel and Marina and her father, Pete Griegos, back here. Wasn't any sign of McCloud around the plaza, but he may be close any minute."

Shafter nodded. "No doubt in my mind now, Curly, he means to kill old Manuel."

"He'll kill Marina an' her father, too," Curly said with tight conviction. He struck the saddle horn. "It's McCloud or me now. He ain't breakin' my girl's neck like he cracked that rustler's neck I brought in. I mean to gun him down on sight."

"Don't try it," Shafter said flatly. "We know now McCloud's a killer. He'll be hard to stop. Miss him and he'll be at you."

"Do I wait till he kills my girl?" Curly demanded passionately.

"Where's her father, this Pete Griegos?"

"Pete went across the river to their house by the coal mine. Means to slip back here after dark and bunk with Manuel tonight. They've got the notion they're safe here at the Wolcott house."

"Is Miss Wolcott still at the bank?" How safe was Joanie Wolcott now with McCloud near and dangerous?

"She started to the burying," Curly said. "A coroner's jury ain't met yet, but they've got to be put under." Curly's own worries rushed back. "What about McCloud?"

Shafter had been thinking. "It'll be near daybreak, or sometime tomorrow morning, before Blaisdell gets word at the far end of the ranch and rides here with his crew. Until then I want the town quiet."

"How much noise does a breakin' neck make?" Curly said bitterly.

Shafter gathered the reins; he was calm. "McCloud is mine, Curly. I want him alive, if possible. He'll probably keep away from this house. In case he doesn't, you stay inside and keep the doors locked. Bar this yard gate on the inside. If McCloud comes, don't unlock."

"Suppose he tries to get in?"

"Keep him out."

Curly's young, tense face mirrored his thoughts—coffee in the kitchen, a little swaggering and courting while protecting his girl. "Wel-l-l, if you think so," Curly yielded.

"I think so."

As he was riding away alone, Shafter's wryly envious smile came. Curly had it all—young, in love, all the eager future beckoning. And for Mike Shafter? Today he felt old, burdened with crushing responsibility. The feeling of being solitary and alone as he rode now to the doctor's house had never been stronger. Joanie Wolcott's future, even her life, was in his hands.

In the same whitewashed inner room, smelling of carbolic and chloroform, the gaunt young stranger lay on the narrow table under two blankets, eyes closed.

"Exactly how is he?" Shafter questioned closely.

Dr. Jim Kelton pushed fingers through his red hair. He looked tired, harried.

"Well . . . exactly . . . I'd say he has *commotio cerebri.*" Shafter looked blank, and Kelton said: "Call it commotion of the brain. More precisely, the frontal, temporal, and parietal areas of bone were fractured by your bullet, with resulting cerebral edema."

Shafter said wryly: "You'd better just tell me."

"His skull," Kelton explained, "is fractured on the line of glancing impact. Blood from shocked and damaged tissue is collecting underneath. Keeping him warm and stimulating him is about all that can be done at the present. The turn he'll take is still uncertain."

"But there's a chance he may talk?" Shafter pressed.

"If he lives, he'll talk," Kelton agreed. He was blunt again. "If you want this man kept isolated from any forcible intrusion, I'll remind you again . . . the responsibility is yours."

"Brad Hampton is going to stay on in your waiting room," Shafter said. "I want to know the minute this fellow can talk."

The five dead men Shafter had brought in yesterday were not being buried with a formal funeral. Three were unidentified rustlers; the two men from the ranch crew lacked close friends or kin in the territory. Just before Shafter reached the small graveyard on a sunny slope at the west edge of town, he noticed a thin lift of smoke over east of the river and thought nothing of it. Trash was probably being burned at Lyd Adams's coal mine over there.

His thoughts were intent upon Con McCloud and Joan Wolcott at the moment. She should be guarded while McCloud was around. Fury at McCloud had not yet set in. He had not left Colorado seeking revenge for anything. Even knowing now that McCloud had killed his father twenty years ago had merely compounded the mystery behind Johnny Carr's letter. Why had Rufe Wolcott held old Manuel Griegos to silence so long? Not to protect McCloud. Of that Shafter was certain. Rufe Wolcott's reason had been far more important. But what reason? A hard, mounting excitement was taking hold of Shafter. If he could stay alive long enough, he knew now he would have the truth about Johnny Carr's fantastic letter, Johnny's death, and all the tangle of mystery he had been trying to unravel.

A scant two dozen people, some of them women, had come to watch the mass burying. Mostly out of curiosity, Shafter supposed as he left his horse with other horses and buggies and walked up the slope to an unpretentious wagon from which a plain pine box was being unloaded.

The large, broad-faced figure of Lyd Adams, dressed plainly today, was standing soberly near the open grave. Joan Wolcott and Priscilla Ross were with her. Off to one side, Vince Wolcott and his sallow friend, Jess Parker, were watching in bored silence. They saw Shafter and watched him with furtive closeness.

Priscilla Ross, ignoring staring eyes, hurried to meet him. "Mike! I heard. You were almost killed this morning in the livery barn." In her dark-blue suit and blue hat, butter-gold hair and warm red mouth, Priscilla had the radiance that not even her present pallor could subdue. Her searching look was dark with worry as she touched his arm.

Shafter pulled off his hat, smiling in reassurance. "Not a scratch, ma'am."

"Who was he? Why did he do it?" When he shrugged, Priscilla said under her breath: "Mike, I'm afraid of what's going to happen to you."

Joanie Wolcott was watching them with cool interest. Slim, young, always disliking him and suspicious, she differed in all ways from Priscilla Ross. She saw Shafter reassuringly pat the hand that Priscilla had dropped on his arm, and her expression did not change. But when Lyd Adams said something to her, Joan came with the big woman to them.

Lyd Adams was grimly sober. "That feller who tried to shoot you still alive, Shafter?"

"Still unconscious."

"Ain't found out who he is?"

"Some young drifter." Past the big woman's old green hat with its jaunty, faded red ribbon, Shafter noted again the dark smoke across the river, greater in volume, climbing higher.

"I didn't hear about the bank until I come back from the coal mine," Lyd Adams said. "All tush an' nonsense about Henry Peck doing it. Henry was a prayin' man. Anyway, he was too rabbity to clean out the bank an' run away from his wife. If you ask me, Henry's dead."

"My idea, too," Shafter agreed.

"Then who done it? Some of the riff-raff hangin' around town now?"

"Someone who wanted more than money did it," Shafter said. "Someone who was thinking. The note file was taken, in an attempt to cripple the bank for good."

"Joanie tells me you've sent for Art Blaisdell an' the men on the ranch. You think it's gettin' that bad?"

There was so much this vigorous Lyd Adams did not know, and it would not help at the moment to tell her. "I think it's just starting," Shafter said. "And McCloud's back. Anything can happen now." The smoke was still increasing across the river. "Burning something at your mine?" Shafter said.

"Not as I know." Lyd Adams turned to look.

A flat voice by the open grave said: "Preacher, you can read over him now."

Shafter heard a horse coming fast, and Joanie Wolcott spoke with sharp conviction: "Something has happened."

A clumsily galloping horse, throwing foam, rushed through the cemetery gate—a thick-bodied wagon horse, still wearing a heavy leather collar and brass-tipped hames. Knife-slashed traces were dangling and flapping. The bare-headed rider, using reins improvised from a length of jerk line, was a comical sight. Bouncing, jouncing on the horse's broad back, he held one hand awkwardly pressed down on the top of his head.

Lyd Adams blurted: "That's Hack Wiggins!" And she followed Shafter's run to meet the rider.

Wiggins hauled the winded animal to a stumbling halt and half fell off, clutching frantically at the mane with the hand that had been pressed on the top of his head. Half his long-haired scalp fell forward off a bloody skull. He pushed the great hairy flap up off eyes that were staring wildly.

"C-crazy . . . crazy man!" Wiggins gasped hoarsely. "Over t' the mine . . . McCloud!"

Other men were running to them as Shafter demanded: "What's McCloud done?"

This Hack Wiggins was middle-aged, his stubble-rough face streaked with coal dust and blood. Holding his scalp down again, he stammered wildly: "D-dragged me offen m' wagon, yellin' I was hidin' someone from him!" Dirty tears rolled down the man's drawn cheeks. "He g-grabbed the coal scoop offen the side of the wagon an' tried to cut m' head off. Left me. . . ."

"Hold easy," Shafter soothed the trembling man. "What's burning over there?"

"Burnin'?" Wiggins repeated stupidly.

Priscilla Ross was staring at the man with something close to sick horror. Joanie Wolcott's pallor was intense, but she was calm.

"I've seen Con McCloud half kill men before," Joanie said quietly. "He has these rages." She stepped to Wiggins. "Hack, you're safe now. He won't get you here."

"Did McCloud say you were hiding Pete Griegos?" Shafter asked tersely.

"That's it . . . that's what he said!" Wiggins moaned.

"Is the man over there?"

"If Pete was, he kep' outta sight," said Lyd Adams.

Shafter was curt to Joanie Wolcott. "I'll handle this. Go to your house now and stay inside. Curly Ames is there." And to Lyd Adams he said: "Make sure she does exactly that."

The big woman nodded. "You aimin' to go over there alone, Shafter?"

"I'm going." His grin was mirthless. "If you can find someone to follow, send him along. Or them." He ran to his horse, throwing on so fast and heedlessly that pain stabbed through his bandaged leg. As he reined hard toward the gate, he noted with sardonic interest that not one man in the cemetery was following him. With McCloud on his mind, he had forgotten Vince Wolcott and Jess Parker, who were staring after him.

Parker was speaking coolly under his breath: "Don't go back to the house. Get on your horse and head for Azul, and stay there."

"McCloud," said Vince, shaken, "ain't apt to come after us."

"I'll do the thinking," Jess Parker said softly and viciously. "If McCloud's killed now . . . and that Shafter's going after him to do it . . . you'll be on hand-outs forever, unless something's done."

Vince's suddenly uneasy look went furtively to Joan. "Jess. . . ." Vince licked his lips. "I don't want anything to do with schemes like you've got in your head now."

"Never mind schemes. Just get going," Jess Parker said savagely under his breath. "And don't leave Azul until I send for you."

"I need money," Vince said uncertainly.

"I've got money, plenty money now. Let's get out of here and get you started."

Vince looked once more toward Joan, and hesitated, fearful and undecided. Jess Parker's grip closed hard on his arm, urging him. Vince drew a breath; he looked sick. "I'll go," he mumbled, and went with Jess to their horses.

The green, wild *bosque* growth along the river was damp, hot, silent when Shafter's hard-running horse sheeted water in the river ford and crossed in plunging lunges. He had by-passed the Grenada plaza. The injured teamster must have been directed to the cemetery from the plaza. This empty road cried its own bleak story; in Grenada, long ruled by McCloud's ruthless authority, men had no wish now to face McCloud's plainly murderous temper.

The rutted road ahead was deserted as it snaked up through

the low, cactus-studded hills east of the river. Smoke still boiled up from the fold in the hills where Lyd Adams's coal mine was located. Shafter's leg, easy after the long night's rest, held stabbing pain again from slamming impact against the hard saddle leather. Scabbarded carbine was ready—revolver had been checked. The decision he had put off, Shafter knew now, was on him.

The loaded wagon that Wiggins had been driving was standing deserted in the road near the coal mine, off leader missing from the long, five-span hitch. The wide coal scoop McCloud had snatched from straps on the side of the wagon lay beside the road; why McCloud had used that clumsy shovel instead of a gun lay in the fierce murk of the man's twisted mind.

Warily Shafter rode on with the carbine across his lap now. When he sighted the weathered loading bin of the mine, the dark smoke was on beyond, around the bend in the hillside, where the small adobe houses of the miners clustered. McCloud was not in sight—but McCloud had been here.

A body in the coal-blackened jeans and shirt of a miner sprawled face down on the sun-baked earth beyond the loading bin. In the streaming sunshine, peaceful quiet lay over the mine entrance, the low adobe office, the smaller adobe shack across the wide mine yard where old Johnny Carr had lived. Beyond the bend in the hillside visible sparks laced the smoke now. Adobe houses could burn; log-and-plank ceilings, doors, window framing, plank floors if any, could burn with the fury of long-dried, pitch-rich wood. Slowly, cautiously Shafter rode up the ascending roadway to the higher, narrow terrace where the mine office backed against the hill slope.

The door was closed. Carbine in hand, he stepped down and looked into the single, deserted room. The sweating horse snorted uneasily as he mounted again and rode on toward the gaping tunnel entrance. The soft *crackle* of the distant flames was audible now—and like a sudden quirt slash against taut nerves a cry cut eerily through the silence. "He kill you!"

Shafter's fast-sweeping glance found nothing. A punching shot, wasp shrill of a bullet so near his waistline that he jerked back, pinpointed McCloud. It had to be McCloud inside the open doorway of the small shack across the mine yard where Johnny Carr had lived. The spurred horse bolted ahead, and a second shot was another close miss.

The running dismount Shafter made shocked pain through the bandaged leg as he stumbled across the light mine rails into the tunnel mouth. Again the warning cry shrilled eerily: "Run quick!" McCloud's carbine shots were fast, savage, splintering dry planks of the loading bin just under the outer edge of the terrace.

The horse had run on. Shafter moved in a crouch out of the tunnel entrance until he could see the open doorway of Johnny's shack. His two swift carbine shots sent more racket batting off among the hills.

"McCloud! Twenty years is enough! Come out!" The man's twisted mind might react to that.

Shafter raised up slightly to watch the doorway, and froze. Bloody fingers had curled over the edge of the loading bin from inside. Another hand gripped beside the first hand. A bullet-torn face, jaw smashed, mouth ripped grotesquely wide, rose into sight. The jaw moved; the gasping gobble that came out had a choking sound of despair. That man had cried warning and McCloud's shots had found him. The eyes were dulling as the head sank from sight again, and the hands let go and vanished.

Shafter was already ducking forward, going prone by the timber stop barrier at the end of the mine rails, where he could look down into the huge, half empty bin. The man—another miner—had collapsed on the coal, both hands at his jaw. Still keeping flat, hidden from the open doorway, Shafter slid down into the bin, dropped the carbine, and whipped out his bandanna. "Let's see it!" he was ordering when the taut quiet erupted in a deep-toned roar. The big bin started to lift almost leisurely, shuddering as it tipped. Then, overhead, blown from the mine tunnel as from a giant cannon barrel, burst the full, howling blast of the explosion. The sun was obscured by spewing dust and earth, rocks, coal, chunks of mine timber, and billows of acrid smoke. Torn masses of the hillside were arching high, disintegrating. The wounded man, dark-brown and wiry, staggered up, eyes rolling wildly, as timbers underneath the rear of the bin collapsed. Coal was shifting underfoot as Shafter gave the smaller man a violent boost up to timber supports of a catwalk around the top sides and front of the bin.

The blood-smeared hands grabbed a support and held with desperate instinct for survival. Shafter caught the adjoining support as the big bin tipped back and crashed against the sheer earth and rock rise of the terrace. Tons of coal in the bottom of the bin pitched forward under their dangling feet. It would have buried them.

McCloud had been waiting in the shelter of Johnny Carr's hut for the mine explosion. Débris was *thudding* down on the heavy bin planks; cascading earth and rock were filling space between the bin mouth and terrace wall and spilling in. Dragging at the man's shoulder, Shafter clawed, scrambled back into the narrowing space. Gasping, groggy, ears ringing, he sprawled on the sloping side and listened to the last rocks and earth pelt down outside and quiet come. Gruesome, shuddering quiet.

They were in gray, dusty half light, cut by tiny shafts of clearing sunlight between bin planks, and three fresh holes where McCloud's bullets had splintered through. *I should have killed McCloud the other night in Johnny's house over there,* Shafter was thinking in dazed rage when he heard the quick run of a horse pull up outside the bin and a chilling sound—McCloud's harsh voice calling: "You watching me, Shafter?"

Shafter groped for his revolver, knowing it was a futile gesture. The smashed jaw and torn mouth of the dazed miner huddled by him were a smeared promise of what heavy slugs from McCloud's carbine would do after ripping through the bin planks.

Joan and Lyd Adams were in the walled stable yard behind the Wolcott house when the dull, punching echoes of a huge explosion rolled across the sky. Lyd's alarmed guess came as they halted. "My powder house! Only thing over there'd blow like that!"

Joan looked back at the small adobe bunkhouse where old Manuel Griegos had cleansed his conscience to them before the end, which Manuel was anticipating now with fatalistic calm.

"More of Shafter's work?" Joan guessed also. Her hostility had reached a peak after Manuel's story. Lyd shook her head. Joan's resentment pressed the thought. "Isn't it clear now what the man is doing?"

Under the old green hat, Lyd's weathered face was soberly grim as she watched a dirty-yellow plume of smoke and dust lift high, east of the river. "We'll talk about it later. I got to get over there." She started toward the house.

"Lyd, you can't go alone . . . not with McCloud over there!"

"I got men workin' over there. They need me," Lyd said simply.

"Take Curly Ames with you," Joan urged as they hurried past the bright flower beds in the rear patio.

"That young feller stays here with Wolcott business, where he belongs," said Lyd flatly. "I'll take a rifle an' go by the upper ford, which McCloud ain't likely to use."

There was an indomitable quality about the big, weathered

woman, Joan thought, watching Lyd whip her buggy horses into a reckless run from the front of the house. When she walked slowly back inside, the house seemed filled with waiting tension. Priscilla Ross was pale, preoccupied. Curly Ames was restless, frowning when he came from the kitchen to look watchfully out the front door.

"Curly," Joan decided abruptly, "you're needed across the river."

"Mister Shafter told me to stay here," Curly muttered.

The new anger since talking to old Manuel Griegos heated Joan's face. "When Judge Dixon returns from Azul," she said sharply, "this man Shafter will be sent packing. Go by the upper ford and stay with Lyd Adams. If you see Shafter, ignore him."

"Yes'm." Curly's dark-weathered young face was unhappy. "He ain't a man to ignore," Curly said, "but I'll tell him you'll explain, ma'am."

"There's nothing I'd like better," Joan said emphatically.

Her resentful thoughts spun on after Curly had left. After twenty years Shafter had returned with old hates against Mc-Cloud and the Wolcotts—and his smiling, ironic scheming had put him where he wanted to be, with disaster happening everywhere he appeared.

Those ragged bursts of shots she was abruptly aware of were in the plaza. Joan hurried out front and listened to more shots, distant whoops, laughter. The man running toward her was Sam Gilman, red-faced and beefy, who always looked like he was sweating, and was usually in belligerent argument with someone.

"What is it, Sam?"

Globules of perspiration glistened on Sam's meaty face as he halted. "Them no-account strangers in town swillin' booze, shootin' out windows, runnin' decent folks off the streets!" Sam panted.

"Can't the marshal stop it?"

Sam's angry challenge struck back. "Ain't you supposed to tend to trouble in town, like Rufe Wolcott did? Bank busted! Gunslingers takin' over!" Sam glowered at her, scooped sweat off his forehead with a bent forefinger, and hurried on, to stay inside, safe and fuming.

More whoops and scattered shots racketed in the plaza as she went back inside. Sam Gilman was right, of course; this couldn't have happened in Grenada while Rufe Wolcott was alive. On impulse, Joan looked into Rufe's plain, almost shabby bedroom, across the hall from her room.

His presence still seemed to hover inside. Memories rushed back as she looked at the cheap wooden bed, the old rag rug. During one of the infrequent times he had shown awareness that she existed, Rufe had told her why his room lacked the luxury in the rest of the house. "I've watched folks get fat in the head from living high on the hog," Rufe had said in this doorway, his thin-lipped grin contemptuous. "The fools pop their eyes at frills like this big house, an' get careless . . . but in my room here I ain't changed. Don't you forget, Joanie, like Vince has forgot . . . hungry and hard inside keeps you sharp."

In many ways he had been a remarkable man, Joan thought as she closed the door. Hard, hungry, sharp—and expecting the same of her. She was entering her own room to change clothes when she heard the frantic beating of fists on the solid front door—and then a hysterical voice she recognized.

"Where is she . . . that schemin' girl who tricked herself into Rufe's will?"

Joan ran—that was Lucy Wolcott, nagging wife of solemn Tibbons Wolcott, the vague relative of Rufe's who clerked in Rufe's general store—her own store now, Joan remembered, as the woman's shrill hysteria reached through the house.

"She that's brought us all to this! Don't hide . . . you . . . !"

The last was a scream as Joan entered the long, cluttered front room and stopped, appalled, as was Priscilla Ross, who stood, stunned and mute, staring at the woman.

Hair disheveled, heavy face blotched with fury, Lucy Wolcott was glaring, screaming hatred. "Hidin' in this fancy house you stole, while a hard-workin' man like Tibbons has his head beat in tryin' to protect what ought to have been his in the first place!"

Joan said coldly: "Talk sense, Lucy. Is there trouble at the store?"

"Trouble?" Lucy screamed again. She was a gross woman at best, who ruled the silent Tibbons with contempt. "Robbin' and killin' us while you hide here rich an' safe! I saw the schemin' on your little face when Rufe first took you in!" Hands, pudgy and soft because they seldom worked at home, lifted claw-like as Lucy advanced, shrilling: "Lyd Adams's coal mine is blowed up . . . serves her right . . . and gunmen loose in town . . . and McCloud in the Palace spendin' fistfuls of money, bragging how he killed that man Shafter you hired, and how he means to take away all you stole from Rufe! You . . . don't touch me!"

Close to her, voice shaking, Joan said: "Stop it . . . or I will show you who's boss here! Is Lyd's mine really wrecked?"

"McCloud claims so." Lucy was snuffling as her mottled face began to work.

"And . . . and Shafter is dead?"

"Them hooligans who come in the store and took over said McCloud was bragging about it," Lucy sniffled.

"Dead!" Joan's mouth felt queerly stiff as she added under her breath: "So McCloud killed him, too!" They couldn't know she was thinking about another man named Shafter, killed by McCloud twenty long years ago.

Priscilla asked in a tight voice: "Where did McCloud get the fistfuls of money he's spending?" Her mouth looked feverish-red against pallor. "Could McCloud have robbed the bank last night?" Priscilla appealed to Joan.

"McCloud was west in the hills long after dark last night," Joan said. "He couldn't have reached the bank in time."

"Money he's saved?"

"McCloud's savings were in the bank, which didn't open this morning," Joan said. Her quick thought came as a guess: "More likely he got it from someone who did rob the bank."

Lucy Wolcott wailed accusingly: "Tibbons bleedin' on the floor . . . and those drunks laughin' at him and me! What about us?"

"Did they shoot Tibbons?"

"Hit him with a gun barrel!"

"Go home . . . or get coffee in the kitchen," Joan said thinly. "But if you start screaming again. . . ."

She ran toward her room, leaving the threat hanging. Lyd's mine destroyed, that ironic, stubborn Mike Shafter unbelievably dead. Con McCloud was the only believable thing now. Joan almost shivered as she remembered McCloud's brutal furies that had sickened her when she was younger. McCloud taking charge—and what would stop him, with Mike Shafter dead? Dead! As she changed clothes, Joan tried to think what could be done. Art Blaisdell and his crew wouldn't arrive from the far end of the ranch until tomorrow. Could Art stop McCloud, who always had given Art orders? Art was pleasant to have around; he carried out orders exactly—but he had never faced down McCloud.

This, suddenly, was savage, cruel, destructive—like the heaps of cattle under the Blind Cañon drop—where Mike Shafter had worked alone in the gray dawn, haggard, red-eyed, sweating at his macabre task. Could Art Blaisdell ever have the cold, reckless fury of Mike Shafter, facing quick death from Bud Holland's gun before watching eyes in the plaza? The sheriff and help from Azul, Joan knew as she left her room, would take even longer than Art Blaisdell's uncertain coming.

Rufe's closed door reminded her how oddly calm and safe the house had seemed last night with Mike Shafter sleeping in there, where he'd never be again. Priscilla, listless on a French brocade sofa in the front room, took in with quick apprehension the brown wool pants, soft-leather riding boots, man's blouse open at the neck, cartridge belt under the trail jacket, and the carbine in Joan's hand.

"I'm going out," Joan said. "You'd better keep the doors locked." She looked at Priscilla's eyes and the damp handkerchief balled in Priscilla's hands. "Crying over Mike Shafter?" she guessed.

"In part," Priscilla admitted.

"He turned your head in a hurry," Joan said coolly.

Slowly Priscilla unfolded the small, damp square of linen and looked at it. "So useless . . . killed trying to help you . . . when you didn't want it."

"There was more to it than you know," Joan said, stung to sharpness.

Priscilla's look was miserable. "More, probably, than you know, Joan. Please don't leave the house. It isn't safe."

"That," said Joan, "is why I'm going. Someone has to give orders now."

She was still strangely irritated when she had saddled her horse out back and was riding toward the plaza. What could a girl like Priscilla, soft under her honey-gold, Eastern bloom, know of the brutal realities of this harsher country? Brutes like McCloud? Smiling, stubborn, tough men like Mike Shafter? In that frame of mind her eyes made a measuring sweep around the ominously quiet plaza. Shot-out windows gaped silently; townspeople had vanished. Sid Lutz's Palace Bar seemed to be the only busy place around the plaza, with men standing out front. In there McCloud was buying gunmen.

Windows of the Wolcott store on the west side of the plaza—her store—were smashed. Men were laughing inside as Joan swung off and ran to the door with the carbine. Two men inside, and Tibbons Wolcott, on his feet now, behind the counter. Two tough drunks, listed probably on sheriff's dodgers. Revulsion struck her—canned goods hacked open and emptied on the floor—molasses barrel shot through and draining—clothing tried on, discarded—candy, food, boxes of opened shells littered the counters. Tibbons, silent and pale, had been obeying jeering orders.

The two men stared, grinning. "Now we'll get fancy service!"

Joan stepped to one side. "Out! Get out!"

"That gun'll hurt you, gal." He was bowlegged, unshaven, hat on his head, grinning as he started toward her with a slab of cheese in his hand. "Hand it over, an'. . . ."

Hungry and hard, Rufe would have been flint. Joan shot the cheese out of the hand, and the hand, too—and, as the store shuddered with the report, Tibbons made a frantic reach under the counter and brought up a heavy revolver, and leaned across the counter and thrust the muzzle hard into the other man's back.

"Out!" Joan said thinly.

Tibbons's voice cracked warningly: "Gun belts, Joanie!"

"Yes! On the floor! Both of you! Don't talk!"

The hand was turning red. Gun belts *thudded* on the fouled floor. Wordless, they sidled out—and a drunken yell came back: "You wait, gal!"

"There was more of them," Tibbons said, staring with fascination at the revolver. "Just took over. . . ."

"Go to my house," Joan said. "Lucy is there. And, Tibbons . . . you're a brave man. Keep Lucy remembering it."

"Well, now. . . ." Tibbons looked at the revolver again, and drew a breath. "Lucy can't abide a gun. . . ." In any other man the ghost grin of anticipation that warmed Tibbons's long, solemn face would have been evil anticipation.

"Did . . . did they say Mike Shafter is really dead?" Joan had to ask.

"Seems so," Tibbons said. He came out from behind the counter, carrying the revolver. "What'll McCloud do, Joanie?" He tapped his head apprehensively.

"Help will be here," Joan said. "I'm going to the smelter and warn Buck Manning. Just stay inside, Tibbons."

"Got to lock up," Tibbons remembered nervously.

Joan smiled; she could still smile. "With the windows broken? Just go."

Alone, she went to the opened boxes of cartridges on the counter and filled her pockets, and ran out to her horse. And when she saw Priscilla's brother hurrying toward her, she waited in the saddle.

In the gray Eastern suit he looked more Boston than Priscilla as he swept off the narrow-brimmed hat. "Bad news, Miss Wolcott. The coal mine has been destroyed."

"I've heard," Joan said, forcing calm. She disliked the man, and not because of his mashed cheek bone and broken nose; when he smiled, the twisted face warmed with an odd charm that could be appealing. But after Rufe's funeral, his bait had been too obvious, his flattery too expansive when he spoke smoothly of money in immense sums, of the travel, luxury, finest clothes waiting for her. High on the hog, soft in the head. He had seemed to think so.

Ross said: "And your man Shafter is dead." Was the sound satisfied? His eyes had a cold, close stare now. When she merely nodded, Ross added brusquely: "Con McCloud has taken over everything."

Joan quieted the nervous horse, looked around the plaza, and at the broken windows of her store. "Not everything," she said coolly. "Only some drunken hoodlums and drifters. Con hasn't taken charge of me."

The twisted face staring up at her looked harder as muscles tightened. "I don't think you realize what is happening, young lady," Ross said coldly. "You have no coal for your smelter. Your bank has closed. Payrolls can't be met, or creditors paid. In my judgment, McCloud is not sane. He obviously intends to destroy you and everything you own."

Joan nodded. "Con may try, and you think I should sell at once to your syndicate?"

"It's the only sensible thing to do while you're safe and have anything to sell."

"Then I'm not sensible," Joan said, and reined away from the visible disbelief and anger in his stare. *He was certain I'd be glad to sell now . . . he's been staying on in Grenada,* waiting. Joan caught breath as bits and pieces fell into place. McCloud had gotten money from some source, which must be waiting. . . . Almost despairingly, Joan wished suddenly for Mike Shafter, to hear what she suddenly believed about this George Ross. When she made the turn out of the plaza, Ross, hat still in his hand, was staring after her, his broken face like a chiseled gargoyle, forbidding, threatening.

She was gone, spurring into a run, when George Ross turned back toward the Palace. Joan never did know that he halted again, watching the sallow figure of Jess Parker riding at a trot across the plaza, making the same turn toward the smelter, following her.

George Ross drew a slow breath. This morning, on a calculated impulse, he had given money to Parker—money from the bank—to help Vince Wolcott, he had told Parker confidentially. And Parker's grin had been sly, wise, as if they understood one another. Ross had guessed then what might happen. Now he had the abrupt conviction that it was going to happen, and quickly now—somewhere out west of town, away from all witnesses. It would settle everything in the easiest way. Suspicion—if there was suspicion—would turn toward Vince Wolcott and Parker. A madman and a greedy young relative doing it all. Ross was smiling at the twist of humor in it as he went on. Now McCloud, he decided, had to be held back, before the burly maniac destroyed too much.

VIII

Shafter had thought it a miserable way to die—crouching in dusty murk under an overturned loading bin, a crazy man outside, taunting him. With helpless fury, he had waited silently, hammer of his revolver thumbed back, braced against McCloud's first shot and the splintering smash of the slug through the bin planks. Beside him the wiry, dark-skinned miner panted softly through a bullet-torn mouth. The man's eyes were glassy when Shafter glanced at him. And then, outside the bin, a gruesome thing happened. Con McCloud chuckled.

"Hear me, Shafter? Blowed you sky-high, didn't I? To busted-up pieces!" It made skin crawl—and McCloud's next words were worse. "Keep watching, Rufe. I ain't failing to do what's right. You'll see."

It stirred primeval emotions—that voice sounding genial and sane—and talking confidentially to two dead men—to Mike Shafter and Rufe Wolcott, promising more to come. Softly Shafter spat grit from his dry mouth and listened to McCloud ride away, back toward Grenada.

Light streamed through a fist-sized opening in the piled dirt that blocked the mouth of the overturned bin. Shafter holstered the revolver and crawled there, driven now by the bleak knowledge of what had to be done quickly, and without mercy. Finger ends were raw when he finally clawed out. In the open mine yard, he looked around at desolation that had been a coal mine. A jagged crater yawned in the hillside. Rock, dirt, débris littered the wide yard. Not even steaming sunlight could make the sight less than disaster. Smoke still streamed up from the houses of the miners around the bend in the hillside. Shafter limped that way, and halted when he sighted a figure standing up cautiously on the hill crest, warily surveying him.

He beckoned. The man waited a moment and started slowly down, and came faster, until he was running in goat-like leaps down the steep slope. Other men showed themselves and followed. They were Lyd Adams's native miners, still shocked and fearful. But when Shafter rasped orders, they broke toward a tool shed still standing, and with picks and shovels attacked the small opening he had made out of the bin.

McCloud's fury, he got from them in jerky snatches as they worked, had been savagely destructive when he had failed to find Pete Griegos, who had furtively come home and had left. McCloud had set fire to Pete's house and the house beside it, and then, on his horse, carbine cocked, McCloud had ordered the contents of the powder house piled in the mine tunnel. The man hiding in the loading bin had been afraid to show himself, but not afraid to cry warning to a stranger. A dusty buggy appeared at a whipped run around the turn in the hillside, and Shafter limped out to meet it.

Lyd Adams pulled the hard-driven team to a wheel-cramped stop and blurted: "McCloud around?"

"Should be in Grenada by now," Shafter guessed.

Winchester in hand, she emerged from the buggy, nimbly for so large a woman. "You look," she said critically, "like you were blowed out of a badger hole." Soberly she surveyed the great crater in the hillside, the dead man sprawled face down near them. "McCloud done this?"

Briefly Shafter told what he knew, and indicated the feverishly working men. "The poor devil under there has to reach the doctor fast."

Without hesitation she said: "We'll take him across the upper ford, like I come. Ain't apt to meet McCloud that way."

Shafter glanced past her. "That man seems to be bringing my horse. I thought the horse had been killed." He looked down at himself. "I'll clean off a little of this dirt, and ride to Grenada the way I came."

"After McCloud?"

"Yes . . . but McCloud," he said evenly, "isn't the real danger. McCloud didn't clean out the bank or hire that gunman, Bud Holland, to kill me. Or try again with that young drifter this morning. Someone with more intelligence than McCloud is trying to smash the Wolcott holdings. If that drifter in the doctor's office talks, we may know who's guilty."

"But you aim to kill McCloud," Lyd Adams persisted calmly.

"Not if I can help it." He saw her disbelief; he hesitated. "McCloud," he said reluctantly, "killed my father when I was a small boy. Only McCloud can tell me why."

"I've been waitin' to hear you say it." The half smile on her broad face was satisfied. "Old Manuel told Joanie an' me when we got back from the cemetery." When Shafter made no comment, her half smile faded to soberness. "Drags the cat out in the open, don't it?"

Shafter lifted a brow. "What cat was hiding?"

"A gold-plated, witch-spittin' heller of a cat, I'd say," said Lyd Adams dryly. "Seein' that Rufe's two mines are on land that Rufe bought from your mother."

Shafter stared. "You're certain?"

"Manuel says so."

"I was too young to think about our boundaries," Shafter said, frowning. "Never occurred to me that our land could have reached up the mountain as high as the Wolcott mines."

"Seems like it did," said Lyd Adams, dryly again. "Knowin' McCloud, I'd guess there was an ore outcrop your folks didn't suspect. It was a Spanish grant land, carryin' mineral rights. Your folks could have claimed any ore on the property, no matter who found it. So McCloud made sure your father would never claim anything, and the land could be bought quick and cheap."

"Bought by Wolcott?"

"McCloud was workin' for Rufe then, Manuel says. Rufe didn't have much, but he was gettin' on."

"It was poor grazing land," Shafter said, thinking back. "I know my mother didn't get much for it. She told me."

Watching him closely, Lyd said: "Rufe got rich off the two mines, built everything else on that money. Ain't easy to take, is it . . . someone else rich, when it should have been you?"

"I didn't know . . . so it didn't worry me." *Johnny Carr must have known.*

"Joanie Wolcott thinks you knew," said Lyd Adams bluntly. "McCloud was upset when he saw you in Azul. Trouble's been flarin' around you ever since. If Judge Dixon had knowed. . . ."

Shafter's reminder was brief. "As a co-executor, you can fire me." At the moment he didn't care.

"I never chop off a nose to pretty up a face," said Lyd Adams calmly. "But don't think Joanie will believe any young stranger would risk his neck to help a girl who got the money he should've had."

"She'll be right." His candor was cool. "I was helping myself. Any benefit to her merely happened."

"Benefit," said Lyd Adams dryly, "ain't a gift horse to flog." She turned her head. "Looks like Curly Ames comin'. He can go back with me."

"After," Shafter said, hardening, "I take his hide off for not staying near Miss Wolcott, as I ordered."

As she rode to the smelter, Joan did not look back. There was reassurance in the dark smoke from the tall, brick smelter stack, in the racket of the mill stamps, the heavy *hrrrumph-hrrummph* of the ore crusher. And comfort in Buck Manning, an old friend.

She drew a breath of relief—even found a brief, wan smile—at sight of Buck's short, lean whip of a body hurrying out into the smelter yard to meet her. "Buck," Joan said as she pulled up, "we're in trouble!"

Seen close, Buck was not so reassuring. Pouchy circles lay darkly under his eyes. He had a haunted look. "That new man you hired . . . that Shafter . . . is dead," Buck said. "Some mule-skinners came by and told me. The coal mine's wrecked. McCloud's running wild and loose." Buck swallowed; he looked more haunted. "Anything else?"

"McCloud may come after the smelter and mill next . . . then our mines," Joan said. "Give your men guns, Buck, and hold off McCloud and anyone who comes with him."

The hand Buck pushed through his sandy hair was unsteady; he was not the cocky, grinning Buck Manning she had known. "Joanie," Buck said huskily, "I've known you for years, haven't I?"

"I thought we were good friends, Buck."

"Listen to me then, Joanie . . . go home, lock in an' . . . an' wait."

Joan stared. "Buck," she said, convinced, "you're crawling inside . . . frightened!" She swallowed bitterness. *Buck, too.* "I'm going on to the mines," Joan said, "and warn the men there. Then I'm coming back. If you haven't held off McCloud, you're fired."

Buck's pallid grimace was white at the corners. "I'll be out of a job anyway if the smelter goes." Then, with unsteady fierceness, Buck pleaded: "Sell out, Joanie. Get out of this while you can. Let Ross and his syndicate worry about it. He'll deal with you. Even now."

"You're sure of it?" Joan asked, unwillingly, because this was Buck Manning, who she had known almost since the day she had come to Rufe Wolcott's house as a small girl.

"I'm sure of it. I know," Buck said with the same husky fierceness; his haunted eyes were pleading.

"Buck, listen. . . ." She bent toward him in her stricken intensity. "No matter what happens, I won't sell. This smelter will run again . . . the mines will be worked . . . the ranch will go on. Understand?"

"Plain enough," Buck muttered.

"Then tell Ross he can leave Grenada . . . and go with him, Buck, where you belong!"

She looked slender and young, riding astride like a man, as her running horse passed the line of beehive coke ovens and up the slope beyond, toward the mines.

Number one oven was still cold. Word must have spread that McCloud was back, and dangerous. No more wood wagons had come in from the mountains. Buck walked slowly toward number one oven. There might be enough wood inside to burn clean and final—everything to ashes. Then, at least, the corrosive threat of a hang rope might go away.

He was almost to the domed oven when he saw the rider passing the smelter. Buck halted, watching Jess Parker—Vince's close friend—ride on over the rise where Joanie had gone.

Buck licked dry lips. He could guess, because he had warned Ross against it. Parker meant to see that Vince inherited. Suddenly Buck found himself running toward the open front shed where the smelter horses were kept. He was running, Buck vaguely realized, back toward the alert, satisfied pride he used to have in Buck Manning.

Inside the Palace, the racket clawed at George Ross's taut nerves, and there was nothing he could do about it, sitting at a rear table, listening with suppressed anger to McCloud repeat himself for the third or fourth time.

"Rufe," McCloud said heavily, "knows Shafter took his place an' meant to kill me." It sounded reasonable—until a man realized Rufe was dead.

Ross tried again. "Shafter," he reminded tightly, "is gone now. Forget the fellow. Enjoy yourself."

Slowly McCloud rubbed his forehead, and seemed to listen. A small chill touched Ross as the man nodded slightly. Across the table, confidentially, McCloud said: "Rufe knows I ain't afraid to do what he wants."

It sounded completely, infuriatingly normal and sane. Until one remembered, then nerves crawled. Ross persisted desperately: "Why not take these men to Azul?" And then went rigid as McCloud's muscular face hardened.

"You trying to stop what he wants, trying to run things?" McCloud asked heavily. His big hand was clenching on the table, knuckles paling as muscles corded.

"No," Ross said through stiff lips. "No . . . no!"

"Stop talking then!" McCloud growled as he lumbered to his feet and went to the bar.

Ross put his right hand on the table and stared at the broken knuckles, forcing calmness. Whatever that bull-built maniac destroyed today belonged to the Wolcott girl. The ore in the Queen would be safe. He looked up as the man named Bud Holland stopped by his chair.

"Lady outside wants you," Holland drawled. In the dark, neat broadcloth suit, and touches of gray at temples, the man looked like a banker instead of the notorious gunman he was.

" 'Tis a drink I owe you when I'm back," Ross said, smiling mechanically. Already Priscilla might have word of the Wolcott girl. McCloud, he noted with another crawl of nerves, turned at the bar, staring suspiciously, as he hurried out.

In front of the adjoining building where she was waiting, Priscilla was oddly pale and abrupt as she indicated the damage around the plaza. "You're responsible, aren't you, George?"

"How could I be?" Ross said coldly. "Go back to the Wolcott house. This is no place for you."

"I've already moved back to the hotel," Priscilla said evenly.

Anger diminished in Ross when he thought of Jess Parker riding toward the smelter, also. "Stay at the hotel then," he said. "But keep inside. I'll take you to the door."

"You needn't," Priscilla said in the same even tone.

She walked rapidly toward the hotel, and Ross shrugged and turned back into the Palace. He had no doubt she'd come to heel, and manage the large Wolcott house for him with the flair for luxury ingrained in her.

The Grenada plaza had an empty, ravaged look when Shafter rode in, carbine ready on his lap. No women in sight—a handful of men staring in disbelief as he stepped off the blowing horse in front of the Palace and limped in. The same stunned silence fell inside. His flat question sounded loud. "Where's McCloud?"

Not many were in the Palace. The long backbar mirror was shattered at the front end. Bud Holland, leaning lazily against the bar, spoke first with amusement. "McCloud took a crew to the Wolcott mines. You walk solid, Shafter, for a dead man, which you're supposed to be."

Even Ross, the Boston man, had shock on his broken face.

"I heard I was dead," Shafter said dryly, and let them guess where he'd heard it. "McCloud do all the damage here?"

"Give the devil his due," Holland drawled. "Loafers got some money and celebrated."

"Money from where?"

Holland chuckled. "I didn't see 'em get it."

"After yesterday, you wouldn't," Shafter said. "Where's the marshal?"

"His health," Holland said sympathetically, "took him somewhere when it got rough."

Shafter was remembering how close this man and himself had been to killing each other yesterday. The glint in Bud Holland's eyes suggested he was thinking the same thing. Every man in the long room was watching, listening; Shafter let them hear the abrupt thought he had. "Be the marshal, Holland, for a week or longer . . . at your own price."

"To help you?" Holland asked lazily.

"So a decent woman will be safe in town. I'll help myself."

"The ladies?" Bud Holland considered, and chuckled. "I've been called a ladies' man. Put it that way . . . well, I'm marshal, I guess. Two weeks."

Shafter grinned briefly; he liked this man who could look into a gun muzzle with amusement. "Two weeks should be enough. Whiskey," he said to the moon-faced bartender. He scooped coins from his pocket, and was sorting through them, his hand resting on the bar, when the bartender said: "That drilled double eagle . . . where'd you get it?"

"This one?" The gold coin with a tiny hole at the edge bounced on the polished wood. "Drilled for a necklace," Shafter guessed. It had been among the coins he had found in the pocket of the man he had shot in the livery barn.

"Sid!" the bar man called.

Shafter glanced at the door as a man shouldered in—young Brad Hampton, who had been watching at the doctor's office.

When Shafter met him, Hampton said: "Heard you were dead." He was panting. "Then heard you'd ridden in. Thought you'd want to know."

"The man die?"

"Talked!" Hampton gestured Shafter over by a wall table, and lowered his voice. "I couldn't believe him!" Hampton was excited, grim, too, and angered. "Had him say it over three times . . . Buck Manning . . . two hundred this morning . . . eight hundred more after you were dead."

"So," Shafter said thoughtfully. "Manning." He shook his head. Buck Manning! "We're having a drink. Join us."

Sid Lutz, the rapier-straight, elegantly dressed owner of the place was impassively holding the drilled coin.

"No mistake," Lutz said across the bar. "The date is the same. One side slick. Gus showed it to me yesterday. I deposited it with the cash just before Peck locked the bank doors. This couldn't have been paid out. This was stolen last night when the bank was cleaned."

Shafter reached for the coin, looked at it, and dropped it in his pocket. "Now we'll have the bank money back . . . and Peck, alive or dead." His thin smile came briefly. "A woman had a necklace . . . so a man will probably hang."

George Ross, walking slowly, but in blind, frantic, inner haste, heard the last as he reached the door—and the rough feel of a hang noose was at his neck as he went out. Buck would talk; there was no doubt that Buck Manning would talk quickly if Shafter found him alive, Ross knew as he reached his hitched horse down the street. One tiny hole in a single gold coin. Before he was halfway across the plaza, Ross used the rein ends with a frantic slash.

This, Shafter was thinking as he rode away from the Palace rack, would be a blow to Joan Wolcott. He was out in the plaza when his name was called.

"Mike . . . Mike Shafter!" He reined back, dismounting quickly as Priscilla reached him. "They said you were dead!" Her pallor was startling; her hand caught his arm for reassurance.

The fingers were icy when his hand covered them. "Never believe all you hear," he said lightly. "Everything safe at the house?"

"I suppose so. Joan went to the smelter."

His voice sharpened. "While McCloud was in town?"

"Yes . . . but, Mike . . . "—Priscilla swallowed—" McCloud isn't the danger."

"Buck Manning is?" He watched Priscilla close her eyes against his hardening stare. Her hand trembled under his tightening fingers.

"Mike. . . ."

"Yes?"

Eyes closed, she was barely audible. "Rich ore, Mike, has been found secretly in the Queen Mine."

"How rich?"

"Very rich," Priscilla said unsteadily.

"How long have you known?"

"For some days."

"While staying at the Wolcott house?"

Priscilla swallowed again. Her nod finally came—and her eyes opened as he lifted the hand from his arm and stepped back into the saddle. "Was it worth it?" he asked, looking down.

Priscilla said nothing; she was standing there, watching, as he rode on, not glancing back. Another blow for Joan Wolcott. And now, if the Queen was a rich mine again, her danger was more acute.

IX

The hitch rack outside the smelter office was empty. Shafter bolted in at a limping run. The office was deserted. He was back in the saddle again when he recognized the rider topping the rise beyond the black slag heaps and domed coke ovens. The narrow Eastern hat marked the man. One of the smelter men was sloshing water from a bucket into the front port of the first coke oven. Shafter spurred there, calling: "Where's Manning?"

The man, in bib overalls, sleeves rolled back on hairy arms, put the empty bucket down and fished in the bib pocket with grimy fingers. "Manning went to the mines," he said without interest.

"Has Miss Wolcott been here?"

"She went to the mines ahead of Manning."

Coal oil, not water, had been sloshed into the oven, Shafter's nostrils told him as he asked: "Did that dude who just rode off stop here for Manning?"

"Stopped to say Manning wanted this oven lit off right now." A match, fished from the bib pocket, swiped into flame on the brickwork beside the port.

Shafter's curt—"Hold it!"—stopped the blazing match from being tossed in. "If Manning went to the mines, how could Ross come from town with an order from him?" Shafter asked sharply, swinging off his horse.

The man stared, match burning to his fingers. "Never thought of that." He dropped the match hastily, and blew on the fingers. "We been waitin' for more wood to fill 'er, but when he said that. . . ."

Staring at the domed oven, Shafter decided: "I'll go in through the charging hole for a look. Bring that ladder here."

This was not the first beehive oven he had been in. Grimacing, he slid feet first down through the sooty charging hole, and found uncertain footing on the haphazardly piled chunks of wood inside. Oil fumes reeked up from below. Crouching in the dim light, bandaged leg throbbing, he moved the heavy chunks of wood, peering down into the maze, and finally saw what he was expecting—the pale patch of a man's cheek.

Soot-smeared, he hauled himself out of the charging hole and called to the staring man: "Get the wood out . . . and have a wagon ready for Henry Peck's body!"

Anger—fear, really, for the girl somewhere ahead—drove him after Ross now. From the rise beyond the coke ovens, the dust of Ross's horse was a distant, hazy drift. Shafter eased the spurred gallop; a ridden-out horse might fail when needed.

Ross stayed ahead, dropping out of sight in the folds of the land, but always reappearing, keeping to the pounded mine road. This long reach to the mountains was mostly barren country covered with scanty grass, greasewood, stunted cactus. And all of it increasingly familiar. He had not consciously avoided riding this way before now, for there were happy memories as well as sad ones. The memories closed in with every dusty mile as he followed Ross, and only two low-circling buzzards off to the right, ahead, brought premonition of what might be over there.

He let Ross continue toward the mines, and reined off the rough road, punishing the horse now, riding recklessly down across dry arroyos, spurring up the slopes. A saddled horse, nipping at the sparse grass tufts, was the first thing he sighted. The gun boot was empty. He caught the reins and led the horse back on its tracks—and under the circling buzzards he found Buck Manning on the dry earth. Yards away was the saddle gun Manning had dropped. A few feet away was the revolver Manning had drawn just before he fell, shot through rib cage, shot again through the stomach.

Other horse tracks went on. The blood-crusted rope had

stayed coiled at his saddle horn since Blind Cañon. Manning was not heavy. Shafter roped the body over the saddle Manning had been using, and took the horse on lead as he followed the deep-gouged tracks of the two horses Manning had been following. He knew now where they were heading. The cottonwoods came in sight first, their high, leafy crowns lifting from the small, sheltered flat beside the narrow run of water that came, cold and clear year around, from a slit cañon in the mountain, not far away now. There had been a corral, two adobe sheds, a home with stout adobe walls.

Shafter pulled up short of the final rise and advanced cautiously until he could see over. The corral was gone. Half walls of the sheds were there. The house walls had crumpled at one rear corner and the roof logs sagged down there. But the other rain-eroded walls still stood, broken windows gaping, back door silently yawning. *Home.* The word passed through his mind with a curious lack of emotion. The Wolcott girl was filling his thoughts, along with the hard, persisting anger driving him.

The first rider had raced down the short slope to the house. The second horse had stopped here. Empty brass shells were on the ground. And blood had dripped. This rider, Shafter found, had ridden along the crest, shooting from three different positions. Still bleeding. Then, unexpectedly, the sign of many horses came in from the south—and went on down to the house. They were gone now. Shafter rode down—and only then sighted a dead horse, still saddled, at the front of the house where it had been invisible. He brought Buck Manning in a last spurred run past the end of the house—and pulled up, staring at the Wolcott XR brand burned on the flank of the dead horse. His bandaged leg almost crumpled as he launched off recklessly and bolted, limping, through the open front door, fearing what he would find. A moaning cry broke from the room corner to the right—the ear-buffeting blast of a revolver shot followed as he lunged on across the room, belatedly catching for his handgun. He'd been certain the place was deserted.

He bounced off the crumbling whitewashed wall, dropping to a crouch—and held there, staring at a shaking hand trying to cock the other gun again, and lacking strength. Jess Parker, sitting in the shadowy angle of the wall to the right of the fireplace, let the gun sag uselessly. He had the look of death, sallow face gone gray and sunken, but blue lips peeled off teeth in a grin as Shafter went to him.

"Where is she . . . Miss Wolcott?"

Parker's grin held. But his eyes hated. His coat was dark with blood on the left side; from under his hip blood seeped across the blown dust and pack rat litter on the floor.

"What happened to her?" Shafter asked again.

Parker's eyes hated; Parker's peeled grin watched Shafter's fear. An empty whiskey pint lay by Parker's hand. The gray face looked drained, fading. All but hate. Burning hate was sustaining the man now.

"I'll guess what happened," Shafter said. He kicked the revolver skittering to the fireplace—and the memories rushed in. There—where Parker's grin, Parker's eyes hated—his mother's walnut rocker had stood. Winter evenings that small boy he had been had sprawled on the carpet before the snapping cedar fire while she knitted or mended. And Big Mike—usually in the room, also—talking to them, laughing. All real—the room for an instant transformed—then he was standing again on the litter of years, speaking with harsh calm to the peeled grin, the poisonous eyes.

"She was riding ahead. Manning's tracks were last . . . so you were in between, following her. Or taking her off the road, to make sure Vince Wolcott got everything. Manning evidently caught up and shot you, trying to stop it, and you killed him. She got away . . . and you put a bullet in her horse. But she made it here and held you off."

Parker was breathing shallowly through the grin—fast, strained, throaty panting—while his eyes gazed fixedly.

"Only one bunch of men is out this way. Not the ranch crew. They'd have taken you in." Shafter heard his voice going thick, in spite of himself. "They must have heard the shots and investigated. And they took her, and left you some whiskey for the end. McCloud's got her, hasn't he?" After a moment, Shafter said bleakly: "Have it your way." He limped out.

Jess Parker's stiff grin was still there when Shafter returned with Buck Manning over a shoulder.

"Here he is," Shafter panted, putting his burden on the floor beside Parker, "waiting for you to join him tonight. He tried to help her," Shafter said, looking down at Manning, "so I'll guess he won't like the company."

When he looked at Parker's gray face, the grin was stripped away. Wildly, thickly Parker began to curse him as he walked through the gaping doorway, and pulled saddle and bridle off Manning's horse.

He could hear Jess Parker until he was in the saddle, rounding the corner of the house. Then the clubbing reality of McCloud took over—McCloud and Joanie Wolcott. His own oath came, softly bitter, driven by anger so virulent it was near anguish as he tried to guess what was best to do. Not for Mike Shafter now. For that girl. Joanie Wolcott.

He had to be right. Had to be certain. But could any sane man guess exactly what a madman would do? The afternoon had raced out. Night was near—and she was with that fierce, twisted mind. With the riff-raff, the scum, riding with McCloud. She would be alone in the night with them. This, Shafter realized, was merely scourging anguish with vivid—and starkly logical—imagination. Had to stop it. Had to think sanely about a madman's viciously unpredictable decisions.

He was trying to think when a gunshot's punching echoes overhead made him yank the horse sharply around. At sight of the rider lining toward him at a gallop, he lowered the quickly raised carbine. The second rider coming on easier made him stare.

The tongue-lashing Curly Ames had received at Lyd Adams's coal mine made Curly sheepish as he brought his sweating horse in.

"Seemed like you'd want me," Curly said defensively. "Picked up your tracks at the smelter."

Bud Holland, when he came up, regarded Curly reproachfully. "He said the ladies in town were safe . . . and, before I thought, I was riding with him," Holland said accusingly.

From the glinting amusement in Holland's eyes, Shafter guessed it had not been exactly that way. Curly's face was getting red.

"I can't chouse you both back," Shafter said. His mirthless grin welcomed them. "I'm guessing McCloud took Miss Wolcott up to the mines," he said. "We have to get there. I'll explain."

Curly riding on the left, Holland on the right, they listened to what had happened. At the finish, Curly objected: "This way don't get us to the mine road."

The sun had approached the mountains while he had been in with Parker. From here the smeared mine dumps high up were not visible. The mountain, close now, lifted in sheer escarpments banded with purple shales and bluish-green sandstones.

"We're short-cutting," Shafter said.

"To where?" Curly was gazing ahead at the near-perpendicular rises, cut by slant ledges, studded with isolated shafts and tilted slabs of bald rock.

"Faster to the mines this way."

"Up that?"

"There's a way up." Twenty years ago there'd been a way up. He was outguessing a madman. Trying to. "Powder isn't stocked at Grenada," he told them. "Lyd Adams didn't keep much across the river . . . but McCloud blew her coal mine with what powder was there." He was chopping out the words—trying to guess the gruesome labyrinths of a twisted mind. "He's turned to destroying. He'll keep destroying everything he resents. He's used powder. He'll use it again. And the big stock of powder is up there at the Wolcott mines."

"You make him sound like a mad dog," Bud Holland said.

"Worse!" Shafter was bleak, grim. "McCloud's thinking, planning. If the miners up there give him trouble. . . ."

Curly said: "They're hard-rock men. Real tough. Some have wives and kids up there."

"How many men with McCloud?" Shafter called over to Holland.

"A bunch for you to tackle alone . . . ten . . . fifteen." Bud Holland's grin suggested that, back in Grenada, in the Palace, he must have known he meant to be along. Holland's return question was blunt. "You sure about this way you're taking?"

"I've used it." Twenty years ago. No long grades of a mine road far to the south then, no mines up there. Only Chupadera Joe's son leading the way up an ancient trail of his Navajo people, until two small boys, kindred spirits, looked out over all the world. About where the Queen Mine was now. The towering mass of the mountain came at them.

Shafter led the way into a high, narrow cleft where purple shadows closed around. A band of sky far above flamed with sunset. A crystal stream raced past them, and would reach, finally, the sheltered flat where Big Mike had built a home. Shod hoofs striking rock echoed hollowly.

The wall on the left finally drew back. Over damp ledges the horses climbed laboriously to a sweep of sloping terrace where pines grew. A mule deer buck raced out of the trees into a wider cleft, taking a narrow trail that curved sharply up out of sight.

Behind Shafter, Curly Ames said: "Ain't much doubt he knows the way up. I wouldn't have thought it!" Farther on, higher up, with light fading, Curly held careful silence when ledges they followed fell away beside him.

Still higher up, they had to lead the horses over tilted, smooth rock, then they labored up faint deer trails through brush and conifers on dizzy slopes. Tension drove Shafter grimly now as the shadows turned sable, and high country chill closed around them. Had he guessed right about McCloud?

Bud Holland drawled: "For a ladies' man, I had the damnedest notion . . . trying this."

Shafter grinned and the tension eased. A little later they topped out, and Curly's grunt of satisfaction soon came. "There's the Queen ahead."

Shafter looked with distaste at the dim blotches of sheds and ore cars they passed in the first starlight. New, rich ore in the dark drifts of the Queen, deep in the mountain, had only triggered greed, violence, murder. Rufe Wolcott had left wealth—great wealth—all of it seeded with the sins of an old man's long life—and Joanie Wolcott had the harvest. Beside him Bud Holland said coolly: "Looks like a fire at Jacktown."

The miners lived at Jacktown, the little settlement between the Queen and the Big Jack Mine. As Shafter stared, a small, crimson glow in the distance ahead grew brighter.

"McCloud!" Shafter said, and said it all in the word—his father, twenty years back—Johnny Carr—Joanie Wolcott now—and destruction loosed even on these high mountain slopes. "Keep together!" he ordered, and put the horse into a run.

The reins, he realized, were slick in the sweating palm; he wiped the palm on his leg and touched his holstered gun mechanically. The Boston man, George Ross, should be with

McCloud. And Joanie Wolcott. With luck she'd be there, too. Still safe. If not. . . .

He tried not to think further. In pale starlight the road was dropping away before them, curving, bending. Curly called over: "Powder house is up the gully ahead!"

Beyond a high cutbank and sharp bend, the narrow road to the powder house struck sharply up to the right, and Shafter's warning was abrupt and harsh. "Man in the road there!"

He swung hard to the right after the figure running off into brush. Bud Holland and Curly smashed into the growth, also, and they hemmed in a panting figure. Swinging off, Shafter demanded: "You with McCloud?"

"Him?" The panting stranger's shirt was open at the neck; canvas pants were tucked into heavy miner's boots. He was peering up at Curly. "I've seed you with the ranch fellows," he decided, and asked thickly: "McCloud out of his head, doin' the way he is?" It had a shaken sound, still unbelieving, as if terror had clamped on the mountain without reason.

"What's McCloud done?" Shafter asked calmly. He listened silently to still incredulous anger. McCloud's men had herded them—women and children, too—into the road in front of the store. Two wagons from Jacktown had been taken to the powder house, with miners to load them. The first wagon had returned to Jacktown, where McCloud was waiting with about eight men.

Shafter stepped thoughtfully back into the saddle. "Can you hold that bunch at the powder house off our backs?" he asked Bud Holland. "There must be about seven of them."

"Seven of that kind?" Holland was lazily humorous again. "If Jacktown blows up in your face, I'll know you guessed wrong."

Curly Ames rode with Shafter, watching flames and sparks now spewing up from the burning building. "Looks like Ma Pelton's boarding house," Curly decided.

They rounded a final curve and Shafter pulled down to a

walk. All the mountainside ahead, the small, scattered houses of Jacktown and larger structures along the road, were bathed in the red glare. A wagon—a bulky ore wagon—had halted on the left side of the street, where the road widened through the little settlement. Beyond the wagon—distant figures on a fire-lighted stage—were women, small children, and men, held in the street by armed riders. And McCloud, on foot—no mistaking that thick-chested, bull-shouldered figure—striding about, gesturing with a carbine in one hand, a pick handle in the other.

It was Curly's keen sight that located Joanie Wolcott. "On the wagon," Curly said suddenly. "See? Miss Joanie an' that fellow Ross with her. . . ."

Shafter looked intently. "Ross must be guarding her." Ross—who had ordered the coke oven lighted, with Peck inside. Anger gathered so violently it constricted his chest. "That long building across the street from the wagon . . . ?"

"Warehouse for the mines."

"The smaller building to the left of the wagon . . . ?"

"Blacksmith shop."

"Can we leave the road here, and come in behind the shop, without a fence or a gully stopping us?"

"I think so." Curly's voice was lean. "That wagon's got the powder."

"I know."

"She's on it!"

"Let's get her off."

Hat brim pulled low against the leaping red glare ahead, Shafter led the way off the road, through low brush, over uneven ground studded with boulders. Finally the low blacksmith shop shielded them.

The yard behind the shop was littered with rusty mine iron and wagon parts. The building was open in back and front. Forge cinders crunched softly underfoot as they walked between the leather bellows and the anvil. Out front the big wagon loomed beyond the hitch rack. From the wide shop doorway, he saw her on the wagon seat, slender in man's pants and shirt she'd put on again, looking even smaller in a too-large coat someone had given her against the mountain night.

The fire glare was on her face—a young face, stripped now of all hint of temper and anger—drawn, tense against the unknown. She looked small and lost, he thought, as if all her rebellious strength and confidence had finally run out. When she stirred, he saw why her hands were behind her back; her wrists were bound and tied to the seat grab iron. And Ross, too, was tied the same way. No mistaking the savage moroseness on the broken face as Ross stared along the street.

A second man stood by the middle span of the long three-span hitch, jerk line held loosely in his right hand. Shafter pulled back a step as that man's head turned. "Look at McCloud, gal. He's workin' up to burnin' the store next." She ignored him and his jeer was a promise. "When we start back to town, I'll sit by you . . . an' down the road in the dark, your high pointy nose'll come down. I got the cure for it."

She looked then—and saw Shafter in the opening of the blacksmith shop. Her mouth opened silently; in rigid shock, she gazed at him as he moved silently out.

McCloud's man was looking toward the fire again. Shafter leaned his carbine against the shop wall. The sullen *pop* and *crackle* of the flames covered sound as he reached the man's back. His left arm snapped around the neck; revolver muzzle gouged the spine.

Curly Ames joined him. "Tie that jerk line to the hitch rail," Shafter ordered, and backed the gasping man off balance, arm clamped across the throat, into the shadows of the shop. Deliberately, with cold thoroughness, he slammed the revolver barrel behind the ear and let the slackening figure drop.

"Not down any road," Shafter said. Wasted words, but anger had never shaken him before like this. Sheath knife in hand, he stepped up fast on the high wheel of the wagon, and heard Ross thickly blurting: "Shafter, isn't it? Shafter?"

The keen blade parted the cords at her wrists while she was saying thinly: "He said you weren't dead. He insisted to McCloud . . . and McCloud had him tied here, too, for the ride back to Grenada."

"One sane thing," Shafter said; he was curt, hurried. "Get into the shop there before someone looks this way."

Ross pleaded: "Cut me loose, Shafter!" He sounded frantic. "This wagon is loaded with powder, caps, and fuse! If sparks fall . . . or there's shooting. . . ."

"Can't think of a better place for you." Hostility thickened his own voice.

"Mike." Joanie was unsteady, words tumbling out desperately. "Don't leave him helpless with McCloud. Priscilla's brother. Not on this wagon. . . ."

Common sense took over; if abandoned, Ross might shout warning. "Cut him loose," Shafter said, giving her the knife. And when she did so, his order to Ross was rough: "Don't get off on that side. You'll be seen."

Already sliding to the wheel, Ross jumped, and ran forward beside the long spans of horses, shouting: "McCloud, Shafter's here! Alive like I said! Shafter!"

"Jump!" Shafter said savagely. He caught her as she dropped off the wheel rim. Against his chest she sobbed in dismay: "How could he? After you helped him, Mike!"

He could see McCloud swinging around in the street, hatless, carbine and pick handle in his fists—a massive, unshaven brute of a man in the crimson fire glare, ghost voices driving inflamed passions. "Get her on my horse!" he told Curly. "Get her away!"

She clung. "What about you . . . without a horse, Mike?"

"Don't argue!" He had to be harsh as his hands whirled her away and shoved her into a stumbling run. Curly caught her arm and urged her on through the blacksmith shop.

Carbine in hand again, Shafter looked along the glare-filled street. Ross, still shouting, was pointing back at the wagon as he reached McCloud. And McCloud swung the pick handle and struck him down.

McCloud's shout filled the street. "Givin' me orders! Lying!" To his staring men, McCloud bawled: "The girl's loose, too! Get her!"

They had been visibly hilarious—scum of the frontier country—who must have been at the Jacktown saloon bottles already. No law here on the isolated mountain but their own impulses, and McCloud. Now three of them spurred hastily toward the wagon as Shafter ran back into the blacksmith shop.

Ahead of him, Curly and Joanie Wolcott were leaving in a rush; they were receding shadows riding back toward Bud Holland as Shafter crossed the littered yard, running behind the buildings, away from the powder wagon, toward McCloud.

Timbers plunged down in the burning building ahead; gouts of flame and sparks rushed up. And yells lifted back at the blacksmith shop as he was sighted in the brighter light.

Guns opened up; when he turned, all three riders were spread out, spurring toward him. Panting, he took time to aim the carbine, and knocked the lead man out of the saddle. The other two reined back, and he ran again, and stepped into a small, weed-hidden hole that threw him staggering and wrenched his ankle.

Another rider broke from between two buildings as he ran on, favoring the ankle. This one shouted, yanked his horse rearing, and threw shots from his revolver. A bullet hit the carbine as Shafter brought it up, and splintered the stock, driving wood and lead fragments into his shocked hand and wrist.

He dropped the useless gun, pulled his revolver left handed, and in sudden, overwhelming rage ran at the man. The first awkward shot missed. The second, also. But as his limping run continued, the other's nerve broke; the horse pivoted to a neck-twisting yank—and, targeted broadside, close, a third bullet went in. The man was bent over, holding mane, as the horse raced back between the buildings.

Shafter went on. All purpose had narrowed down to McCloud. For the first time, the calm words of old Manuel Griegos had full meaning: *A man is not killed until his sons are dead.* He was Big Mike Shafter's son—Big Mike's blood, flesh, face even, hunting McCloud down now after twenty years.

He was not, Shafter dimly sensed, quite sane himself as piled-up wrongs and anger, and the threat of McCloud, whipped him in the hobbling run to the back of the burning building. Past the fire-wreathed side of the structure, through smoke and sparks, he sighted McCloud in the street. More roof fell in. The large frame building was vomiting smoke and flames toward the night sky as his lurching run broke through smoke and searing heat toward the street. Numbness was passing from the bleeding right hand. He transferred the gun; the smeared fingers of his right hand fell into place on hammer and trigger.

In the street, McCloud turned and saw him bursting, gun in hand, out of smoke, sparks, and fire glare. The burly figure stopped short, eyes bulging, and seemed to shrink. A howl broke from McCloud as he took a step back. "Rufe . . . he's back from fire, Rufe!" McCloud turned, fleeing, and stumbled blindly over Ross's sprawled form and fell heavily.

He scrambled up out of the scuffed dust, only the pick handle in his hand, and looked again with wild eyes. The scream that broke from McCloud was sub-human out of tortured nightmares and fears as he ran at Shafter, swinging the club.

Gasping for breath, Shafter threw a shot—and missed; he shot again without halting the screaming, bull-like charge.

Beyond McCloud he glimpsed the frozen silhouettes of McCloud's four remaining riders who were guarding the Jacktown families in the street. The running leap of a wide-shouldered miner was dragging one man from the saddle, grabbing his revolver.

Tough men, Curly had said. More miners were breaking toward the three remaining riders as Shafter fired again and the revolver *clicked* empty. He'd forgotten to reload. The pick handle struck his upflung arm as McCloud's frenzied charge reached him. The man was slobbering, gibbering.

Pain leaped through the arm as McCloud crashed into him and carried him staggeringly back. The wildly swung club glanced off the back of his head as he chopped the useless revolver at McCloud's ear. His left shoulder was clubbed as he struck again, desperately, with the heavy steel—and, when McCloud's rabid mouthings broke into a mewling gasp and went silent, Shafter staggered aside.

Through dizzy mist he saw the massive figure caving, falling. He lurched in a half circle around the spot, waiting. McCloud lay there.

Miners were running through the flame-brightened mist to them. Gasping for breath, sick suddenly, Shafter stood watching them dully. They didn't know him; some were still dirty from their shift in the Big Jack, but they were grinning—they were friendly, sane, decent men.

"Tie McCloud and Ross so they can't get loose!" Shafter ordered thickly. "Get guns, anything, and hunt the other men!"

He was getting sicker, and he walked unsteadily toward the other side of the street, and began to reload the empty revolver with shaking hands.

In a dull, pain-laced daze, he was standing there when Joanie

Wolcott wheeled her horse—his horse—into the street. She must have circled back past the houses up the mountain slope.

She rode to him, dropping off like a boy, light, fast, despite the too-big man's coat. "Mike . . . are you hurt?"

His grin cracked a stiff face. "Scratched hand." The thick voice, labored, was a stranger's voice.

She caught the hand, looked closely, pulled a blue bandanna from the coat pocket, and tied a crude bandage around the hand.

"There's been gunfire toward the powder house. Curly is watching the road. Sit down here and wait." She looked closely at his face before she turned away, pulling off the coat.

He looked at the hand, and stood in the painful daze, watching Joanie Wolcott giving orders, taking charge of women and children. Her forlorn look, her lostness had vanished, and would never return, he suspected.

He sat down awkwardly on the edge of the walk, closing eyes, fighting the sick dizziness. Sometime later her voice asked: "Mike, are you all right?" She was calling him Mike.

"Fine," he said agreeably. That stranger's voice, thick, groping.

"Take a swallow from this pint of whiskey." He obeyed—and coughed, choked, sucked deep breaths as she said: "I'll be back."

Curly Ames came in at a hard gallop and pulled up. "Bud Holland scattered that bunch on the powder house road!" Curly blurted from the saddle. "Some got away, but they won't stop!"

"Tell Miss Wolcott," Shafter said. He sat watching the flames across the street, burning lower now, and musing on what they'd have done in a strong wind. Burned the town, set the mountainside afire. Presently he put the bottle down carefully, and got up with an effort, not so sick or dizzy.

He was limping slowly back and forth in front of the store, pain receding in head and arm, when he saw riders and a buggy coming on the Grenada road. And Joanie Wolcott running out to meet them. More of it? He started after her, instinctively fumbling at the holster with his bandaged hand.

The large, unmistakable figure of Lyd Adams getting out of the buggy stopped him. But the threat and leaping pulses had cleared his head and brought strength surging.

He limped on, slower, and smiled ruefully as the buggy came on by him, Dr. Jim Kelton waving. Grenada men rode past him. Lyd Adams, wearing her old green hat with its faded, jaunty ribbon of red, was grim when he reached her and Joanie Wolcott.

"When Grenada learned what was goin' on," the big woman said, "enough men got gumption up to start this way an' take a hand." Keen eyes in the broad, weathered face surveyed him. "From what Joanie says, if you wasn't so hard-headed, McCloud would've ruined you, but looks like you'll be makin' her life miserable as usual."

"I doubt that," Joan said calmly.

Shafter grinned wryly; by the minute he was feeling better. "She doesn't know it, but she'll feel very good. High-grade ore seems to have been opened up in the Queen, and kept quiet. By Manning, evidently, for Ross's benefit."

He saw Joanie Wolcott shiver slightly.

"I think I've pieced together most of it," she said in a low voice. "Rich ore . . . money." She sounded bitter. "When I see what it's done . . . when I think. . . ." She drew a breath. "Buck was my friend . . . and I can remember him that way now."

"It'll help," Lyd Adams said. "Joanie, you get Shafter fixed easy until Doc Kelton can look at him. I got to see what needs to be done."

Shafter chuckled wryly under his breath as the big woman left them. "She'll give the orders now until Blaisdell gets in from the ranch and takes over."

"Is Art taking over?"

"I suppose so." They were moving along the street toward the dwindling flames in the gutted boarding house. "Not much left for me to do," Shafter said. "The law will take care of McCloud and Ross, one way or another. I want to talk to McCloud before I start back to Colorado."

Joanie Wolcott looked quickly at his face. "To a little mine working three men?"

"It may work three hundred someday."

"And the little stageline?"

"I'll make it a large stageline." His grin came briefly. "Like you, I have plans."

"Not like my plans." She was cool. "I asked the men not to tell you. McCloud is raving, repeating . . . 'No Shafter probate, Rufe . . . only a quitclaim . . . only a quitclaim. . . .' "

His startled stare turned frowning as he tried to grasp the meaning. "No probate court? Rufe Wolcott bought a quitclaim to our property?"

"Evidently, and then your mother vanished. The county records will show . . . and Rufe's papers."

He muttered: "I was too young to know such things. Mother sold quickly and left at once. I remember that. She couldn't bear to speak of those years again."

He remembered more. Old Johnny Carr had known about Big Mike's murder. Johnny must have pried into the dead past here in Grenada. Asked casual questions. Probably had searched the records in Azul. Old Johnny's brilliant legal mind had ferreted out the truth.

"Your mother," Joanie Wolcott said in the same cool voice, "evidently gave a quitclaim deed . . . all she could give . . . for her community interest in the property."

"I suppose so," Shafter muttered again.

"The law is plain," Joanie Wolcott said evenly. "I think Judge

Dixon has stumbled on this. He explained the law to me, casually, as if merely talking. I'm sure now he wanted me to know, because he saw this coming. A widow gets one half of her community interest, plus one fourth of a minor child's half. So a son inherits three-eights, held legally for him until ten years after his majority. Are you past thirty-one?"

"Twenty-eight." *We're rich, Michael . . . if we aren't killed.* Rufe Wolcott must have sweated through the years—and made certain old Manuel Griegos held silence about the old days. And McCloud, suspicious evidently of Johnny Carr, had silenced Johnny after sighting Mike Shafter in the Azul plaza. All the tangle of mystery was falling into logical order. And cool logic filled Joanie Wolcott's words.

"Your share of all the ore taken from these two mines, plus interest over the years, must amount to a good part of what I inherited. So I doubt if you can leave very soon for Colorado. You'd better give Art Blaisdell his orders, since you'll be most concerned from now on. Even the Grenada house, and everything in it, will probably be yours." She dusted palms together in a brisk gesture of finality. "At least I'll know now that I'll never be married for my money."

They had stopped in front of the burned building, both watching the rising smoke and remaining flames.

"Only one thing in the Grenada house I'd want," Shafter said absently. When she looked quickly, he was gazing at the smoke, thoughts elsewhere.

"Priscilla Ross?" Joan guessed. When he was silent, she stood very still, watching the flames. "Priscilla?" she asked again in a smaller voice—and this time, when she looked, his faint smile was reminiscent.

"I was thinking," Shafter said under his breath, "of how you were in the Azul plaza. . . ."

". . . covered with dirt, tricky, deceitful . . . ," Joan remembered under her breath.

"The prettiest girl," Shafter recalled. "The nicest armful." His grin was apologetic. "What did you say?"

He watched her draw a breath. When she smiled like this, he thought, she looked at peace, utterly contented.

"Never mind," Joanie Wolcott said, and there was contentment in her voice as she looked at the red, lazy flames. "Just keep talking, Mike."

ACKNOWLEDGMENTS

" 'What Color Is Heaven?' " first appeared under the title "Those Fighting Gringo Devils" in *Dime Western* (5/42).

ABOUT THE AUTHOR

T. T. Flynn was born Thomas Theodore Flynn, Jr., in Indianapolis, Indiana. He was the author of over 100 Western stories for such leading pulp magazines as Street & Smith's *Western Story Magazine,* Popular Publications' *Dime Western,* and Dell's *Zane Grey's Western Magazine.* He lived much of his life in New Mexico and spent much of his time on the road, exploring the vast terrain of the American West. His descriptions of the land are always detailed, but he used them not only for local color but also to reflect the heightening of emotional distress among the characters within a story. Following the Second World War, Flynn turned his attention to the book-length Western novel and in this form also produced work that has proven imperishable. Five of these novels first appeared as original paperbacks, most notably *The Man from Laramie* (1954) which was also featured as a serial in *The Saturday Evening Post* and subsequently made into a memorable motion picture directed by Anthony Mann and starring James Stewart, and *Two Faces West* (1954) which deals with the problems of identity and reality and served as the basis for a television series. He was highly innovative and inventive and in later novels, such as *Night of the Comanche Moon* (Five Star Westerns, 1995), concentrated on deeper psychological issues as the source for conflict, rather than more elemental motives like greed. Flynn is at his best in stories that combine mystery—not surprisingly, he also wrote detective fiction—with suspense and action in an artful balance.

The psychological dimensions of Flynn's Western fiction came increasingly to encompass a confrontation with ethical principles about how one must live, the values that one must hold dear above all else, and his belief that there must be a balance in all things. The cosmic meaning of the mortality of all living creatures had become for him a unifying metaphor for the fragility and dignity of life itself. *A Bullet for the Utah Kid* will be his next Five Star Western.